My heartfelt thanks t
mornings – those tirel
inputs – this book cou

Jack Galvin, Vinny Fraion, and Michael Grossman. Thank you,
Ed Weyhing, my favorite convert. Gone, but not forgotten. And
thank you, Tom Harper. You know why.

LEITH C. MACARTHUR is the author of the William Snow
series of thrillers, as well as various other short stories and
poems. He lives with his life partner in the quiet of Rhode
Island's western woods.

THE DEATH OF HARRY CROW

LEITH C. MACARTHUR

SilverWood

Published in 2020 by SilverWood Books

SilverWood Books Ltd
14 Small Street, Bristol, BS1 1DE, United Kingdom
www.silverwoodbooks.co.uk

ISBN 978-1-78132-944-3 (paperback)
ISBN 978-1-78132-945-0 (ebook)

British Library Cataloguing in Publication Data
A CIP catalogue record for this book is available
from the British Library

Page design and typesetting by SilverWood Books

The Death of Harry Crow

Enjoy,

1

The Driver

Leaning into the gale, The Driver plows through knee-deep snow toward the back of his truck. When a blast of icy wind cuts into his face, his eyes clamp shut. *Good.* If he can't see beyond two feet, no one can see him.

He leans against the liftgate and allows the storm to pummel him. Lowering his head, he wonders why he's being subjected to this obstacle. His other hauls had gone off without a hitch – each late-night drive, each boat ride through freezing waters, each delivery to that mass of unforgiving stone.

To soothe The Driver's grief and agony, God came to his bed one night and whispered details of a MasterPlan into his ear. Since then, the plan has been unfolding perfectly. *But this fucking storm could ruin everything!*

His anger with the elements raging, The Driver feels the urge to smash his head against the truck!

Make it stop!

He knows he's losing his mind. No matter. He's committed

to the plan. If it takes his life to complete it, he'll gladly give it.

Son of a bitch! The Driver screams. Then he unlocks the padlock on the steel bar, yanks the icy handle and pushes the heavy door upward till he hears the clank of the safety latch.

Hoisting himself into the truck's empty cargo box, he has a strange feeling. He pushes his hood back, eyes adjusting to the dark. Satisfied nothing has changed, he pulls the door down with a clang.

Outside, the wind screams back at him.

His flashlight beam pierces the darkness. There's a box at the base of each side-wall, the size of a freezer chest. To the untrained eye, the two boxes look like the truck's wheel wells. The Driver did the work himself, adding the extra length, doubling the space inside. Installing heating ducts to feed warm air into the custom wheel wells had been critical. January in Maine, the mercury can drop below zero.

The Driver goes to the right wheel well, takes a small, cordless screwdriver from his parka, kneels and begins removing screws. The whine of the cordless tool in the empty space strikes a nerve in his psyche. He stops. Listens.

Only the howl of the storm.

Gloves off, hands freezing, he switches the tool from one hand to the other. When the last screw falls, he lifts the sheet metal and is immediately knocked back by the smell.

Taking a deep breath, he bends forward and plays the flashlight's beam into the space. His heart pounds as he pulls a woolen blanket out and throws it to the floor. The heat-duct-system worked well on his previous runs, but those nights weren't viciously cold like this. The Driver has been out of his

8

heated cab only a few minutes, yet already he's shivering. What if it's just too cold?

After pulling a second blanket out of the well, he sees the bright orange of the *Minus-Thirty* sleeping bag. Grabbing the big tab at the corner, he slides the zipper open and moves the flashlight closer. Twin orbs bounce the light back at him like little mirrors.

Inside the coffin-like space, lifeless eyes stare at him. The Driver jerks back. Stark, grey, frozen, the eyes hold him. As he watches, a drop of liquid forms in the corner of one eye. With agonizing slowness, the drop leaks out, then slides down the frozen cheek.

The Driver holds his breath. He waits.

The eye closes.

When the eye opens, The Driver lets his breath go. *It isn't dead.*

He takes a leather case from his parka, unzips it and removes a long syringe. With his teeth, he pulls the cap off the needle and, once again, leans forward into the well.

2

Laura Crow

Home is an old tugboat, 100 feet long, 25 feet wide. Displacing 300 tons, *Paralus* is my personal leviathan.

I'm tall and wide and I'm surrounded by steel – above, beside, beneath me. My bare feet slide across it. My shoulders brush against it. My knuckles graze across it. I reside within a universe of iron bolts, diamond plate, welds, rivets. There's even bulletproof glass.

On my good days, living within the constancy of a steel-plated hull makes me feel safe. I'm comforted by its coolness, its solidity, its absolute unwillingness to yield.

But on the dark days, steel turns to lead, and time grinds to a halt. I am oblivious to the outside world. *Don't answer the phone. Don't get the mail. Ignore the tapping at the door.* I could be living in a cave, or on an abandoned planet.

Thursday.

I notice the corner of a pale green envelope sticking through the bottom seam of my ninety-pound front door. I know it's from Paula.

A single piece of pale green stationery carefully folded inside a matching envelope. A handwritten note with the letterhead: *Morning Star Kennel*. At some point she must have quietly slipped it underneath my door. She'd neither tapped nor rung. The woman knows me.

The note reads: *Laura Crow is a friend. Her daughter has gone missing. When she calls, <u>answer the damn phone!</u>*

Paula knows how committed I become when searching for a child. Her referral implies urgency.

When I begin a search, clues don't come to me, and I rarely experience what you might call intuition. Others call what happens inside my head 'a gift' – truth is, what happens in there is mostly chaos and confusion, so disturbing it sometimes makes me crazy. You could call the images I receive puzzles, signs, or even metaphors; but they're more like deconstructed concepts tossed into a blender. Which is just about what my head feels like after I get them.

But regardless, I'm in. Because it's a missing girl. Because it's Paula asking. And because I can never say, "No".

The following day. Four in the afternoon.

Low on the horizon, the sun scatters a trillion tiny lights across the surface of the cove. It's so beautiful, it's hard to look away. The ocean breeze brings the smell of salt and mud through portholes, open for the first time in weeks.

The prospect of working again stirs me. Anxious for spring, I feel my energies gathering. This is good. It's been a hard winter. I don't like cold and I'm glad it's almost over. I long to get back to scraping, sanding, and painting my tugboat's hull.

11

I hear the crunch of tires in the gravel parking lot that abuts the docks. Looking through a small starboard porthole, I see a white Chevy sedan, pulling up to my gangplank. The glare on the windshield makes it impossible to see inside.

I don't go to my door. Instead, I watch.

The engine shuts off. The driver's door opens. A woman steps out, leans against a fender and raises a hand to shade her eyes.

I'm guessing she's five and a half feet. I wouldn't call her skinny, but she looks thinner than I'd imagined. Perhaps even delicate. Suburban mom. Mid-forties. 2.5 kids. In her casual jeans and dark, waist-length coat, Laura Crow is a fine-looking woman.

Balanced against her car, staring up at *Paralus*, Laura Crow looks hesitant. Maybe she's wondering what kind of person lives in a rusty old tugboat. Or maybe she's trying to decide if such a person should be involved, in any way, with her family.

Maybe she'll change her mind. Turn away. Get back in her car. *Leave.* That would be fine with me. There's more than enough work to be done on *Paralus*. I've got a little money in the bank. Enough to keep me out of trouble for a good long time.

Laura Crow drops her hand and curls around the front of her car. As she's doing this, the other door opens and a younger version of her steps out. Laura's daughter has the same body stance, the same coloring as her mother. Together, they begin walking up my gangplank. It appears Mrs Crow has made up her mind.

Life has been tolerable lately. Why do I feel that's all about to change?

3

Amanda

Amanda believes she's in a bed. She thinks she's asleep. There are blankets all over her. She's wrapped in them. Engulfed by them.

Suddenly the floor drops and there's a loud bang. Amanda wakes. Her first thought is, *I can't breathe!* She's being suffocated by the covers! She tries to throw them off, but she can't move her arms!

Her senses seem to go on and off, like a lighthouse in the fog – in and out, like a radio station warbling in a storm. She hears rushing water. Smells gasoline and oil, dead fish, and the caustic stink of fiberglass. She tastes her last meal, her bile, her fear. Feels her hair being pulled from her scalp, her shoulders arched and aching, the roughness of wool scraping on her skin.

She is conscious. Then unconscious. In and out.

More sounds.

An engine thrumming. Moving water.

I'm so cold!

Amanda Crow's head slams into something hard and she goes out again. This time, she doesn't come back.

13

4

The Crows

Laura Crow has an expressive face and intelligent brown eyes. Shoulder-length brown hair brushes against her beige turtleneck sweater. Next to her, Annie looks just like Laura, minus ten pounds and twenty years.

We're in the salon on board *Paralus*, sitting across from each other in the dinette; a booth like the ones in old diners. There are dark circles under Laura's eyes. As she tells her story, her fingers twitch and her right foot taps on the cool steel floor. Annie Crow looks as if she hopes I might produce her missing twin sister from behind a screen.

As Laura tells me about Amanda's disappearance, Annie's slim fingers twitch and her eyes moisten. The look in Annie's eyes suggests boldness and strength, but her body does not. It looks frail, as if a precisely directed scream might cause it to shatter.

It's apparent that Laura and Annie both think I look familiar. I get that a lot. It's also apparent that Paula has spoken highly of me. The look in Laura's eyes mirrors Annie's – mother and daughter envision me as the hero of their story. They see me bringing Amanda home, safe and sound. I've worked with enough desperate families to know; this kind of misplaced familiarity can be a problem.

Laura begins by telling about a tragic incident that occurred four years ago. Her husband, Harry, was a recovering alcoholic. Hadn't had a drink in years. For some reason unbeknownst to Laura, Harry fell off the wagon on June 6, 2002: the twins' fourteenth birthday. It started in the morning in his workshop, out in the old barn behind the house. By the afternoon, when Harry came into the house to join in the celebration, he'd obviously had a slip and gotten drunk. An argument ensued. Laura demanded that Harry leave, thinking he would go back to his workshop in the barn. She imagined he might even sleep it off in the apartment above. Instead, Harry roared off in his Cadillac and got into a horrible accident. Five people died, including Harry himself.

As Laura finishes this part of their story, Annie's shoulders fall and she closes her eyes.

"Amanda became distant after her father's death," Laura says, softly. "Her grades crashed. She stopped hanging out with her friends and started running around with these kids I'd never seen before. She got hard and crass and had a constant chip on her shoulder. It seemed almost every day she and I would fight. It was chaos. About two years ago she moved out of the house and into the apartment over the workshop. We rarely spoke. She'd have those awful friends of hers over, but the barn is far enough behind the house that it didn't cause too much of a problem. You know, out of sight, out of mind. Things stayed pretty much that way until a few weeks ago when I noticed that Amanda just wasn't there anymore."

She turns her head and looks at Annie.

Annie opens her eyes. As she speaks, two perfect tears spill softly onto her cheeks. "Her friends weren't even from our school. I'd never seen them before. They were very…dirty. They would come and go, and I just tried to ignore them. But then it was quiet out there for a couple of days. When we checked the apartment, she was gone."

"It was obvious," Laura says. "She hadn't been there in a while."

"It must have been hard," I say.

Neither of them responds. There's an uncomfortable silence.

Then Laura steals a glance at my dog. Annie does the same. Sitting on her haunches, backed into a corner of the salon, Bradley is huge – 180 pounds. Her fur is brown and black, and short. Her head is lopsided, like it's been walloped with a lead pipe. Ever since Laura and Annie arrived, Bradley has been fixated on them, her blind eye unblinking, her seeing eye unwavering. Every so often, Bradley's tongue shoots out and snakes across her nose.

Laura and Annie look back at me. "She's really something," Laura says.

I nod.

"She looks…" Laura struggles for a word. "Formidable. She must be quite the watch dog."

"She is," I say. "Try coming in here without any warning and you'll get all the *watch* you can handle."

Annie's lower lip begins to tremble. Nice move, Snowman. Subtle.

"I'm sorry," I say. "I didn't mean to put it that way. I know Bradley's disfigurement can be unsettling. But she's really a sweetheart. You have no idea what a little softie she is."

Annie gives me a look.

"Okay." I smile. "She's a *big* softie."

Laura shakes her head, as if trying to shrug off an old memory. "I was bitten by a big dog when I was a little girl. Ever since, I've been... I've never seen a dog like her. She's...umm..." Laura's lips barely move.

"Scary," I say.

Laura gives a tremulous smile. "I didn't want to offend you. Or her." She nods at Bradley. "But yes. She's scary."

"What happened to her?" Annie asks.

Laura bristles. "Annie!"

"No, it's all right," I say. "A few years ago, I was throwing some garbage into the dumpster when I heard whimpering. I climbed in and found this little puppy, stuffed inside a trash bag. Her head and face were disfigured, which is probably why they threw her out." I pause, feeling it in my bones – the ancient anger. "I wanted to find them and..." I look over at Bradley's sweet, crumpled face.

"What is it?" Laura says. "What did you want to do?"

I look back at Laura. "I wanted to find the person who put her in that bag and kill them."

"Kill them?" Annie seems to approve. "Literally?"

"Figuratively isn't worth much."

Annie looks at me like I've answered a question not yet asked.

"The way she looked at me. With that one eye, like her life depended on me."

"You saved her," Annie says, with admiration.

"Mm," I say. "She was adorable, with that one little ear pointing straight out. And those sounds she was making. Kind of mewing, almost like a kitten. From then on we were a couple."

"A couple." Annie smiles. "That's so cute."

Annie may be warming up to me.

Laura looks relieved. "I see why Paula was so adamant about you. It certainly feels like you're the one to help us. You know, you look a lot like…"

I raise a hand. "Bridges, yes. "

Laura nods. "Have you ever felt utterly helpless?" She lifts her chin toward Bradley. "Like she must have felt when she was inside that dumpster?"

I look at Bradley, then at Annie and Laura. Reminding myself of their losses, I say nothing.

"This feeling of helplessness, of not knowing what's happened to Amanda. It's awful."

I wait.

"Do you have children?"

I shake my head, no.

Laura looks at Annie, then at me again. "Paula told me you're a powerful man. Just sitting across from you, I feel it. She says you have hard bark."

I say nothing.

"Paula says that when you're looking for a child, nothing will stop you. That you're fearless. Is that true, Mr Snow?"

"I wouldn't say that," I say. "But the only thing that matters is whether or not I can bring your daughter home." I look at Annie. "If I can save your sister."

"You know, I just realized..." Laura says. "I remember reading an article in the *Providence Journal* a few years ago. Something about a teenage runaway. The reporter called you The Finding Man."

No. It was a little girl who called me that. She'll be with me forever.

"I suppose I should tell you about *this*," I say, tapping the warm mahogany table.

Laura looks at where I am tapping and then to me, curiously. "The wood is stunning. But I don't see..."

I cut her off. "This table was built by Bob Shaw. He's a shipwright. A legend among local artisans." I stroke the smooth surface with my hand. The joiner work is flawless, and the finish shines like glass. "You may have heard of him," I say.

Laura shakes her head, no.

"A few summers ago, I helped find Shaw's missing niece, Kelly. Kelly's parents – Shaw's brother and sister-in-law – are heroin addicts. Shaw was certain Kelly took off to get away from them, and he was afraid she'd end up with the wrong people."

I have Laura and Annie's full attention now.

"I enlisted the aid of an acquaintance, a man named Mooney."

Thinking about Mooney, I pause and glance out the salon window. My eyes track along C dock, all the way to its end, to Mooney's shack. My gliding awareness stops and hovers a few feet above the shack's roof. I close my eyes. Mooney's not inside.

Feeling Laura and Annie's stares, I open my eyes. "Sorry," I say, and reel my awareness back into the dinette. "Mooney found Kelly, along with two other girls, in an abandoned tenement house in South Providence. Kelly didn't want to go with Mooney. He took her anyway.

"I don't know how Mooney did it and I don't want to know. But the encounter with him scared Kelly so badly, she gave up drugs and stopped hanging with the people who use them. Kelly's back in school today and doing all right. She's living with Bob Shaw and his wife, while her father rots in jail. No one knows where the mother is."

I pause again. Give my story a moment to sink in.

"A few months after Kelly was *saved*," I smile at Annie, "Shaw built this dinette. His way of saying thank you."

Laura's reaction is both grave and comprehending. "Please help us find Amanda."

I look across the table at the Crows. Their desperation is brittle and bright. My gaze settles on the daughter. She holds my eye. In the midst of this moment, it occurs to me that I know very little about identical twins.

"Annie," I say. "Help me understand what it feels like to be a twin."

Annie responds without hesitation, "Amanda and me. We can't imagine what it would be like to be you. You know what I mean? Just *one*."

I get a sense of something, like a sacred garment being torn; a separation. Somehow, I know this is the right moment to ask. "Is she alive, Annie?"

Laura gasps.

But Annie doesn't flinch. "Yes," she says. "I'd know it if she wasn't."

"Mm," I say, almost to myself. "I think I'd know it, too."

I speak directly to Annie. "I'll need to know more about Amanda," I say.

"Amanda is amazing. Even though we look alike, she's different from me. She's strong. Did you know she plays ice hockey? And that she's a gymnast? Last year she was state champion in the floor exercise. She's really smart. So smart she doesn't need to study. Everyone likes Amanda. She's always smiling. The most popular girl in school." Annie bows her head again. "At least she *was,* before all this happened.

"Amanda was closer to Dad than I was. She did things with him that I didn't. Skate. Go to ballgames. Stuff like that. Dad was…" Annie looks down.

Laura takes Annie's hand and squeezes gently. "It's okay. If Mr Snow is going to help us, he needs to know everything."

Annie lifts her head, eyes glistening. "Dad was…a guy. He liked to do guy stuff. Watch football, hockey, work on his car. He went to Amanda's hockey games, her gymnastic meets. I think that my sister was…" Annie looks down again.

Laura pats Annie's hand. "Annie's got this idea that her sister was the son her father never had."

When mother and daughter look into each other's eyes, I feel the love and pain of both hearts. And I feel the disappointment, like alternating currents of heat.

Laura and Annie hold each other's hands on the tabletop. When Annie looks at me, her eyes seem small, her resolve even smaller. "But it's true, Mr Snow. Amanda was Daddy's girl. Without him she was lost."

"What about the police?" I ask.

"I went to them," Laura says. "The first time, they said she had to be missing at least twenty-four hours. The second time, they said she was eighteen, an adult, and had the right to go wherever she wanted."

Cops who don't care. That's just what I need to hear.

I reach across the table and put my hand on top of theirs. "Try not to worry anymore. We're going to find Amanda."

5

Crazy

The Driver always arrives ten minutes early for a pickup. He parks, gives himself extra time to determine traffic restrictions, evaluate escape routes. He sits in his van, head touching the headliner, six-and-a-half-foot frame overwhelming the seat. He also uses the time to think through potential obstacles. A civilian walking his dog. The appearance of a random police cruiser.

In the morning, people are alert. At the end of a long day, they just want to get home. In the middle of the night, cops can pull you over and ask troubling questions: "What have you got back there?" So, dusk is the optimum time.

When he'd first called Rosalie Tam and made his unusual offer, The Driver heard the caution in her voice and understood her distrust. He wondered, what if a stranger called *him* and said that *he* might be entitled to a lot of insurance money because Harry Crow had, in a drunken state, *intended* to cause mayhem the day of the accident? The Driver would have doubts, too. Absolutely.

But he called each victim to provide them with something they needed more than money – *the reason their loved one had died.* What The Driver offered was closure. How could anyone say no to that?

Heritage Hills is an unremarkable plat of modest homes. You get in and get out, using the same horseshoe-shaped road. Side streets branch off the horseshoe, with names as phony as that of the development itself: River Road, Hemlock Valley Road, Pine Needle Road. The Driver knows there are no rivers or valleys anywhere near Heritage Hills. And there isn't a pine tree in sight.

The Driver heads straight for 16 Green Meadow Lane. He knows the house because he's cruised the place. Reconnoitered. Not in his van but in a car, with license plates that would trace back to no one.

He knows when Rosalie Tam leaves for work and when she gets home. He knows she always uses the side door that opens onto the driveway. Never the front.

He remembers there's a walkway that leads from the driveway, across the backyard, to the back door. He's thankful for Rosalie's twelve-foot stockade fence; her neighbors can't see into her backyard.

The Driver is confident he'll be able to pick up Tam, even though he knows he's losing his mental faculties. After twenty years dealing with criminals and their lunatic associates, he knows what crazy is, and he's headed there.

Over those twenty years, The Driver looked, acted, and talked like a regular human being. Underneath that façade, he was a tuned machine, coldly executing a long string of contract killings. But, ever since Harry Crow's careening Cadillac interrupted the robotic sequencing of his life, he has begun to *feel*. Now, driven by a newly discovered organ – his heart – all aspects of him lurch with passion and purpose toward one act of divinely demented genius, powered by humankind's most powerful engine – the need for revenge.

The Driver wheels his van between stone pillars made to look like sentry posts, goes right at Weeping Willow, left at Stony Drive, then right onto Green Meadow Lane.

A shark cruising shallow waters, The Driver slips past house after house, imagining the people inside as they share their dinners – moms, dads, kids – all blissfully unaware of the danger.

Shouldn't someone warn them?

This thought occurs in an old segment of his brain; a tiny chunk of gray matter not yet touched by his madness. The Driver is aware the thought occurred, yet he remains separate from it by focusing on what he believes to be a fact: not one person in the history of mankind has ever done what he is about to do.

There are fewer lights on in Rosalie Tam's house than in others. Hers is a house of one, her family destroyed four years ago by Harry Crow's selfish act.

Rosalie Tam could be eating dinner or taking a shower after her long day at work.

She could be feeding the dog.

This thought induces a mild shock, a tiny electrified twinge in a different place inside The Driver's skull. With it, his mental processes seem to skip, like the needle on a vinyl record, bumped forward to lyrics yet unheard.

She could be feeding the dog?

25

There it is again! But it's *wrong*. There's no dog in that house! The dog – the last item on The Driver's list – resides in a *different* house, in a *different* town. It's in a different *state,* for fuck's sake. He'll steal that dog later.

The Driver grits his teeth. As if this might keep his brain from bursting.

Rosalie's ridiculous-looking little Mini Cooper is parked in the driveway, facing out. The Driver parks the van in front of the driveway, blocking the car. He shuts the engine off, reaches into the glove box, and removes his leather case. He slips the case into his jacket pocket, grabs a slim briefcase from the passenger seat and throws open the door.

For the moment, The Driver stands before the house in his new clothes – beige cotton slacks, tan sports jacket over white cotton dress shirt, light beige tie. He walks down the driveway, past the silly-looking Mini Cooper, and stands at the side door, a low-watt bulb casting a pale circle of light around him. When he pushes the button, he hears the soft chime of a bell inside.

The upper half of the door is a grid – six panes of glass. The Driver pushes the button again, leans closer and peers inside. He can see most of the kitchen. On the far wall, a dark opening to a hall, a soft light glowing at its far end, and a lone figure slowly turning into the light's arc. The figure appears to grow taller as it glides toward him.

The Driver's body surges with adrenaline.

The silhouette of a woman emerges from the hallway and appears to float across the kitchen toward him. From the tiny wedge of healthy cells at that distant point in his brain, an uninfected thought emerges – *What good will this do?*

Rosalie Tam stares at him through the glass, looking him up and down. Six foot six. Three hundred pounds. A man who could tear her door from its hinges. He knows the sight of him frightens her.

The Driver works up his most masterful smile. "Hello, Mrs Tam. I'm Chester Ramsey."

Rosalie Tam stares at The Driver a moment longer, her eyes looking especially big through the glass. Decision made, the curtain falls back and the lock clicks. The door opens a few inches but stops at the end of a chain.

When The Driver glances at the useless chain, a blade of pure current slices through him. Fighting the urge to warn the woman, he holds his waxy smile.

Rosalie Tam speaks through the gap. "Mr Ramsey?"

"Yes." The Driver nods. "I'm here for our seven o'clock appointment."

There's a hesitation, but then the chain comes off, the door swings inward, and Rosalie Tam steps aside.

How could she let him in?

"I was just doing a little reading. Come in."

Rosalie Tam has sandy hair, warm brown eyes that seem to dance with lights and a pleasing face etched with delicate laugh lines. A light maroon skirt, short sleeved beige blouse and tan sneakers compliment her fair complexion. The Driver realizes she's more than petite – she's tiny. Just a hair under five feet, although she's definitely fit. He can see definition in her arms, the curve of her biceps.

The Driver steps into Rosalie Tam's house. He inhales the faint aromas – tomato sauce, oregano, lemon.

Rosalie gestures toward the kitchen table. "Make yourself comfortable. Can I get you anything? A glass of water?"

"I'm fine," The Driver says.

Next to Rosalie, he's gargantuan.

The Driver knows a lot about his hostess. Rosalie and her husband, Jonathan, led a quiet life. He had a desk job. Insurance. She taught tennis at the local Y. In her college days, was some kind of phenom with a racket. There were no children, no extended family. Since Jon was killed in the wreck, Rosalie still teaches, but does little else. Spends her evenings at home, alone.

A real tragedy, The Driver thinks. And here is the cruelest of ironies. It was due to the actual manner in which Jonathan Tam died that a madman now stands beside his widow, chatting with her calmly, as if he were, in fact, a regular human.

Mindful not to touch anything, The Driver nudges the chair aside with his hip and sits down. As he does this, he looks at the doomed woman and thinks, *I could do it right now...*

The Driver reminds himself to focus. Do not deviate from the plan. He wonders, would it help if he smashed his carefully crafted rules into his head with a hammer?

The pickups must be flawless. Do not deviate from the plan!

He casually glances around the room, ignoring its details. He has a camera for that. When his eyes come back to Rosalie, she's standing by the sink, looking at his hands. The operations were successful, but they still don't look right. The skin is stretched tight and it has a glossy sheen. The absence of imperfections makes the hands appear not real.

Rosalie's eyes come up.

The Driver nods. "Again, I apologize for having to schedule our meeting for such a late hour, but this week has been...well, I've just been swamped. This isn't my territory, and it takes almost an hour to get to this neck of the woods."

"I see," Rosalie says. "I'm hoping this won't take too long? I've had a long day myself, and I'm pretty tired." Her smile is warm and genuine. Real.

The Driver feels a little rattled. Something about this woman is different. He feels some kind of *energy* emanating from her, and it's affecting him in the strangest way. Suddenly The Driver realizes what it is – *gentleness*. Rosalie Tam is one of those people who will go out of their way to help you. She is a good woman.

Jesus Christ.

The Driver doesn't like what's happening to him. In a process he cannot arrest, this gentle, trusting widow is reminding him of Rebecca, his own wife, dead, four years, two months, seventeen days. Rosalie Tam doesn't look like her, but the quiet woman's spirit, her *gentleness,* is so much like Rebecca's that it makes him want to turn around and run out the door.

Yes! You can leave now!

The big man takes a breath and grinds his teeth. Carried forth on a wave of momentary sanity, The Driver feels something akin to compassion. But his moment of clarity is short-lived. The feelings of mercy quickly dissipate, eradicated by his surging illness.

"Mr Ramsey?"

The Driver realizes he's been staring at Rosalie. He decides to tell her the truth. "Yes. I...I'm sorry, Mrs Tam. It's just that you…ah, you reminded me of someone…ah, my niece. My sister's youngest daughter, Rebecca. The resemblance is startling. Rebecca has been gravely ill, and the family is having a hard time coping. Ah…seeing her in you kind of jarred me."

Rosalie Tam takes one small step backward, a defensive maneuver that does not go unnoticed by The Driver. He knows there is a good chance, no matter how trusting this gentle woman is, she could be sensitive to anything he says that is not truthful. If Rosalie Tam realizes he's bullshitting, her defenses will come up and he will have to subdue her. He doesn't want to do that. He must not make a mess. It's time to play his trump card.

The Driver looks around the room, avoiding eye contact with the woman. "Well, let's talk about what matters, shall we?"

Rosalie takes another half-step away from him.

"Mrs Tam. Let me run the particulars by you, give you a general idea what we're talking about, so you can decide whether or not you'd like to join with us. Then I'll leave you to your evening."

At the mention of his leaving, Rosalie seems to relax. And just like that, they are back to the subject most important to her – what happened to her poor, dead, Jonathan.

The Driver places his briefcase on the table and unsnaps the clasps.

Rosalie takes a chair across from him and gives him a wan smile.

The Driver feels that damn gentleness coming from her again. "You know," he says. "On second thought, I think I would like some water."

When Rosalie gets up and turns her back to The Driver,

he reaches into his jacket pocket, deftly unzips the case and pulls out the syringe.

Rosalie gets a glass, takes a plastic container from the refrigerator and begins filling the glass with cold water. Watching this, The Driver realizes he actually *is* thirsty. He slides the syringe back into his pocket just as Rosalie turns around.

Rosalie places the glass of water in front of him and regains her chair.

The Driver looks at the glass. He can't pick it up. Not yet.

"Hmm," Rosalie says. "What makes you and your group feel so certain this can be brought to court? It's been more than four years and nothing's happened. Why now? Has something changed?" As Rosalie speaks, she angles her body slightly away from The Driver and looks out the window. "Is that your truck out there?"

When she looks back at him, he knows it's almost time.

"Yes. I normally use it when I'm doing on-site investigations. But my car is in the shop. You know..." The Driver lightly taps the table. "Your kitchen set-up. Cabinets. Countertop. It would all look great in our kitchen. We're remodeling. I'd be willing to bet you a quarter, if Rebecca saw this kitchen, she'd agree with me."

Rosalie Tam frowns. "I thought you said Rebecca was your niece."

"What I'm getting at here is, would you mind if I took a few pictures? I'd like Rebecca to see this for herself." The Driver stands and reaches into his jacket pocket.

Rosalie looks confused. "But didn't you just say...?"

The Driver has already taken the tiny camera out of his

31

pocket and begun shooting. He points first at Rosalie, clicks, then turns and quickly clicks off a half-dozen other shots of the table, cabinets, countertops, the camera giving off these unsettling little pops of brightness.

"But you just said…"

The Driver slides the camera back into his pocket. His massive body leans toward Rosalie.

Rosalie seems stuck in her chair.

"I'm glad you're sitting down, Mrs Tam. The police received an anonymous tip a few months ago. A diary was unearthed. It belonged to Harry Crow, the driver of the Cadillac that swerved in front of your husband's truck. The man who killed your Jonathan."

Rosalie Tam's eyes are bright with fear. "Wait. You're going too fast. I thought…"

"It will soon be public knowledge. Due to an entry in Crow's diary, the authorities will have to alter the cause of your husband's death."

Rosalie slowly shakes her head as she rises from her chair. "I have no idea what you're talking about. This isn't…"

"Mrs Tam. Harry Crow left his house that day and drove onto that highway for one reason. To crash that big Cadillac of his into an oncoming vehicle at a high rate of speed."

Rosalie Tam gasps.

"That's right," The Driver says. "To kill himself."

Rosalie reaches out and grabs the back of the chair. She begins to tremble.

"However, the police now believe that when Harry Crow saw a van parked on the side of the road, he made a split-second decision. He veered out of his lane and smashed into that van at full speed. There were no skid marks. He never touched his brakes."

It's easy to see that Rosalie Tam has forgotten all about Rebecca. Her face has gone white. She has a death grip on the chair, as if only this will keep her from leaving the earth.

"Yes, Mrs Tam. Harry Crow *intentionally* crashed his car into that van. You can see how this changes everything. Instead of an accident, it was a willful act of suicide. Which, of course, means he also committed *manslaughter.*"

At the word, Rosalie turns from the chair and walks slowly toward the window. Her head is tilted back, her eyes shut as if to seal in the tears.

"I'm sorry that I have to dredge this all up again, Mrs Tam. But your husband's death was not an accident."

The Driver begins moving slowly toward Rosalie, her back to him once again.

"We, the survivors, have formed this group in order to file a unified lawsuit against Harry Crow's estate. The man left behind substantial assets, and we believe every person who has lost a loved one deserves a portion of that estate."

Rosalie seems unaware that The Driver is now close enough to touch her. Which he does. He puts his hand on her shoulder. She flinches, but only slightly – after all, he's merely trying to comfort her. As he gently removes his hand from her shoulder, he glances at his watch and takes note of the time. His right hand goes into his jacket pocket, and again produces the fully loaded syringe.

As The Driver removes the safety cap, Rosalie begins to softly cry. With her eyes closed, she will not see it coming.

Wrapping a massive arm around Rosalie Tam, The Driver plunges the needle into her soft flesh.

The tiny woman convulses but does not scream.

In the time it would take anyone to realize they've made a terrible mistake, Rosalie's legs turn to mush.

A roaring sound fills The Driver's head.

Like a piece of discarded cloth, Rosalie Tam settles into The Driver's iron arms.

6

Ray

Ray Driscoll is a detective with the Providence cops. He's also an old friend. When I call to ask if he knows anything about the disappearance of Amanda Crow, he tells me it's his day off. Translation? *Buzz off.*

I don't respond. There's a long pause, after which he asks if I want to meet for lunch.

I tell him I'm giddy at the prospect. Watching him eat two large pizzas while I eat a salad is more than I'd hoped for.

Ray and I are sitting in a booth at a pizza joint. We've just finished our lunch. There's cheese and napkins and bits of crust all over the table. The lunch crowd is gone. The heady aroma of pizza sauce and bread dough lingers in the air. 1960s tunes play softly from the retro jukebox in the corner. There's an occasional clang from the kitchen, but otherwise, it's quiet.

A shade over six feet tall and almost as wide, Ray Driscoll looks like a Hummer in street clothes. He's wearing jeans and sneakers, an open, paper-thin leather jacket and a faded Mickey Mouse T-shirt. His short, dark hair is concealed under a Red Sox baseball cap.

Ray has the broad, disgruntled face of an old beat cop.

Laura Crow gave me the names of a few of Amanda's new friends. A few hours ago, I called Ray and asked him to do a little digging. Now I ask him if he's learned anything about them.

"Listen up!" Ray barks. "The only one I got a hit on was this cheeseball, Vinnie Iannucci, aka Slo-Mo. Thirty-four. Not much of a sheet. At least nothing he'd wanna brag to his scumbag friends about. I don't know what your girl was thinking when she connected with this creep."

"Okay," I say.

"This is what I got on Amanda Crow. She's your average kid, aside from being a twin. She was headed on the straight before her father bought the farm. But her old man's death screwed with her head."

Ray goes on to tell me much of the same stuff I got from Laura and Annie – Harry Crow abruptly leaving Amanda's birthday party, the accident, etc. The one new piece I get is that Amanda blamed her mom for her father's death.

Ray's voice sounds like shoveled coal. "You already know a lot of the guys on the force have a hard-on for you. When they didn't find that Sweeney girl and you did? All the media shit that followed?" Ray hooks air quotes. "*Rescued Girl Calls Local Hero The Finding Man!* You can't blame the guys who think you one-up the force. They think you make us look bad."

I raise my hand. "I never try to—"

"Hey!" Ray barks again. "I couldn't care less about that crap. The girl's body was returned to her parents and a useless piece of shit got nailed for it. Enough. But now, here you are with another missing kid, and I'm thinking it might be best if I'm not seen talking to you."

"So, you invite me to lunch in a Pizza Hut," I say. "Crafty."

Ray chuckles, then his eyes skate away. "Yeah, well, what can I say? There's something about you, Snowman. You get your hook into me some way or another. Make me feel guilty about these kids that're always getting themselves lost."

"There's no hook," I say. "You're just easy. These kids need help. Your help. My help. Our help. Why should anyone care which?"

Ray points at me, and for the first time he almost smiles. "Don't you fuck with me, Snowman. I will drop-kick your ass." Then his eyes go hard as iron. "It's obvious you don't know this. I was on the scene of the crash that night. Rolled up right after it happened. I've seen some bad ones, but this was the worst."

I'm confused. Why would Ray – or any homicide detective – be called to the scene of an automobile accident?

"So, you're telling me you were sent to the scene of an accident that killed the father of a girl who would go missing four years later who I would then be hired to find?" As I hear my words, the extent of the strangeness hits me. "What are the odds of that happening?"

"You're asking the odds?" Ray's face tightens. "Jesus, Snow. When you get involved in something, the odds that it will turn into a clusterfuck are *even*." Ray grimaces. Possibly for effect. "And the fact that our trajectories would eventually collide within the same forensic dimension of facts? That doesn't surprise me one bit."

That our trajectories would eventually collide within the same forensic dimension of facts. This is how Ray Driscoll can surprise you.

Ray takes a pull from his root beer. As he tilts his cup, his faded blue eyes grin at me from across the rim.

I take a drink of my root beer and wipe the foam from my lips. "Am I missing something?"

Ray settles back in his seat. "Yes, you are, my friend. It was my day off. I wasn't on duty. I just happened along a few minutes after the crash."

Something dark erupts in Ray's eyes. He's been through wars, but it's obvious, the Harry Crow wreck is still with him.

He takes a breath. Then, he tells me.

Van, with family inside, pulls off highway into breakdown lane so husband, who's driving, can switch places with wife. Husband gets out. Goes around to passenger door. As he's opening door, Cadillac, travelling at excessive speed, hits van from behind. Van is flipped over on its roof. Cadillac caroms across highway. Crosses into high speed lane into path of speeding pickup truck. Impact kills driver of Cadillac. Harry Crow.

Ray places his glass carefully on the table. He's suddenly weary. It shows in the slump of his shoulders, in the bulge of his aging eyes. "It was bad. The M.E. said the family in the van got bounced around. Whiplash, lacerations, like that. But they were wearing their seatbelts, and the air bags went off. He said there were no serious injuries resulting from the initial impact."

The M.E.? "Why is a medical examiner involved in an automobile accident?"

Ray ignores my question. "Like I said; the family survived the initial contact. But not the dog. The dog wasn't in a harness."

I love dogs. I have the most amazing dog on the planet. I don't want to think about any dog flying around inside any flipping van.

Ray purses his lips. Gives me grim. "*So.* This is how I imagine it went. And this is what I can't get out of my head. The family members are a little banged up and they're probably freaking out but they're okay. They're getting out of their seatbelts, trying to figure who's hurt and who's not, when this pickup truck goes sliding by on its roof."

I shake my head. "What?"

Ray slides his hand horizontally through the air above the table, mimicking an object sailing peacefully by – though I'm not sure the peaceful aspect is his intention. He's still looking at me, but his eyes are fuzzy, like he's back out there on that highway that night.

In my head, I see a man standing alone on the side of a road. He has this look on his face – like he's just seen a skyscraper fall over with his family inside.

Then it hits me. "The gas tank."

Ray nods. "The van's gas tank is spilling gas all over the road. The pickup goes sliding by the van on its roof. It doesn't hit the van, but it's throwing sparks. Two seconds later, the van is an inferno."

The lining in my stomach burns.

Ray nods again. "They couldn't get the doors open. The crash jammed everything."

I look out the window.

"The husband tried to pry open the doors."

"My God," I say. "This must have been all over the news. Why didn't I hear about it?"

Ray grunts. "Because you're a hermit living in a tugboat. You oughta read a newspaper. Watch the news. Maybe even try the Internet."

I can't imagine what it must have been like for the husband. I look at Ray. His eyes are dead.

I take a few slow breaths. "What about the driver of the pickup truck?"

Ray Driscoll blinks. He's a cop's cop. He likes to go after bad guys. But there are none in this story. No chance for a happy ending. "The pickup driver died in the ambulance on the way to the hospital. The father from the van was the only survivor. That is, if you don't count the kid."

I'm not sure I want to hear about the kid.

"A lot of people pulled over. A few of us had fire extinguishers. We managed to suppress the fire a little, enough so we could get one of the back doors open. We got one of the kids out. But as soon as I saw him, I knew he wasn't going to make it."

Ray doesn't have the face for tears, but right now, it's close.

"By the time we got the boy out, it must have been a thousand degrees inside. I've heard screaming, but I've never heard anything like that. If I live to be a hundred, I won't forget it."

Ray picks up a napkin. Wipes the sweat from his forehead.

I need to change the subject. "Tell me about Slo-Mo," I say.

Ray looks exhausted. "Kid's a punk. Gangster wannabe. He hangs at The Corner Pocket, a dive down on the river. Got

40

a rap sheet, but it's mostly nickel-and-dime beefs. Wouldn't have figured him for an abduction. But hey, nothing surprises me anymore."

"Have you talked to Laura Crow?" I ask.

"Not directly, but I know she's been pushing. Thinks the State Police, National Guard, Feds and the CIA should all be looking for her kid."

"You can't blame her," I say. "Why aren't you guys taking this seriously?"

"There's no evidence of foul play. Besides, her daughter is an adult. Adults can come and go whenever they please."

"Is there anything you can do?"

"I already made a few inquiries. Seems Slo-Mo has something the ladies like. Every winter he grabs a new one and drives south. So, unless Amanda Crow shows up dead on some beach in Florida, there's nothing to be done." Ray lifts one eyebrow. "It hasn't even been a week, Snowman. Let it go."

As I drive away from the pizza joint, a movie begins playing in my head. This is one of the ways it starts, how my mind can begin to bend. I get intuitions. Hints. Insights that are turned upside-down and inside-out. Rarely do I get a simple clue.

In my movie, it's winter. Snow is falling. Four cars, occupied by four different families, are stopped abreast of each other, blocking a highway. The occupants are about to play a perverted version of a teenager's game from the 60s.

This is how you play Chinese Fire Drill. A car stops in the middle of a street. All the kids pile out, including the driver, and they run in circles around the car. Sometimes they bump into each

41

other and fall over. Everyone laughs. Traffic backs up. Horns blare. After a few circuits around the car, the kids jump back inside and there's a new driver.

I played Chinese Fire Drill when I was a teen, but there are two things wrong with the version that's running in my head. When this game stops, there are new drivers, but family members are all mixed up, sitting in the wrong cars, staring in fear at the strangers sitting next to them.

The other thing wrong with this game is that no one laughed.

There's a message for me here, but I don't know what the hell it is.

I'm almost back to *Paralus* when it occurs to me that I didn't ask Ray the names of the other people who died in the wreck. This realization triggers another process inside my head – questions erupting so fast, I can't process them. Does it matter who the other people were? Why am I even wondering that? Was the Harry Crow crash an accident? Was it something else? Even if it *was* something else, it shouldn't matter to me. Should it? After all, how could five dead people and one dead dog have anything to do with the disappearance of Amanda Crow, four years after an accident that killed her father?

This is what happens within the confines of my skull – what my girlfriend, Paula Starr, calls my "instinctive pseudo-psychic conflicted self".

No joke.

7

The Park

I'm sitting on the edge of the couch, tying my sneakers, when Bradley comes skittering around the corner at hyper-speed, a hip bouncing off the doorframe as she charges into the salon. Nails skittering on the steel floor, tongue a pink flag flapping from her mouth, the expression on her crumpled face is a pure *Yippee!*

When Bradley wants to play it's best not to ignore her. "Okay!" I laugh. "I guess you want to go out, huh?"

At the word *out*, her eyes bulge, her tongue snaps back into her mouth, and her face gets all serious, like, *You wouldn't kid me, would you?*

When I tell her that we are indeed going out, she woofs and, with her hips waggling, backs up and knocks over a floor lamp.

"Nice," I say. "That's my girl."

When I get off the couch, Bradley rears up, thumps her front paws onto my shoulders and looks at me, eye to eye. I smell her musk, and see the love beaming in that one beautiful eye.

"Want to go to the *park?*"

At the word *park*, Bradley peels away and goes skittering out of the salon in a reversal of her grand appearance. As she clamors for the door, I hear her tail thwacking the walls.

In the truck, Bradley sits in the passenger seat. Given her size, it's a spectacle – particularly on warm days when she hangs about ninety of her pounds out the window. We drive to Smithson Park and I shut my truck down in the picnic-area parking lot. Smithson has a beach, a baseball diamond, a big field of cut grass and miles of hiking trails that snake through the dense forests and skirt the shores of Narragansett Bay.

Sitting next to one of the picnic tables in a custom-made electric wheelchair is Eddie, a wounded veteran and a friendly guy. He lives in a shelter downtown and can often be seen in his wheelchair on the road to the park, smiling, twin American flags fluttering at his back. Thanks to an IED in Iraq, Eddie lost the use of his legs and has moderate brain damage.

I grab a Frisbee from behind the seat and let Bradley out. She immediately runs to Eddie and sits politely next to his chair. Eddie gives her disfigured head a rub, then pulls a treat from his pocket. Bradley licks Eddie's face, grabs the treat in her teeth and gallops off across the field, dipping her nose here and there to breathe in the latest news. Finding the perfect spot, she lies down in the grass and begins nibbling on the treat.

I walk over to Eddie. "Eddie," I say. "How's it going?"

Eddie speaks, not in sentences, but in word groups. The spaces give his fried synapses time to connect. "It's the same… as it is…every day, Mr Snow. It's…a good day…to be alive."

"It is," I say.

44

Long-bodied, lean and clean-shaven; dressed in wrinkled tan cargo pants, a red wool shirt and a baseball cap, Eddie has the oval, smiling face of a priest. His body looks perfectly normal, as if at any moment he could step out of his chair and do an easy lap around the field. If not for the wheelchair and the hitches in his vocals, you'd never know that on his second tour in Iraq, he was blown twenty feet into the air.

"Couldn't ask for a better one," Eddie says. "No point in it." He gazes across the field at Bradley and his smile widens. "You got yourself...some...dog there."

"Couldn't ask for a better one," I say as I head off toward the field. "You take care of yourself, Eddie."

"Yes sir. I...I will."

After finishing her treat, Bradley bounds to her feet and searches the perimeter, looking for her friend. Lady is a nine-pound Shih Tzu with the silky white fur of a kitten and the soft brown eyes of an otter. Her owner, Tom Harper, a local business owner and philanthropist, often brings Lady to the park. Bradley and Lady's playful greetings are not just heartwarming, they're hilarious.

I don't believe Tom and I have ever had a meaningless conversation. He's one of the most curious men I've ever known, and his provocative questioning of our species' capabilities, and his conclusion that it suffers from a collective, incurable madness, has earned my unwavering respect. I'd hoped he'd be here so we could discuss the ins and outs of my case – but he's not, which means Lady is not, which means Bradley is disappointed. She stands in the middle of the field, chest heaving, her half-good eye casting about for her little friend.

But she doesn't want for long. Just as I let the Frisbee fly,

45

Tom pulls into the parking lot. When Bradley sees his car, she ignores the incoming disc, letting it bounce off her head as she bolts. At the edge of the field, Lady makes her own mad dash and the two dogs meet and begin prancing in circles, taking mock lunges at each other. As Bradley rears and leaps, as Lady feints and dodges, they communicate using delicate little huffing and pleading sounds. The dance looks risky – if Bradley fell on Lady, the tiny dog might be crushed. But Bradley's movements are precise. She wouldn't hurt a hair on Lady's body.

"Hi there." Tom shakes my hand. "Look at them," he says, chuckling. "The lion and the mouse."

"It's a beautiful thing," I say.

Directly across the field from where Eddie sits in his wheelchair reading, Tom and I sit on a bench and allow our dogs to do their thing.

Run. Circle. Pounce. Play dead.

Pounce. Run. Circle. Play dead.

"How's life?" I ask.

"Good."

"And Barbara?"

"She's good. She's been having some arthritis flare-ups lately, but otherwise good. And you? How's the rentals? Tenants driving you nuts yet?"

"My tenants are great," I say. "I guess I'm one of the lucky landlords. I have no vacancies, and everyone pays on time. Well, *almost* everyone."

"I still say you should raise your rents," Tom says. "Your rates are below average and you don't make enough profit. That's risky business."

"Most of my tenants can barely afford what they already pay. And I get by all right."

"You're a good man," Tom says, smiling. "But maybe not such a good businessman. How's the other thing going? You staying out of trouble?"

"Not exactly."

"I keep telling you, my friend. You keep pushing your luck and—"

I cut him off. "You're beginning to sound like Paula."

"When others tell you the same things, maybe there's an opportunity to learn something about yourself."

I tell Tom about Laura Crow and her missing daughter, Amanda, making a point of the fact it was Paula that sent Laura to me. "Paula's giving me a bit of a mixed message, wouldn't you say?"

"She is," Tom says, "and that's not at all like her. She must be really worried about her friend's daughter."

Suddenly we hear shouting from across the field. A car has parked near my pickup, and four guys are marching toward Eddie. The biggest of them is a tall, rangy young man, maybe mid-twenties – he's the one yelling, while Eddie sits quietly reading his book.

I look over at our dogs. After thoroughly exhausting themselves, they've fallen asleep in the grass next to each other.

The tall guy is getting louder.

"Oh boy," Tom says, under his breath.

When Tall Guy reaches the wheelchair, he leans over and screams into Eddie's face. "You coulda fucking *killed* us!"

I get up.

"Oh, shit," Tom says.

Tom and I cross the field just as Tall Guy says to his friends, "We gotta teach this fucking fraud a lesson."

"What's the problem?" I ask.

Tall Guy turns, startled. "What the fuck?"

I look at Eddie. "Eddie?"

Eddie smiles. "Hey Mr…Snow. You back…so soon?"

I take a step toward Tall Guy.

"Who the fuck are you?" he yells. "This is none of your fucking business!"

"What's the problem?" I repeat.

"This *fraud* here," he gestures at Eddie, "was driving his stupid chair on the *road!* I had to swerve around him and almost ran into a fucking *truck.* We almost got killed because of this *fraud.*"

Eddie looks up at Tall Guy. "You didn't…have to…swerve. You were going too…fast…and you…weren't paying…attention. I was…on the side…where I belonged. I was almost…in the sand."

Tall Guy seems confused by our insertion into his moment. He looks at Tom and me and jabs a finger. "You guys get the fuck outa here. This is between me and him!" He points the finger at Eddie.

"What this is," I say, "is four guys threatening one guy in a wheelchair. Is there anything about that that sounds okay to you?"

"This disabled act of his is bullshit!" Tall Guy says. "I see him all over the place, rolling around in that little go-kart of his like he owns the fucking road! Always in the way, flying those stupid flags. But look at him! He doesn't have a mark on him. I'm betting his whole act is a scam. Just another money-suck, living off the government." Tall Guy seems pleased with his elocution. "Sucking off of our tax dollars," he adds.

"You pay taxes?" I say. "You work?"

Tall Guy moves closer. His eyes are red with anger, glassed with alcohol. His breath smells like scorched tobacco and regurgitated beer. "This is none of your fucking business, big mouth. Get the fuck out of here." He curls his right hand into a fist. "I'll knock you the fuck out!"

"You're bullying a man in a wheelchair," I say. "That alone makes you a coward."

Tall Guy clenches his other fist. "You say another word and I'll—"

I smile as I interrupt him. "You know, my mother was right. She used to say, when it comes to bullies, 'the tallest are the smallest'."

Tall Guy is doing his best to look tough, but it's not working.

I continue to smile. "There are four of you, and two of us. What do you say we even up the sides? You wouldn't threaten me if you were alone." I turn and yell, "Bradley! *Come!*"

Bradley leaps to her feet and comes galloping across the field toward us like a small horse. Tall Guy's eyes brighten with fear and he takes a step back. "What the *fuck?*"

Bradley halts at my side and promptly sits, her head almost even with my shoulder. She's excited. She thinks we're going to play. Of course, with her damaged face, she doesn't look the least bit playful to Tall Guy. In fact, I think he thinks Bradley wants to eat him.

"How we doing now?" I ask.

There's a noticeable shift in Tall Guy's body stance. He's already leaving. "I'm not gonna waste my time on a bunch of losers like you."

I look him in the eye. "One word from me and this animal will tear you to pieces."

"*Jesus*," Tall Guy says. He glances at Eddie, gives Tom and me a pathetic, watered-down 'evil eye', then gestures to his friends. The four of them go to their car and climb in. As the car slowly idles past us, Tall Guy stares at me through the half-open driver's window.

"Let me guess," I say. "You want my address."

Tall Guy mashes the accelerator and the car tears off in an explosion of dirt and gravel.

"Damn," Tom says, looking at me. "The tallest are the smallest?"

"Yeah. Well. So I made that up."

Tom chuckles.

"Let's go play," I say, to no one in particular.

As Tom, Bradley and I head back across the field toward the still-snoozing Lady, Eddie calls out, "Hey, Snow."

I turn.

"It's a…good day…to be…alive." Eddie's smile is as good as it gets.

"It is indeed," I say.

Cantering along next to me, Bradley says, "Woof."

8

Big

You get to The Corner Pocket by going down a set of stone stairs, next to a crumbling foundation – what's left of a bridge that once spanned the Greene River. The steps deliver you to the riverbank, and a group of old brick buildings along the river's edge.

The three structures were once textile mills. Now, a pool hall and bar occupy the first floor of the first building, while the remaining two are just empty shells tilting precariously toward collapse.

It's a cloudy day. Fog rises like smoke off the surface of the polluted river.

I enter The Corner Pocket through a green door, into a miasma of odors – sweat and testosterone, scorched cooking oils, stale beer pooling in rotting rugs. Despite the potpourri of aromas, it's easy to distinguish cigar and cigarette from the heady odor of marijuana. In defiance of state law, layers of the forbidden pollutants hang over the dozen or so billiard tables – charcoal clouds floating above islands of green felt. At the far end of the room, a bar serving booze and finger foods is barely discernible through the choking haze.

I stand still, allowing myself time to adjust to the remarkably unhealthy environment.

A handful of men are playing pool at various tables; most of them working stiffs. No prison tattoos. No gang colors. No one behind the bar.

To my left, behind an elevated platform that may have once been a stage, is the office. A sign above a door says so. In the middle of the platform, a podium. Behind the podium, a man, his face hidden behind an open copy of *Barely Legal*. To hide the rest of him would require more than a magazine filled with obscene photos of women made to look like little girls. As I'm processing this, the enormous man lowers the magazine and pins me with his beady black eyes.

He's in his late forties or early fifties, sweaty, bald, unshaven, and stupendously large. Massive arms covered in thick black hair poke out of his skimpy white T-shirt. His body appears to be a unified mural of sinister-looking, interconnected tattoos. I estimate his weight is between three and six hundred pounds.

I will never underestimate the physical prowess of a man simply because he's obese. Under all the fat on this man, I see enough defined musculature to suggest that he was once a physical specimen. In my mind, I call him *BIG*. His size says offensive line. His nose says super-heavyweight boxer. The number of kinks in his nose says super-heavyweight boxer with a losing record. I shudder to think who could have beaten him.

I smell Big before I reach the platform. When I look at him, he stares down at me with those little, black pig-eyes as if I'm beneath him. Which, physically, I am.

"Hey," I say.

Big looks me over. He doesn't answer.

"Got a minute?" I give him Dazzling Smile # 3, which I usually reserve for the charming of older ladies. I use it because I know it will piss him off. Sometimes I just can't help myself.

In a show of contempt, Big lowers his magazine slowly.

I hold my smile.

"Do I got a minute?" Big says in a heavy New York accent – Danny DeVito in the South Bronx. "Lemee see." He brings a ham-hock of a hand to his chin. His show of further contempt. "Yeah, I got a minute. You want a beer? I got a minute to take your t'ree bucks. You want a rack an' a table? I got a minute to take your twenny bucks. You want anything else? You got ten seconds to get the fuck outa my face."

I continue to smile, even though my stellar wit has failed to disarm him. Maybe the glare from my teeth will throw off his equilibrium.

"You," I say, "give new meaning to the phrase *customer service.*" Like I said, I can't help myself.

"Uh, Jeez," Big mutters as he begins lifting his massive bulk off his chair.

Now, ladies and gentlemen, if you move just a little closer, you'll witness a water buffalo extracting itself from a mud hole.

Big is even bigger than I thought. Yet he takes the steps down to the main floor with the agility of a gazelle.

I glance again around the room, at the men leaning over the tables poking at perfectly round balls with slightly crooked cues.

Big intimidates. My guess is, none of these guys are his friends. If there's trouble, it will be me against the three of him.

"I'm looking for someone," I say.

"Isn't everyone," Big says. His attention span goes right to zero.

"His friends call him Slo-Mo."

Upon hearing the nickname, Big's immense face constricts, like he's just taken a whiff of something rotten. "You a cop?"

"No," I say.

Big gestures toward the podium. "Does my station here look like an information booth? Do I look like a…" His expression goes blank when he realizes he doesn't have the punch line. Setting his jaw, he says, "Get your ass outa here."

I want to tell him what he *does* look like but decide against it. "I'm not here to cause a fuss. I'm just looking to talk to the guy. Maybe you could help me with that."

"You don't wanna cause a fuss?" When Big grins, skin wobbles above exposed, yellow teeth. "Cause a fuss. That's rich."

I'm undeterred. "So. The guy in question? His friends say he hangs out here a lot."

"The guy in question?" Big's smile is gone and his eyes are slits. It's clear – he knows Vinnie Ianucci. "Slo-Mo ain't got no friends. The fuck you want with him, anyway?"

I've annoyed Big by distracting him from his fantasies, by disrupting the curdling of his juices while he wallowed in his sexual proclivities, fired and shaped within the diseased cauldron of his magazine. His reaction to me is so aggressive, so potentially volatile, I wonder how hard I can press before he explodes.

Big steps toward me and balances his weight. As subtly as

I can, I shift an inch to the left, slide my right foot back a touch, shift my weight onto my left leg. This is the perfect stance; at least it has been in other situations like this. Yet in truth, I've never been in a situation quite like *this*. Big's mass changes the physics.

"I just want to talk to him about a girl. She's supposedly his girlfriend. Her name is Amanda Crow. You know her?"

The sound of Amanda's name perks Big up. "*Sweet* thing," he says. His eyes seem coated with a sickening sheen. I half expect him to drool.

Still, he seems on the verge of detonation.

"So. You *do* know her."

"Why should I tell *you* anything? I don't like your smart-ass mouth. And I don't like how you think everything you say is so fuckin' funny."

Once again, I'm unable to stop myself. "Well. I've never really been a disciple of absolutism."

The look on Big's face is priceless. I don't know if he knows that what I just said is meaningless. I don't know if he thinks I've insulted him. But I'm guessing that none of it matters because it feels like what I just said may be the straw that broke the water buffalo's back. And the buffalo is about to make that clear.

"I'm charmed," I say, before Big has a chance to act.

"Huh?"

"I said, *I'm charmed*. You know, as in, *I'm blessed*. As in, *I'm fortunate*; as in… Aw, never mind. No matter how you look at it, I've always been lucky in matters such as these. In fact, I've been on a lucky streak lately. So, believe me when I tell you, I'd really appreciate it if you don't take offense. That would break the streak. Not to mention the mess we'd make. What do you say you just tell me what you know."

I feel it coming a half-second before Big lunges at me. I shift my weight and fire my right leg, the foot pointed like a blade – like kicking a field goal, but without a ball. The energy in my leg is tremendous. Just before my foot makes contact, I take a little off. I don't want to cripple the guy. My boot catches Big square in the groin. The impact stops him in mid-lunge. Air whooshes out of him. He grabs his crotch and slowly bends forward, his skin turning gray. In slow motion, he tumbles forward.

I step back and watch Big go down, a cartoon giant, falling slowly onto his face. When he hits the floor, the floor vibrates and a little cloud of dust rises from the boards.

Everyone in the place freezes. The guys at the bar have their necks craned. The guys at the pool tables are stuck in mid-stroke, their balls rolling to stop.

Big slowly curls over onto his back. A single word wheezes from his pinched lips, said over and over. "Uh, uh, uh, uh..."

I kneel down next to him. "Don't try to move. Just take deep breaths, slow and easy."

Big is a brawler, and I'm guessing he's been kicked in the groin before. No man of his ilk can reach middle age without taking at least one grand slam to the stones.

"The pain will go away in a few minutes," I add.

My words of reassurance are for my sake as much as his. Necessary as the kick was, I didn't like delivering it. The pain from a point-blank groin shot is epic.

Big's eyes are clamped shut and he's still going, "uh, uh," though more quietly now. As he slowly windmills his legs, the bottoms of his shoes scrape back and forth on the floor. The grimace on his face does nothing for my conscience.

I keep my voice low. "Look, I just want to know where Slo-Mo is, that's all. I mean the guy no harm. I want to ask him about the girl. She's gone missing. Anything you can tell me would be helpful."

Big looks at me and says, "uh."

I wait.

The big man has a look of genuine surprise on his face – like it's been a while since anyone has bested him like this. He raises his hand and, with a finger the size of a bratwurst, makes a *come here* gesture.

Of course, I do not *come here*. In fact, I take a step back, out of the range of his long, powerful arms. If I was closer, he could easily sweep me onto the floor. And on the floor with Big is a place I never want to be.

"Slo-Mo," he whispers. "Ianucci."

"Yes," I say. "Vinnie Ianucci."

"Dish," he says, gulping air into his lungs.

"Dish?" I repeat.

Big makes no attempt to get up. He shakes his head a few times, looks at me, and says, "Dis...appeared."

I see relief in Big's eyes – the pain is starting to leave, and he doesn't look menacing any more. In fact, lying on the floor he looks like an immense child, eyelids fluttering as he holds back tears.

"Tell me," I say.

Big gulps air spasmodically, then nods. "Haven't seen Vinnie. More than a week. He usually comes in about every day.

Word's out…" Big pauses. "Somethin's up."

Vinnie Ianucci. Now *he's* missing, too?

"Cops are lookin'," Big wheezes. "Even his mom's been in here askin' for him. Why din't you just axe me?"

Big moves like he wants to get up, then gives up.

"What else?" I say.

When he shakes his head his bulbous cheeks wobble and the tips of his greasy hair swoosh on the floor. He's done.

To hell with this.

I turn from the fallen mammoth and head for the green door. Halfway there I stop and turn. Big is still on his back, his massive torso ballooning into the air. No one has come to help him.

He stares at the ceiling.

"Why do they call him Slo-Mo?" I ask.

Big seems to be struggling with the notion of giving me anything else, even answering a question as simple as this. But then he winces and says, "We say 'Slow-Mo' cuz he move so smooth."

Big rolls onto his side, then works hard to get himself up on one knee. It's something to watch. For a few seconds he stays like that, sucking air, head bowed, black hair hanging.

Not particularly pleased with myself, I leave.

9

The Driver

The Driver glances down at Rosalie Tam, calmly exits the kitchen, passes through the living room and goes down the stairs. As he goes, he takes a pair of latex gloves from his back pocket and, with grace born of practice, stretches the gloves onto his massive, waxy hands.

A flick of a wall switch illuminates a partially finished rec room. Big TV. Oversized L-shaped couch. Overstuffed chair. Coffee table with a PlayStation and a bunch of games.

The Driver smiles. He wonders if the games have been untouched since the night the little woman learned her husband was dead. Or maybe they're evidence that Rosalie found a way to escape her pain.

He goes into an area with cement walls. Furnace. Hot water heater. Two bicycles. One lawnmower. The door to the backyard. The Driver opens the door and sets the stop against the piston on the screen door to hold it open. In doing so, he allows the night, his dark companion, to enter Jonathan and Rosalie Tam's house.

As The Driver retraces his steps, the night slips in behind him. He goes back upstairs, strolls past the body and exits the house through the side door. He walks up the driveway to his truck, starts it and deftly backs it into the driveway, stopping close to Rosalie's car. The Driver shuts the truck off, goes to the rear and slides the big overhead door up carefully, keeping noise to a minimum. He climbs into the box, takes a rolled-up rug from the corner, tosses it to the driveway and puts a roll of duct tape in his pocket. He jumps down and hefts the rug over his shoulder. Walking behind the house so no one will see, he re-enters the basement through the propped-open door.

In the kitchen, he unrolls the rug on the floor. Without effort, he lifts Rosalie Tam's limp body onto the rug and rolls her up in it. He tapes the rug, stands and slings it over his shoulder, and retraces his steps through the basement and across the backyard. At the truck, he simply shrugs his shoulder and Rosalie Tam rolls into the empty cargo box.

The Driver passes through the fenced-in yard for the final time. He releases the stop on the piston, locks the back door and goes up to the kitchen. He retrieves the digital camera and hits the review button. A picture appears – Rosalie Tam at the kitchen table, staring up at him, stunned.

Using the pictures for reference, The Driver puts everything back the way it was when he arrived. He notices that a magnetized notepad has slid down the refrigerator door to the bottom edge. He slides the notepad up, matching it to where it is in the picture.

The Driver picks up his glass of water and drinks. He then washes the glass, dries it, puts it back, puts the dishtowel away.

He looks everywhere, comparing everything he sees to what's in the pictures.

He makes a minor adjustment to a chair.

Everything is now as it was.

To confirm he's left no evidence, The Driver does a walk-through, turning off lights as he goes. He leaves a lamp on in the bedroom. Leaves the outside lights on.

The Driver grabs a cluster of keys from a hook, goes out the side door and locks it. The house at 16 Green Meadow Lane is precisely as it was an hour ago, minus one item.

The Driver climbs into the cargo box, removes the lid from the secret compartment, unrolls the rug, slides Rosalie inside. He's careful to position her body such that she'll be able to breathe, despite the inevitable panic when she wakes.

The Driver screws the lid in place. He turns on the cargo box interior lights, jumps down, reaches under the truck's tailgate and flicks a switch. Accompanied by the rhythmic whirring of a hydraulic pump, two steel ramps slowly extend outward from under the back of the truck.

When the ramps are in place, the pump shuts off. The Driver crams himself into Rosalie's Mini Cooper, starts it, leans his head out the window and hits the gas. The little car zips up the ramp and bounces into the cargo box. He puts the car in park, sets the e-brake, gets out, sets chocks in front of, and behind, the two rear wheels.

The Driver hesitates. Goes through a mental checklist. Certain he hasn't forgotten anything, he clicks off the interior lights and pulls down the overhead door. He slides the locking arm into place, clips the padlock on, slams it home, then hits the button to retract the ramps.

When he's behind the wheel of the truck, he pulls off the latex gloves, puts them in a ziplock bag, starts the diesel and slowly pulls out of the driveway.

With its cargo secured, the truck chugs up the incline and out of the cul-de-sac, a large lumbering machine fading into the shadows of an empty street.

Illuminated briefly by a lone streetlamp, the truck turns left and vanishes into the night.

10

The Finding Man

It's rough inside the cove. Wind rips the rain in sheets across the bay. Waves slam against the shore. My head pounds with doomsday thoughts – missing children, whole families burned alive.

I'm having a cup of coffee when the phone rings. I hope it's Paula. I need to commune with someone who can allay my fears for the lot of us.

But no. It's Ray Driscoll.

"Snowman," he says.

"Ray," I say.

"I got something that's gonna throw a monkey wrench into the idea that Slo-Mo might have taken Amanda to Florida."

As I absorb the darkness in Ray's voice, the movie screen in my head blooms open like an umbrella. On the flat screen, across a vast granite plateau, an endless line of people march single-file toward a cliff.

"All right," I say. "What have you got for me?"

"For you," Ray gives me a long pause, "...I've got a corpse."

My heart sinks. In my head a teenage girl walks off the cliff. "Amanda Crow?" I say.

"No. Vinnie Ianucci. Won't know how long he's been dead till the coroner's report. Body was found in an empty building over on the river, next to that dump where he played pool. The Corner Pocket."

As my heart rate slows to normal, I say Amanda's name again.

"There's no sign of her," he says. "Sorry, bud. But that doesn't mean..."

"Any indication she might have been with him?"

"Lotta footprints, like there was some kind of scuffle, but..."

"You have a cause of death?" I ask.

"It's not official but... Looks like someone tried to cut his head off. It ain't pretty. There was blood everywh—"

"I'm good, Ray!"

I imagine Ray's look. *If you can't take the heat...*

"If Amanda Crow *was* there," Ray says. "She either killed him, or knows who did."

He hangs up.

I look out the starboard salon window. Beyond Bullock's Island there's a field of brown grass that ends at a stand of trees. Through the trees, I see the glint of the Greene River as it churns through its final turn before rolling under an old, iron bridge and then tumbling off a shelf into the cove. A cloud of mist hovers in the air above the place where fresh and saltwater meet.

I get a chill. Fifteen miles away, that same river flows past The Corner Pocket, where they found Slo-Mo's body. With the chill come troubling thoughts. I have faith, but does that mean I may actually believe in God? Since Sabrina's murder, I don't know about Him. But I do know something about faith – mine is in revenge.

My father died a month before Sabrina was born. It was around then that my 'daydreams' started. They could happen during class, while playing a game, or even in the middle of a conversation. Suddenly, it was as if I was in two places at the same time: here, and some other place where information seemed to flow over, around and through me. In that other place, I was encircled by hundreds of people, each of them whispering information only I was meant to hear.

The sheer volume of information was impossible to process. Occasionally, all of it would coalesce into something like a film, an old-time movie flickering in the theater of my mind. Sometimes the film played forward, other times backward. Sometimes it played inside-out, as if the images had been imprinted on the inside of an ice cream cone, and the cone was unraveling.

When the information stopped flowing, when I came back from that other place, I would 'know' things – a friend's grade *before* he took the test; the name of the player who would commit an error in a Red Sox game yet to be played. I began to brag about my 'knowings'. There was a buzz about me at school.

I shouldn't have boasted about my 'gift'. But using it made others notice me, and I liked the attention. I felt the subtle current of power. I also felt guilty. If I could tell my friends when a pop quiz was coming, why couldn't I warn my mother her refrigerator was about to die? I guess I was afraid she'd think there was something wrong with me. I figured if she didn't know about my gift, it wouldn't matter. Which was true, until the day it did.

Sitting in the stands at a softball game, it felt as if the seat dropped out from underneath me as I fell into that other place. This time I got a movie. Mom and I were in it.

We're at a butcher shop. When Mom rings a bell on the counter, Mr White, the principal of my school, appears out of nowhere. When Mom asks for hamburger, he smiles, turns on a fan and leans his face against its grille. As the wind makes Mr White's hair fly, he gives a big smile. Then he turns on a meat grinder, forms a big O with his mouth and jams his left thumb into the whirling blades. There's screaming, lots of blood, and Mr White isn't smiling anymore.

Showing off the next day, I told my friends that our principal would be coming to school with a bandage on his hand. They didn't believe me. But they changed their tune when Mr White showed up a week later with a cast on his left hand and wrist.

It wasn't long before we learned the real story.

Mr White had been driving in his car, windows down, air blowing through the car, left hand hanging out the window. Coming from the opposite direction, a pickup truck drifted into the middle of the road. As the two vehicles whizzed past each other, only inches apart, the truck's mirror smashed into Mr White's hand.

Some bones in his hand were broken. His thumb was so badly injured, a nurse said it "looked like it had been put through a meat grinder".

The buzz got louder. The school's biggest bully started calling me a freak and pushing me around, so I figured it was time to stop talking about my gift. I did, and the bullying stopped.

The daydreams didn't.

Like this one:

It's summer. My sister and I are walking on a dirt road in the country. The sun reflects off Sabrina's long hair – gold, with slashes of red. She's laughing, and her eyes dance with green lights. There are a million freckles on her face.

Black clouds fill the sky. A frantic wind skitters across the road toward us, gathering into a column. When the tornado overcomes us, I call Sabrina's name, but my voice is swallowed by the wind.

After the storm passes, a body is found in the middle of a cornfield a hundred miles away. The child is covered in mud.

For some reason, I felt a strong urge to tell my mother about the dream, but did not.

Two weeks later, Sabrina disappeared on her way home from school. She was last seen walking into the woods, on a shortcut that leads to our house.

I burst into tears when I told my mother about the vision. Crying, hugging me, she told me not to worry. Sabrina would be coming home soon.

I don't think she understood.

For two days, while police, firemen, Mom and half the town searched for my sister, I sat in my room with the blinds drawn, my eyes squeezed so tight they hurt. I prayed and prayed for a happier vision to come, but all I saw in my head were those dark clouds.

On the third day, in a town fifteen miles away, in the middle of a cornfield, a farmer found a body, covered in mud.

My sister's killer was never found.

11

Mooney

After hanging up with Ray, I go to the galley, make myself a fresh cup of coffee, then head out to the afterdeck. Just as I'm settling into my deckchair, I notice Beatrice Bullock in her ancient Volvo coming slowly across the iron bridge. After crossing the gravel lot at about 3 mph, she guides her beloved wagon into her designated parking spot with the infinite care of a surgeon inserting a shunt.

Paralus – formerly named *The Beatrice B*, back when Beatrice's husband was the owner – is docked directly across from Mrs Bullock's parking spot, so I have a clear view of her doing what she always does after she parks. Nothing. Before she exits her car, she sits for two minutes. Every time. I know, because I've timed her. When those 120 seconds are up, she gets out, removes her shopping bags and begins the arduous ascent of the steep, painfully long front stairs with the black iron railings. The staircase connects the parking lot with the huge porch that encircles the Bullock house, high above the lot.

I can only assume she sits in her car to catch her breath and gather her strength before taking on the one hundred and thirty-eight steps that will deliver her to her front door.

As always, I'm struck by the sight of this slight woman, plastic bags hanging from each clenched fist as, step by cautious step, she ascends the gray granite hulk known as Bullock's Island.

I have, on two occasions, exited *Paralus* and gone to meet her at the base of the steps. I've offered to take her bags, to assist her up the stairs. Both times she thankfully, and adamantly, refused. "The day I can't make it up these damn stairs that my husband built with his own two hands? That's the day I'm done living."

In the years since I moved onboard *Paralus* I've gotten to know Beatrice Bullock, and I know she takes pride in her iconic house. I often wonder what possessed her great-grandfather to build it atop such an immense granite ledge. To this day, the house is accessible only by the stairs that Hiram built. She's also proud that she's the only Rhode Island resident in possession of her own bridge. Her great-grandfather built that, too. Spanning the Greene River, the bridge replaced the original wooden structure that was little more than a raft.

Built in 1819, the Bullock house is known to locals as 'The Captain of the Cove'. Destroyed by fire in 1923, the 'Captain' was reconstructed to exceed the heaviest standards of the day and deemed strong enough to withstand weather and time alike.

I get out of my deckchair, go to the railing and watch Mrs Bullock until she's safely established inside her home. Relieved that she's made it yet again, I take in my surroundings.

Fifty yards beyond *Paralus'* blunt bow, an old dock, a crumbling finger of decaying wood, juts out into the cove. Beyond the dock, the beach curves gracefully eastward for a thousand yards, then ends in a promontory of sand and rock. Behind the beach, Smithson Park, a forest dense with pine trees and scrub oak, stretches all the way to Narragansett Bay, the second largest body of water on the east coast.

Behind me, off my transom, I have a clear view of Bullock's Marina – outbuildings, boats and docks. C dock, the longest, is the nearest to me. Out at its end, Mooney's shack.

A professional race boat driver, Mooney thinks nothing of blasting across the water at speeds that would make most of us weep. When not racing, Mooney stays in his little house, reading books or working out, or whatever the hell else he does in there. If he's not racing, if he's not at home, he's hunting – a wolf, in search of the child killers.

Mooney is obsessed in the way the Jewish Nazi Hunters were obsessed. He will go anywhere, do anything, in pursuit of deviants. It is for this reason, and a few others, that we've developed a kind of animal synergy.

Because I understand Mooney – because I know how quickly his blood can boil – I think carefully before requesting his assistance. To say Mooney lacks restraint would be an egregious misuse of the word 'lack'. In his day-to-day life, he respects the law and those who enforce it. But when tracking down a pedophile or a child killer, the idea that only public officials should enforce the law goes out the window.

Mooney's eyes are black bullets. His face is a nightmare of gouges, scars and what looks like permanent bruising – gifts from his father, The Psycho. I've never known anyone who, upon their first meeting, wasn't frightened by Mooney.

He grew up in a rotting trailer parked in the woods of western West Virginia, miles from any town. A prisoner until the age of fifteen, he didn't attend school and rarely saw anyone other than his mother and father.

His parents valued him no more than a lawnmower or a set of used tires. As a kid, the abuse was limited to a slap or the occasional kick in the butt. But when he was twelve, Mooney's mother died of a 'strange illness'. After his father dumped her body into the swamp behind their trailer, the abuse escalated. Mooney told me he could have taken the beatings, if not for the belt – toward the end, his father began whipping him with it, sometimes hitting him in the face with the buckle.

One day when Mooney was fourteen, he found his father passed out drunk in the shed behind the house. Mooney saw his chance. He took his father's rifle from the bedroom closet, went to the shed and put a bullet through his father's head.

Because of his age, because of the severity of the abuse, Mooney's sentence was to become a ward of the state, placed with a foster family. He did okay, though he was painfully silent. After two years, for reasons unknown to him, he was removed and placed with new parents; a much older couple. Touched by the sadness in the boy's dark eyes and by the horror carved into his face, the new parents offered Mooney something he'd never experienced. Love.

Mooney was bright and furiously curious. Though far behind in grade levels, he excelled in school and avoided trouble. Because of his appearance, most kids stayed clear of him anyway, with one exception. A hulking, sullen brute of a boy named Buddy taunted Mooney about his scars, calling him Leatherface. Each time, Mooney walked away without saying a word. Then one day, Buddy grabbed Mooney by the shoulders and spun him around. Before Buddy could speak, Mooney head butted the bully, knocking him onto his back. Mooney calmly positioned himself on top of Buddy's chest and proceeded to beat the bully's face to ruin.

Soon thereafter, Mooney's foster parents decided to move. Perhaps they feared retaliation for the severe beating their son had given Buddy. Or maybe they feared something about their foster son. Whatever the reason, they wound up in Rhode Island.

At the age of twenty-nine, after both parents passed away in the same year, Mooney moved into the former fuel shed at the end of C dock, Bullock's longest. He stocked it to the roof with provisions and didn't come out for weeks.

Three years after Mooney settled in, I met Beatrice Bullock by chance. After several conversations, I convinced her to let me buy her husband's abandoned tugboat. She sold it to me for one dollar.

Viewing the world through the ruptured lens of his childhood, Mooney has a unique radar for individuals who get off on hurting others. He is particularly attuned to the deviants. Given a free pass, he'd kill them all. The desire for revenge is burned into Mooney's soul – it's the anchor in his life, and the umbilical the bonds us.

12

Amanda

A thump wakes Amanda. Still in darkness, every inch of her aches, and the pressure in her head is tremendous. After hours of constant restraint, her mind has retreated into a place of numbed horror.

But the thumping stirs a memory. Nine years old. A family vacation on Bock Island. Her father rented a boat and they casually motored around the island. The ocean swells were so long and luxurious, the rise and fall of the boat made her and Annie feel drowsy. They went into the cabin, lay together on a bunk, pulled a blanket over themselves and fell asleep, their arms and legs entwined.

A boat.

Oh, my God! *I'm on a boat!*

Amanda gets sick to her stomach.

Please, God. Don't let me get sick!

Amanda does the only thing she can. She wills herself to stay calm, to breathe.

And the boat thumps.
And the boat rolls.
And Amanda Crow breathes.

13

Rosalie

Rosalie Tam awakes to the stench of rot and decay. Lying in a fetal position, her hair is matted in filth and her clothes are damp. Drool leaks from her mouth. When she tries to move, every muscle screams.

In the distance, the hollow echo of water dripping.

Rosalie feels a point of pain in her shoulder. *The needle! Oh God, he drugged me!*

The memory of the needle makes her nauseous. She rolls over to her other side, inducing more pain. Stomach lurching, lungs pulling air, she feels the damp, musty mixture of mud and grit against her cheek. Rosalie rolls onto her back and groans.

That man! He was huge! And the skin on his hands stretched so thin, she could almost see the bones. Through a haze of pain, she vaguely remembers being lifted onto the big man's shoulder.

Rosalie works herself into a sitting position and looks around. It's dark, the only illumination a narrow strip of dingy light beneath what might be a door. As her eyes begin to adjust, she sees shapes.

A jolt of panic shocks her. *What is this place?*

Rosalie gulps the fetid air and chokes off a sob. She tries to scream, to plead for someone to help her, but no sound comes out.

Think!

She squints into the darkness, wills herself to see.

Why me? I have nothing!

Maybe he meant to take someone else. That's it! This is a mistake! But no. He called her on the phone. He knew her name. He knew about the accident. About Jon's death.

This is no mistake. He wanted me!

Panic crawls inside Rosalie's chest. She feels it reaching up into her throat.

You have to stay calm!

Rosalie works up more saliva in her mouth. She swallows, whispers, "You have to figure out where you are. C'mon. You can do this."

Hearing her own voice gives Rosalie comfort.

Emboldened, she tries speaking again.

"Hello?"

She works herself onto her hands and knees. Palms planted, she settles her butt into the dirt. She feels like a wet dog, sitting on its haunches.

This time it bursts from her. "*HELLO!*"

She waits.

But there is only the water…drip…drip…drip…

Rosalie's eyes fully adjust. She's in a room, the size of a small bedroom. The walls are rough, like concrete. The floor is dust and gravel, muddy in places.

On the nearest wall, there's a kind of platform held up by chains bolted to the wall. Like a cot in an old jail! She reaches out, touches its metal frame. It's cold.

Atop the cot, there's a coarse blanket over a thin mattress. Rosalie runs her hand along the blanket – even this is damp. She yanks her hand away. *"Please! God!"*

With great effort, Rosalie stands. Too weak, she immediately sits on the edge of the cot. She tilts her head back and looks up. The ceiling seems far away. In its center, one naked, unlit bulb, hanging by a single, crooked wire. She searches for a switch, but there's not enough light to see.

Rosalie looks around the cruddy, dirt floor. In a corner, a square wooden stool with four legs, a round hole cut in the middle. Underneath the stool, a dark shadow.

"Oh, my God," Rosalie says. "That's a toilet." Her stomach heaves.

Now she sees that the entire floor slopes toward the hole – anything liquid will flow into it.

Bile burns the back of Rosalie's throat.

There's something else, to the right of the toilet, in the far corner. A pile of…what? Are those blankets? Even though Rosalie is shivering, the thought of wrapping herself in one of them repulses her.

Now Rosalie can see that it *is* a door on the right wall, above the dingy crack of light. She stands and shuffles over to it. She yells, but her voice is cracked, and what comes out sounds nothing like words. "Somebody please help me!"

Rosalie is so weak, she's afraid she'll collapse. When she reaches the door, she grabs a long metal bar. She holds on and breathes. Legs quivering, she inspects the door. It's made of heavy wood planks. The bar is some kind of brace. The door looks bombproof.

There's no handle. This confirms it. Rosalie is a prisoner.

Rosalie leans her back against the door and slides down to the floor. She buries her face in her hands and screams: "*What do you want from me?*"

She feels something like...*pressure*...as if she's being encapsulated by a great weight. The room seems to be shrinking, the walls grinding inward toward her.

Her body is telling her: *she's underground!*

She wails as her composure bursts. "Help! Help me! Somebody help me! Get me out of here! Let me go! I haven't done anything to you! Let me out of here right now YOU SON-OF-A-BITCH!"

Rosalie screams until her voice gives out and her anger runs dry. Face covered in tears and mucus, she straightens her back and runs her fingers through her hair. Using the corner of her blouse, she dries her face as best she can. She stands, staggers back to the cot and slumps onto the soggy mattress.

Defeated.

She looks again at the pile of blankets. *Something about their shape.* She stares for a while, then leaves the dampness of the cot and moves cautiously toward the mound. Close to it, she hesitates. Then she reaches out with an unsteady hand. As she inches closer to the pile, her right foot slides in a puddle of something slippery.

Oh my God, the stench!

She smells something else. *Rank body odor.* Rosalie's heart pounds. *There's someone under there!*

"Hello?" she says, almost a whisper. "Hello?"

Rosalie closes her eyes. As she reaches forward, she starts to cry.

She hears breathing, slow and faint.

Mere inches separate her trembling hand from…who can it be?

The breathing.

The smell.

Almost there, Rosalie turns her head to the side, reaches out blindly and touches it.

Beneath the coarse fabric, she senses mass, energy, warmth. Slowly moving her hand, she encounters roundness. A shoulder?

Part of her fears a response, yet again she speaks. "Hello?" She squeezes, gently, then inches her hand further until she thinks she's touching an arm, then an elbow, then a wrist.

Rosalie can't bring herself to touch the hand.

Going back to the shoulder, she folds the blanket away from the body. It's on its side. Again, she touches the arm, then moves across to the chest. Rosalie's hand encounters something resilient and soft. *A breast.*

Rosalie moves her hand to the throat. Even though the woman is warm, the skin at her neck is cold and clammy. Rosalie feels the pulsing of blood. The heartbeat is slow, but it's strong.

With both hands, Rosalie grasps the shoulders and rolls the woman onto her back. She leans closer, trying to see the face in the near-dark.

"Can you hear me? Are you all right?" She takes hold of the shoulders again and gently shakes. "Can you hear me? You must wake up. We have to get out of here."

Nothing.

She's been drugged, too.

"Hello?"

Only the breathing.

Brushing aside the woman's thick hair, Rosalie leans in even closer. Again, she's assaulted by the smell. *Vomit.* She gags, spits into her palms, then rubs her hands vigorously on the edge of the blanket.

Keeping her head turned away from the hideous breath, Rosalie gives the body a name. She turns, sits and leans her back against Lilly.

14

Back to Big

Tonight, The Corner Pocket is packed. Pool players crowd each table. People mill about everywhere. Men and women at the bar, equal parts sullen, indisposed, hammered. Smoke. Drink. Kill time. Repellent odors – stale beer, scorched cigarettes, unwashed bodies. Only the jungle-sweet smell of the ganja entices.

The air writhes. My lungs ache.

Bodies move through whirlpools of smoke. If not for the twenty-foot ceilings and the sheer immensity of the space, people would asphyxiate and drop like flies. By what miracle has this dump retained its liquor license?

The energy is nerve-racking. Cue sticks slam into cue balls. Cue balls rocket into racks. Sounds like gunshots above the clamor and din. Everyone is *shouting!*

Driven by giant speakers hanging from chains attached to girders, the hip-hop music insults, threatens, degrades. The bass is so powerful, my internal organs tremble.

I get a shock when my eyes adjust to the gloom: Big, up

on the dais. I chose to come back at night because I assumed he worked days. Yet there he sits. I wonder how many guys it took to get him off the floor.

I expect him to react swiftly. Maybe pull a gun or come swinging at me with a bat. Instead he stares. I approach, staring back.

I stop a few yards short of his perch. Wait a few beats. Big doesn't move. Like everyone else, I have to shout.

"*How you doing?*"

Big cups a hand behind a large ear.

I move closer, get louder. "How you *doing*?"

Big gives a single nod. "What do you want?"

I don't get it. Big is acting like we're just a couple of guys. Like, maybe we could hang out for a while, talk sports, tell bathroom jokes, women jokes, women in bathrooms jokes. Big exudes no menace, which is baffling.

"I need to talk with you," I say. "I've been asked to help out with the Slo-Mo thing."

His expression says he doesn't hear me. When he bends forward, I catch the movement as his hand slips under the lip of the podium. "*It's too fucking loud out here!*" he yells.

My guess, Big has pushed a button. Called for reinforcements.

He shouts again, "You wanna talk to me, we can go in the office over there." With this he straightens, jerks a thumb over a shoulder, turns away from me.

Beyond the podium, through the smog, the vague outline of a door. To the right of the door, two large mirrors that look like one-way glass. Anyone on the other side of that wall can oversee the whole place with impunity.

The enigma that is Big expands. Why didn't he push the button the other day? Today, why didn't he come down and clock me as soon as I walked through the door? How comes he's acting as if nothing happened? If I want answers, I suppose I'll need to follow him.

Just as I'm deciding to move, a skinny kid comes skulking around the corner. He looks up at Big, a question on his face.

Big says, "Watch the front for a few."

The kid's wearing a cheap, rumpled T-shirt, filthy jeans just barely hanging off his hips and $300 sneakers. Hollow cheeks, unhealthy skin, unshaven face. Little dents and clefts from acne. On his exposed arms, a half-dozen dark spots, each perfectly round, the size of a pencil eraser. *Cigarette burns.*

"You got it, Boss," the kid says as he steps up onto the raised platform to take the watch. When he passes Big, his eyes avert and his body subtly tilts away.

Turning his back to me, Big sweeps his arm and gestures toward the door – the perfect gentleman. I step up on the platform, walk past the shell-shocked kid. I hesitate at the door. What's waiting inside?

I hold my breath and step past Big. Inside the dimly lit room, I breathe and immediately wish I had not. The reek of incinerated nicotine is even stronger in here than out in the bar. The room is a torture chamber.

I was right. Through two large picture windows on the wall, I can see almost every inch of The Corner Pocket.

Opposite the windows, an ugly green metal desk. Military salvage sale? Piles of papers scattered all over. In the middle of this mountain of paper is the biggest ashtray I've ever seen. An upside-down hubcap overflowing with cigarette butts, cigar stubs, and filled with five pounds of ash.

Two grimy couches and a bunch of wood and metal chairs form a semicircle in front of the desk. Apparently, meetings are held here.

Big goes behind the desk and lowers himself into what looks like a custom-made leather captain's chair. Despite being beefed up, the chair groans under Big's hundreds of pounds.

"Take a seat," he says, gesturing at the semicircle.

"Sure," I say. I choose the metal chair, the one least likely to transfer bacteria.

Big leans back, folds his huge hands over his huge belly, seems pleased with himself. Maybe he feels superior, having let me off the hook.

I'm baffled. "What's your name?" I ask.

"Tony," he says. "My peeps call me Tons."

Of course they do.

"My name is William Snow. I'm not with the cops, but I am helping with a police investigation. It's informal. I'm looking into Vinnie Ianucci's death."

Big puts his hand up. He leans so far forward, the leather creaks like hide being peeled from a carcass.

"The heat was all over it this morning. You'd a thought there was some kinda national security breach over here. One of the cops was your buddy, Driscoll. He grills everybody. Then, just before he leaves, he takes me to the side, tells me to be expecting you." Tony gives me a conspiratorial nod. "Wants me to know who you was. Like, who you *really* was."

"Driscoll," I say, nodding. But I have no idea what he's talking about. I can't wait to hear what Driscoll thinks I *really was*.

Big's face erupts into a murderous grin. "Turns out, we're sorta connected, you and me."

Then it dawns on me. Tony 'Tons' has learned something about me he can brag to his peeps. Something that feels like fame.

"And how is it that we're sorta connected?"

Big's grin could turn your insides to jello. "You remember that dago spic bastard, what's-his-name? Dominic A-yoyo? The wetback you jammed a few years ago that was pokin' them little kids in the projects? Thanks to you, he's in the slam."

I will never forget Domingo Arroyo.

"The heat was hatin' on you like a motherfucker. Hated it was you that busted A-yoyo. Found him usin' that psychic shit a yours. You made the blues look like fools. That was somethin' else."

"Yeah," I say. Arroyo kidnapped two boys and locked them in his cellar. Committed despicable acts. When I got involved, the media distorted things. Made me look like a psychic nut. Portrayed the cops as bumbling idiots. It was rough, but I have a choice memory – the looks on the cops' faces when the boys and their parents were reunited.

Big is worked up. "He was the fuck that capped Dodo. And Dodo and me was good from the get. After Dodo was hit, me and my guys looked all over for A-yoyo. But that dude was gone. Hadn't been for you, he would've stayed gone. So now, *thanks to you*," Big points at me with a giant finger, "A-yoyo is upstate doin' his bit, gettin' butt-banged every day by the soul brothers." Big winks. "Everybody know A-yoyo hate them blacks."

I say nothing.

"Anyways, you gettin' this squared out, man? You the one zeroed my bud's killer. *You da man.*" Big lights up with what just might be genuine pleasure.

I take a moment to process his understanding of the concept of karma, of cosmic balance and its enmeshment in the gears of our lives. It kind of weirds me out to think that Big's take on Arroyo isn't all that different from mine.

Big goes on. "Because you put that skeezball away, you get the Tony Tons pass." He holds up a single, fat finger. "But hear me. I'm talkin' just this one pass for you, my man. *One.*" Big gives me his no-bullshit face – eyes withdrawn behind overhanging brow, mouth slack and partly open, black gaps between yellowing teeth.

When Big sees the look of wariness on my face, he says, "This is how it is. The other day, you made me look bad in front of all them assholes out there. But then I hear from Driscoll how you put Dodo's killer away? And then tonight, you come walkin' through my front door, bold as fuckin' brass? You no longer just some motherfucker kicked me in the stones, brotha. You the man put Dodo's killer on ice."

I nod.

"Wasn't for that, you'd already be folded inside a drum at the bottom of the bay."

"Understood," I say. "I have to ask you about Slo-Mo and his girlfriend, Amanda Crow."

Big is still smiling, making a little too much of his magnanimity. "Ask away," he says.

Just as Big says this, I hear a change in the muffled sounds coming from the pool room below us. Something's happening down there.

Big notices, too. He gets out of his chair and rumbles over to the window. Curious, I join him.

A guy at one of the tables is enraged. He's shouting expletives and holding his cue like he's going to throw it. He does. Launches it across the room, barely missing several people's heads. The cue smashes against the wall and breaks in half. The guy spins around, storms off down a short hallway under a 'Restrooms' sign and disappears into the men's.

We watch as the angry guy's opponent saunters over to the broken cue stick and picks the two pieces off the floor. He carefully fits them together, holds them in both hands and goes to a wall rack. He turns his head around and looks nervously in the direction of the mirrors, as if he's unsure about whether he's being watched.

Still holding the cue as if it's been magically restored, he places it into an open slot carefully, making sure it doesn't fall apart. He again glances in our direction. Convinced he's pulled it off, he goes to a coat rack and snatches his jacket off a hook.

Big goes back to his desk, picks up the phone, mumbles something and hangs up. When I try to speak, he holds up a meaty hand.

We go back to the window. The pool room has gone quiet, and four hard-looking men have appeared out of nowhere. Two of them are dragging someone out of the men's room – the guy who threw the cue stick. The other two have their hands on the guy who grabbed his coat. The four men quickly hustle the two pool players past the bar and out a back door. Play at the tables resumes as if nothing has happened.

I'm stunned that anyone would care that much about a broken cue. I look up at Big. "All that over a broken cue stick?"

"Doesn't have nothing to do with no broke stick," Big says. "It's about respect. Guy breaks my cue and he owns up to it? We're good. But he breaks somethin' a mine and tries to walk the fuck outa here?" Big's single headshake says it all. "Not gonna happen, brotha."

I don't want to know any more.

We go back to our chairs.

"How well did you know Vinnie, Slo-Mo, whatever you call him?"

Big settles in his chair. "Slo-Mo been comin' here for years. A regular. Always pay his tab. Never start no trouble. But don't nobody push him, either. Most guys know, you don't mess with that boy. Of course, I only know him from in here." Big jerks a thumb over his shoulder, indicating the world outside. "Don't know nothing 'bout what he do when he's out there."

"You mean," I say, "what he *did* when he was out there."

Big's face goes cold. He does not like to be corrected.

"Like I *say*, he's been coming in here a few years. Seems like he got a new quif every week, you get my drift? Has hisself a sheet, did a little time in the local joint. But from what I seen lately, he's been toning it down, working things out. What I'm sayin' is, he didn't want to be gettin' no more housing invitations from the county. You feel me?"

No matter the subject, when Big talks, it's pure aggression. His is a perpetual anger; lids that never blink; brow bones that protrude; eyes so black, they make sensors fire off in your brain.

"Not everyone come outa the joint in one piece like he did, so I guess Slo-Mo figure he didn't wanna be pushin' on Murphy's Law. Bottom line, he was a solid soldier findin' his groove. About six months ago, he start bringin' in that young quif."

"Amanda?"

"You don't gotta be a shrink to know they was tight. She was a step up for him. Everyone could see that."

Big likes the sound of his own voice, which is fine with me for now. I want him to keep going. "What did you think of her?"

"What'd I *think*?"

Oh, oh.

Big seems schizophrenic. With little or no provocation, he's shifting back and forth between engaging and threatening. Right now, his anger is evident. I get the feeling he either hates my questions, or me.

Big blinks. "I'll tell you what I *think*. I think she was the sweetest young thing I ever met. She come in here with Slo-Mo a few times before her pops died. Always quiet. Respectful. Had these peaceful *eyes*, man. Like, you could see down inside that she was *good*, you know what I'm saying? She wasn't running no game like most of them that comes in here."

When Big's voice drops down, his words sound like stones rolling in an iron pot.

"After her pops got killed, she started dressing tough, acting tough. You know. But she didn't fool me. She was just a little girl, scared about what life was gonna be like without her pops. She needed someone to step up and take care of her. Protect her. She was a *good* girl."

Hmm.

89

"So," I say, "the two of them got along fine? Is that what you're saying?"

Big's eyes nail me. "They never had no beefs, far as I know."

"What did you think when you heard Slo-Mo's body had been found right next door? What about the cops treating Amanda as a suspect?"

Big looks like he might snap. "That's a load of steamin' *horseshit!* Amanda no more killed Vinnie than I just opened a weight loss clinic in the back room. Cops. What the fuck is wrong with them? There's somethin' about Vinnie's murder those dumb dicks just don't get. But hey, they don't wanna hear nothin' from me, so fuck 'em."

"What do you have to say?" I ask.

Big tilts further forward in his chair. "What do I have to say? *Me?*"

As I try to imagine what insight he's about to share, Big drops his voice down and surprises me. "He say he love her."

I wait.

Big snorts. "Slo-Mo *say* he love her, but he don't know shit about love."

And with the big man's sarcasm, my take on certain key elements of this case begins to shift. Big is saying that Vinnie Ianucci made it known he loved Amanda Crow, but Big didn't buy it. Not only did he not buy it, he didn't like seeing Slo-Mo stringing Amanda along.

From what I've learned so far about Amanda Crow, for her to commit an act of extreme violence would be as unlikely as Big doing a backflip. Somebody else took Slo-Mo's head off, and Amanda saw it happen. I'm certain the killer abducted Amanda.

Given that I'm also feeling she's alive right now, all of this begs the question, *why is she alive?* Maybe Ianucci's killer doesn't *want* to kill her. Maybe he hasn't been able to do it. At least, not yet anyway. The obvious reason for this would be that the killer has feelings for her.

He love her.

I get a shiver. Could it be *Big?*

But if Big is involved, then other such vague conclusions of mine are way off point. What connection could Big have had to Harry Crow before Amanda even met Slo-Mo?

Any normal-thinking person would have a hard time imagining how the death of Vinnie Ianucci, and the abduction of Amanda Crow, could be connected to Harry Crow's accident. It makes no sense, yet that's exactly what my intuition has been telling me the past few days. I'm beginning to feel it in my bones.

Blaming Big would be too easy. Besides, he wouldn't need a knife to take off someone's head. Something's off here. Feels out of synch. Big's voice jars me back into his world. "We're done," he says, anger radiating from him like toxic gas. Time to go.

I say my thanks, but it seems to barely register. Climbing out of his chair, Big looks like a monster.

Outside The Corner Pocket, even the foggy air seems crisp and clean. As I stand by the river, breathing deep to scrub my lungs, a brief scene plays in my head: I'm trapped in Big's office. The door is padlocked, and the ashtray is pumping out funnels of singed gray smoke. With no windows to break, there's no way out.

Just once, I wish I could shut my head off.

I climb the stone stairs, find my way back to my truck.

The next logical thing is the thing I want least to do. Tonight, after The Corner Pocket is closed, I will return to these old brick buildings, go inside and find the place where Vinnie Ianucci bled out, where Amanda Crow was abducted. I will meditate in that place. I will free my mind so it can leave the confines of my body and wander in the dark.

But I must remember to be careful, to not let my mystical wanderings go on for too long. I did that once and wound up in a place that harbored an infinite malevolence. My mind was infected. I came close to melting down.

I can't get one image out of my head: Big, towering over Amanda, his shadow obliterating hers.

15

The Driver

These days, The Driver performs his work with the focus of a neurosurgeon. He does so because he's learned that each minute spent executing his MasterPlan is sixty seconds of anguish, deferred.

In the wake of the tragedy, The Driver's suffering had been intolerable. After arrangements were made for the bodies, he went home, locked the doors, pulled the shades, sat on the living room floor with his drugs and his gun, and didn't move for three days.

On the third day, as he was raising the gun to his temple, God's voice (even though he did not believe in God) filled his darkened house: *As Moses led the Israelites to Canaan, so must you lead your subjects to the compound.* It was then that The Driver came to believe he was an agent of God, a Warrior of Restitution.

Now, when he thought of his family, and his soul became racked with pain, he imagined Moses and the burning bush, and he wept.

To further ease his suffering, The Driver rationalized that (A) if the tragedy hadn't happened, then (B) God wouldn't have induced the epiphany, and (C) without the epiphany, there'd be no MasterPlan, which (D) gave him a reason to go on.

Of course, this train of thought was proof to The Driver that he was insane.

However, every so often he experienced certain moments within moments, tiny slivers of time within which 'normal' thoughts still occurred. These normal thoughts rose up out of some deep vein of gray matter that had somehow escaped infection. But no matter: sane or insane, he was hurtling toward a resolution that nothing on earth could prevent.

16

The Vision

Textile mills once flourished in these three buildings. Now hushed, their cavernous rooms were once filled with sound; the clamor and bustle of the workers; the racking, the thumping, the hissing of the machines; the shouts of the shift bosses, urging production forward. The effect all these people and their machinery had upon these buildings was profound, imprinted into the brickwork from the inside out, more than a hundred years ago.

Today, time and the elements impact these buildings from the outside in. Stirred by river breezes that thread through the open windows and the unlocked doors, brick dust hangs in the musty air. Flakes of paint lie curled upon filthy, wide-planked floors, fragile as the fallen petals from dying flowers. Crumbling mortar dust accumulates in the corners of every empty space. The buildings themselves seem to lean ever more toward the river, as if wearied by their struggle, as if their only desire now is to join with the churning brown waters.

The fact that a pool hall is now the only pulse of life inside the former factory complex seems to add to the gloom, evoking ancient fears long imbedded in our DNA: the unknown; the darkness; *predators*.

On the opposite bank of the river there is another industrial complex, this one thoroughly abandoned long ago, its brick buildings engulfed by massive overgrowth – vegetation gone wild. Vines and bushes and trees have thrust their way into the structures, then grown their way back out again through doors and windows, ceilings and walls. Earth, healing its wounds. As if attempting to escape the suffocating growth, two brick smokestacks reach forlornly toward the sky.

Dark forms lurk beneath the green jungle – evidence that 'the company' once ruled. Loading docks, their wooden frames rotting. The hulk of a massive steel crane, tilted, useless. Rusted, hollowed-out vehicles. A solitary faded yellow bulldozer, a monster of power stilled forever. The overgrown parking lots are fouled with beer bottles and burned-out truck tires.

And garbage. McDonald's, Wendy's, Burger King. Disposable diapers. Cigarette butts. Shredded, black plastic bags, flapping in the breeze. Shredded, white plastic bags, snagged on branches, high in the trees. Human waste, everywhere.

As I stare across the river at the corpse of a once-thriving factory, with the near-dead complex at my back, I feel an encompassing dread. Mists continue to rise like coils of smoke from the surface of the oily, brown river. It's a scene from the apocalypse.

On my side of the river, yellow police tape is strung around the third building on the right. The tape has already been breached in a few places, most likely by kids, curious to see where a homeless guy found a dead guy with his head nearly torn off.

Through a side door, I step into an empty, gutted shell. Most of the interior walls have been ripped apart by thieves scavenging the plumbing and wires for copper. The floors above have long ago collapsed. Aside from the brick walls and the partially collapsed roof, only the interior load-bearing posts remain, like pillars in a bombed-out cathedral.

Dusty shafts of light stab through broken window frames. The place stinks of beer, decay and rot, of human and animal wastes.

In a far corner, a large dark stain saturates the layers of dust on the wooden floor, turning it into thick slurry. Vinnie Ianucci's blood. There's so much, he must have lost every drop. The cops did their work, collected their evidence, but no cleanup crew was called.

Animals will crawl into this building tonight. Hunching over, warily leaning into the pool of congealed blood, their frantic eyes will meet.

In another corner, more piles of dirt, broken glass, shreds of cardboard and a filthy mattress, stuffing poking from ragged vents in its fabric. Next to the mattress there's a dented 55-gallon drum coated with grime. I go to it. The drum and the wall next to it have been blackened by fires. Around the drum, a collection of broken chairs. I imagine homeless people seated around the roaring drum on a freezing winter night. Flames belch above the rim of the makeshift furnace. Shadows dance along the crumbling brick walls. Outside, the winter wind howls.

I twist away from my vision.

I see something on the floor. A broken hypodermic needle, in stark relief atop a dislodged brick.

I've only been inside the building a few minutes, yet already my energy is plummeting. The ether in this space feels saturated with the desperation of lost souls. This is one of my challenges – a liability generated by my ability to perceive the feelings of others, either long gone, here today, or soon to be. As my spirits decline, I have the powerful urge to seek out any outcast, to help any lost soul who would seek to bed down in a lonely place like this.

I'm torn, my emotions at odds. Energy falling, anger rising, my rage directed toward the fates. Why are so many of us destined to fall into hopelessness and despair?

I feel my heart opening.

My mind reels with questions. Why did Amanda Crow and Vinnie Ianucci come to this awful place? Was it for sex? Did he bring her so he could introduce her to drugs? Ianucci lived with his mother, so they couldn't go there. Based on the police estimate of the timeline, it was late at night when they entered. But why didn't they go to Amanda's apartment?

What were they doing when confronted by Ianucci's killer? Why was Slo-Mo slaughtered? According to police profilers, when an act of violence results in a near decapitation, it's almost certain the killer knew his victim.

If Amanda had in fact witnessed the grisly murder, why do I feel her essence, pulsating? I pray I'm not deluded.

Where is Amanda now? With Vinnie Ianucci's killer? What is he doing with her? *To* her?

Forensics went over the area carefully, so I don't expect to find anything. Still, I keep a sharp eye.

I sit in one of the chairs. When the fatigued metal creaks, the hollow sound is amplified in the empty space. I relax, using a technique that drops me into a trance in less than a minute. I locate a small spot on the wall – the head of a nail. I focus on the nail. I breathe deep and slow, counting backward in my head. Within moments the head of the nail is my only awareness. All else falls away.

I feel myself entering the nail, then like osmosis, I pass through the brick wall and float.

And float…

I become the walls, the floor, the sky. I slip further beneath my subconscious, into even more heightened awareness. I am in a state of somnambulism.

A warm bubble of plasma appears. Inside the bubble: letters, numbers, icons. The plasma draws me into it, at the center of pure data; millions of bits of information, spinning around me. As if in response to my wish, the data coalesces into a single point on a screen. This pinpoint of compressed data begins to flower, then blossom into a scene.

It's dark inside the room inside the building inside the mind. Freezing cold. I'm no longer sitting in a chair. I'm crouched in a corner, staring into darkness, emptiness, nothingness.

The ravaged building surrounds me. Through gaping holes in the roof, a star explodes, scorching a jagged pattern across the sky and my retina. Shadows skitter along the walls. A man appears as if he's stepped through a door from another world. He is little more than shape. His back is bent. He's looking for something.

Two dark forms appear to my left. I hear laughter, the clinking of glasses. The man with the bent back turns, moves in the direction of the sounds. Something is dangling from his right hand; I focus my attention on it; a coiled wire with handles at both ends: a garrote.

The bent man's form merges with the other forms.

Chaos. The forms tumble and merge. They move apart, then merge again. A strange odor comes to me, like the friction burn of a dentist's drill.

A girl screams. Her cry fades, as if she's falling down a well.

The chaos ends.

The screaming stops.

The bent man retreats, leaving behind a noxious cloud. Inside the cloud is a girl.

To my left, I see a body crumpled on the floor. In front of the body, a human being slowly grows out of the dust. Bruised lips slide open, exposing a rictus of grinning teeth. Black eyes glare at me, reach into me.

My heart stops.

Silence.

I emerge from the trance.

Afterward, as always, I am empty.

I look around. My vision has dissipated, but the odors linger: fear, sweat, the acrid burn of the drill. There's another smell, and this one has attached itself to me. It's the smell of life.

17

Another One Bites the Dust

As it rains, each drop makes a soft *ping* against my tugboat's skin. Waves gently lap against her hull. Every so often, when I'm down in the Pit, I hear something big brush along the bottom near the keel. Living on the water is a spiritual experience.

Solid ground has its merits; but living on this cove, which is part of the bay, which is part of the ocean, I feel connected to the rest of the world. There are times when the water is so still, I forget I'm floating. Other times it gently lifts, shifts, sways – rocks me to sleep like a child.

It's true, the sea supports us. But it is also true that she never lets us forget we're *not* safe, nothing is, and it would be wise to fully appreciate the moment – here, now.

When the water heaves with undeniable force – as it's doing today – I'm reminded how fragile we are. It's good to be humbled, to be reminded that I'm here at the ocean's innermost edge by grace alone. For me to live elsewhere would be to dull my own edges, to trick myself into a false state of security.

Living on solid ground might induce a kind of insanity. I have enough of that already.

The rain falls. The wind howls. The cold creeps into my ship, finding its way in through chinks in *Paralus'* armor – through leaky portholes, loose doors, hatches whose seals have dried and cracked. Down in The Pit – my engine-less engine room – a diesel-fired furnace quietly pumps out heat.

I'm sitting in the wheelhouse sipping coffee, looking out through foggy windows. All the boats in the marina are heaving and bouncing and snapping at their lines, while here, I am safe and sound. It's dry and warm inside *Paralus*.

Rivets. Iron plates. Cold-rolled steel. The occasional funk of dirty bilge water. The haunting echo of footsteps, creeping in and out of The Pit.

The Pit: the empty, two-story engine room that no longer stables horsepower. This is where Bradley sleeps. The huge diesel engine was removed decades ago, but the fuel tanks remain. When I moved in, I found that each tank was almost full. Thousands of gallons of oil – enough to keep me warm for a hundred years.

I have no TV. There's an overwhelming amount of negative news these days and I do my best to avoid it. I only want to hear about the important stuff. Like when nuclear warheads are headed this way.

With my second cup of coffee I pick up the *Boston Globe*. I've read almost the whole thing when I come upon a small article near the back of the local section: "Woman Still Missing After Five Days. Search Continues".

And to think I almost missed it.

According to the article, a Framingham woman didn't show up for work on Monday. Authorities notified, etc. In the third paragraph of the article is the missing woman's name: *Rosalie Tam.*

The hairs on the back of my neck stand. Rosalie Tam is the wife of Jonathan Tam, the driver of the pickup that T-boned Harry Crow's Cadillac, killing both Jonathan and Harry.

The article points out that Rosalie Tam, now a widow, has lived alone in the couple's modest home since her husband died. A next-door neighbor, having known Tam for years and being familiar with her habits, has corroborated her vanishing. The neighbor told the police she hasn't seen Tam for about a week. Authorities have called Tam's disappearance 'suspicious'.

I think it's suspicious too, but not for any of the reasons the authorities in Framingham might think.

I'm a little rattled when I consider the following: What are the odds that both the wife of the guy that crashed into Harry Crow, and Harry Crow's daughter, would vanish within a week of each other?

I put the paper down. Outside, a gust of wind splatters raindrops onto the wheelhouse windows. The drops strike the glass with such force, they sound like they've been fired from a pellet-gun. As I watch the boats in the marina bouncing furiously against their lines, I think about the random dispersion of raindrops. I know there's nothing random about the disappearances of Amanda Crow and Rosalie Tam. I know they're related.

I feel a little overloaded, as if I have too much information instead of not enough. This double disappearance makes no sense. I can't imagine a scenario in which it *would*. A woman vanishing because she's related to someone who was in an automobile accident? *Zero* sense. *Two* women vanishing for the same reason? *Less than zero.*

Could the two vanishings simply be coincidence?

I think, imagine, guess, speculate. All I get for it is a headache.

And this, that keeps scratching at my brain.

Rosalie Tam.

18

Permission

Laura Crow invites me to sit. I decline. Leaning against a doorframe in her kitchen, I watch her as she carefully prepares a meal.

As Laura concentrates while chopping vegetables on a cutting board, the look on her face touches something in me. During the few times I've spoken with her, she seems to be in an almost constant state of fear. I strongly believe Amanda is alive, regardless of Slo-Mo's murder, and I've told Laura as much. Understandably, my assurances have done little to calm her. Yet I know my belief in my gift is infectious. If things go as they often do, Laura will feel it soon.

I've come here to spend some time in Amanda's room, and I've just told Laura that doing so may yield nothing.

Laura looks at me, eyes wide. "What are you going to do in there?"

I say nothing.

"Or...ah...what do you expect to happen when you do... whatever it is you do?"

In the beginning, I tried explaining to parents what I do. It never went well, so I decided upon a rule – say nothing. "When I go into Amanda's room, I need to do it alone. I'll be spending some time with her things. Computer, books, anything she may have written by hand."

Laura may not know it, but she's turning her head from side to side, telegraphing her doubts. I understand her reluctance: I'm going to invade her daughter's privacy, perhaps by reading a diary, or by rummaging around in her drawers. I may even stumble upon things Amanda has purposefully hidden from her mother.

"It doesn't always happen, but when people touch things, they sometimes leave behind a kind of residue that may be infused with what they were thinking or feeling at the time. I know it sounds corny, but it's like a fingerprint of the soul."

Laura looks startled.

"The last time Amanda was in her apartment, it's possible she may have left something. Especially if her thoughts were either exciting or disturbing."

Laura looks petrified by the notion that some aspect of her missing daughter may still reside in the garage apartment at the end of her driveway. I feel for her and decide to break my rule.

"I can sense numbers, letters, words. I might envision a scene or hear a song. I might get a hunch. A simple hunch can sometimes be more helpful than a hard clue. But my hunches are different from what you might be thinking. When I get a strong hunch, I call it a 'knowing', because the information is always right."

Laura's eyes narrow. "This is just hard to believe. I mean, no offense, Mr Snow, but it sounds ridiculous."

"No offense taken. I don't expect you to accept what I'm saying. I'm just asking for a little time and space. Paula sent you to me for a reason."

Laura nods at the mention of her friend.

"Imagine puzzle pieces spread out all over a kitchen table. For whatever reason, I'm sometimes able to see how the pieces will form, what they will become."

Laura is shaking her head again. "I'm glad you've agreed to help, but I don't understand any of this."

"You don't need to," I say.

Taking a deep breath, Laura removes a key from her pocket and hands it to me. I take the key and head out the back door.

19

Apartment

The Crows' 'garage' is an old barn at the end of a dirt drive, a few hundred feet behind the house. As I'm walking the drive, it occurs to me that you could have one hell of a party out here without anyone in the house knowing about it.

When Amanda moved out of her bedroom in the house to the apartment over the garage, Laura conceded to an increasingly argumentative daughter who had threatened to move out altogether.

I climb an outside staircase to a little deck at the front of Amanda's apartment. I stand on the deck for a few minutes, taking it in. It appears that Laura's concession has not included cleaning up after her daughter. I'm grateful for that.

Two deckchairs. Bamboo coffee table. On the table, three burned-out candles, an empty, crumpled pack of Marlboros, and two ashtrays, both filled with butts. In the back corner of the deck, a large brown wastebasket overflowing with empty beer cans and wine bottles.

In contrast to the mess, the view from the deck is lovely. Behind the barn, a broad field of high, brown grass. A swirling breeze bends the grass into graceful, shifting shapes etched into the field's canvas. It's so peaceful here, I have a hard time imagining kids hanging off the deck, laughing and shouting, while music thumps from inside Amanda's apartment.

Huge spruce trees block most of my view of the house. All I can see is the sunporch at the northeast corner.

Using the key, I let myself in.

The apartment is a studio. The vaulted ceilings, skylights and big windows create brightness and a feeling of openness, even though there are only two rooms. The main room serves as eat-in kitchen and living room. The bedroom is reached through a pair of slatted, swinging saloon doors.

There's a small bathroom – shower, no bathtub – that seems stuffed into the far corner across from the kitchen area. It's so small, the toilet had to be installed beneath the down-sloping eave of the roof. A man could stand in front of it no problem, if he was three feet tall.

The apartment appears to have been lived in by two Amandas – one a neat-freak, the other a slob. The kitchen area to the left is spotless. In the living area to the right, it looks like a bomb went off. Articles of clothing have been tossed everywhere; a shirt draped over a lamp; a sweater dangling from the arm of the couch, a pair of jeans, one leg turned inside-out, lying across an ottoman. Two pink and blue sneakers were apparently catapulted in opposing arcs; one of them lies on the carpet next to a wilted palm in desperate need of water; the other balances on the top corner of a cheap bookcase that divides kitchen and living areas and holds no books. More clothing on the living room floor, precisely where they were removed, I'd guess. Even the shower has a bathrobe crumpled in its corner.

The kitchen is as clean as a surgical theater. Which makes the presence of the single sneaker seem all the more odd. Automatic coffeepot, toaster, salt and pepper shakers arranged evenly on the countertops. Above, all cabinet doors clean and closed. Clean dishes stacked in a drying rack.

The inside of the refrigerator is clean and sparsely stocked. A few food items stored in Tupperware containers. A half-full bottle of an inexpensive Pinot Noir, lying on its side. A shrunken slice of cantaloupe in Saran Wrap. Three bottles of Budweiser. A brown head of lettuce, in Saran Wrap, disintegrating.

I push through the saloon doors into the bedroom. Dozens of posters on the walls. Big-hair rock bands of the 70s. Twisted Sister, Firehouse, Whitesnake, Aerosmith. These bands seem an odd choice for today's eighteen-year-old girl. I'd have expected Britney Spears, Evanescence, Pink.

What do I know.

Perfume bottles, hairsprays and brushes of every size and shape crowd the surface of a small dresser. The full-size bed is half unmade, the corners of the bedding folded over to one side. It appears only one person slept here last.

I rifle through, under and behind everything in the apartment. Finally, in a dresser drawer beneath some blouses and T-shirts, I find three items; a small zippered case containing several pieces of inexpensive jewelry, a nine-by-eleven-inch leather-bound journal, and a thick stack of lottery tickets secured by a rubber band.

I take the items to the kitchen and lay them out on the countertop. First, I hold the tickets in my hands for a while. Then each item of jewelry. I feel nothing. The journal, however, shocks me.

Generally intended as a place to record experiences and feelings, this journal has no such entries. Instead, it's filled with articles cut from newspapers and pasted to the pages.

There are close to forty articles in Amanda Crow's journal. Some lengthy, some brief. They all cover the same story: the spectacular crash that took the lives of three family members, one lone man, one dog and Harry Crow.

Some of the articles are dated the day after the crash. Others are dated days, weeks and, in a few cases, several months after. Many include photographs taken at the scene. For the first time, I see the demolished vehicles from various angles.

The back of the van is caved in like an accordion. The blaze consumed it, leaving a warped skeleton of blackened metal.

The images of the van give me the creeps. There was a family inside. The way they died is etched into my brain. *Incinerated.*

I look at a picture of the pickup that T-boned Harry Crow. Despite the fact that it's on its roof in the grass, unlike the devastated van it looks relatively undamaged, like a big turtle flipped over onto its back.

In the last of the pics I find Harry's Cadillac; gnarled metal, bowed inward at the driver's door, the point of impact. There's a round hole the size of a grapefruit in the middle of the driver's window. This is where Harry's head hit the glass with the force of a catapulted melon striking a wall.

Looking at these pictures makes me want to give up what I'm doing and get a job at Jiffy Lube.

I poke around in the drawers of a computer table and find paper and pen. I take the journal to the couch and read through all the articles in the car-crash album again. I make a list of facts. The victim's names, as well as people related to them. Various facts I learned from Laura Crow and Ray Driscoll.

When I'm done, my list looks like this:

1. *Harry Crow, driver. His Cadillac strikes van and sets off chain reaction accident. Wearing seatbelt, Crow survives initial hit on van. Caddy skids into high-speed lane. Is then struck in driver's door by pickup truck. <u>Harry Crow, deceased.</u>*

2. *Eldrick Creech, owner of van hit by Harry Crow's Cadillac. At time of impact, Creech is standing in breakdown lane. <u>Eldrick Creech, survivor.</u>*

3. *Rebecca Creech, Eldrick's wife, age 38, sitting in passenger seat of van when hit by Crow's Cadillac. Wearing seatbelt. Survived initial impact. Trapped in vehicle. Vehicle consumed by fire. <u>Rebecca Creech, deceased.</u>*

4. *Judith Creech, age 12, daughter of Eldrick and Rebecca. Passenger in van. Back seat. Wearing seatbelt. Survived initial impact. Trapped in vehicle. Fire. <u>Judith Creech, deceased.</u>*

5. *Richard Creech, age 9, son of Eldrick and Rebecca. Passenger in van. Back seat. Wearing seatbelt. Survived initial impact. Rescued. Survived fire. Died at hospital. <u>Richard Creech, deceased</u>.*

6. *'Fergie'. Creech family dog. Rust and white Lab–Collie mix. Passenger in van way back. Likely killed on impact. <u>Fergie, deceased</u>.*

7. *Jonathan Tam. Driver of pickup truck. High speed. Passing lane. Direct hit on Crow's Cadillac. T-boned driver's door. Tam either not wearing seatbelt or locking mechanism failed. <u>Jonathan Tam, deceased.</u>*

8. *<u>Summary</u>. Three vehicles involved in crash. Five people, one dog = 6 deaths.*

Depending on which newspaper article I consult, I find various references to other individuals, not on the above list, that were in some way connected to the accident. I can't imagine why anyone would think this newsworthy, but there's an interview with a laborer on the state road crew, dispatched to clean up the accident debris after multiple tow trucks hauled away the wrecked vehicles. There's another interview (this one has validity) with a tractor-trailer driver considered by some to be a hero. According to multiple witnesses, this driver/hero sustained second-degree burns on hands and arms while trying to put out fire in van, using extinguisher from his rig. The hero was assisted by Eldrick Creech. The two men managed to extricate Richard, age nine, who died later.

I'm startled yet again when I come upon Ray Driscoll's name. Ray is mentioned in one of the later articles, referred to as the first 'official' on the scene. The article fails to mention that he was off duty at the time, that he was there in an unofficial capacity.

A few articles from local papers mention others who either helped or tried to help. An EMT who took Rebecca Creech's body to the morgue in his ambulance. The first on-duty officer to arrive, a Rhode Island State Trooper who became ill when he saw the burned bodies. The tow-truck operator who winched the still-smoking van onto a flatbed truck and hauled it away to the impound yard.

A reporter from Channel Six Eyewitness News described the van as it sat above him on a flatbed. Completely incinerated, windows blasted out, metal skin stripped of paint, tires melted into black pools, jagged metal panels flayed by the Jaws of Life. He wrote that it looked like a Humvee, blown apart by an IED.

I close the journal. Lay it on the cushion beside me. Close my eyes. Amanda's journal is a memorial, not just to her father's death, but to a tragedy that killed five people and a dog. I now think the tragedy may be connected to the death of Vinnie Ianucci.

Seven deaths.

I find Amanda's journal fascinating. Perhaps because I, too, am curious about death. What is the true cause of death? How can any death be untimely – by what clock do we measure? *Why didn't I tell Mom about my dream?*

Screw this.

I get off the couch. Put the journal, the jewelry and the tickets back where I found them. Go back outside onto the deck.

What is the true cause of any death? The only way to combat death is to not live in the first place. The cause of death is life.

With this I feel a loosening, a sense of something relinquishing its hold on me. Sabrina was born. She was happy. She

114

lived well while she was here. She died.

Failing to tell my mother about a dream did not kill my sister. A psychopath did. I'm not obsessed with death. I'm obsessed with the deaths of psychopaths.

I sit down on a deckchair. Lean my head back against the wall. Close my eyes. Breathing deep, I begin the exercises that will take me to a place where questions are sometimes answered, connections sometimes made.

I fall asleep.

...I'm in an elevator. The doors slide shut with a hiss. Interior lights dim to a soft glow, the color of congealing blood. When the room drops, my body floats an inch above the floor.

As always, paradox. Float while plummeting. Rocket while motionless.

Down. Into the absolute absence of light.

...A subtle *thump*.

Music. It wafts in and out as if carried on a serpentine wind. I am energy, waiting to be realized...

A hole opens in the dark and music pours through. Celestial violins. The sound of dunes carved gracefully by the wind.

A prayer reaches out to me from across a void. It's wrapped in a melody I don't know, sung by a voice I've never heard.

Now...
I lay me down to sleep,
I pray...

(she sobs)

115

...the Lord my soul to keep,
If I shall die before I wake...
I pray the Lord...
my soul to take.

Out of neither intention nor purpose,
I sleep.

The heady fragrance of the sea. The sound of wings above a beach. A touch upon my skin. The smell that was the sea is now the smell of the earth. The touch that was contact is now a flutter beneath the earth's skin.

I hear the firm click of two puzzle pieces coming together.
Underground
and
Cold.

20

Missing Pieces

As I hand the album over to Laura, I wonder how she'll react.

Laura places it on the countertop. She turns the pages slowly, absorbing the implication of its construct, the morbidity of its focus.

"This is unbelievable," she says, looking up at me. "I had no idea Amanda was so obsessed with the accident."

Laura cradles the album to her chest and pads solemnly into the living room. I follow. She sits on the couch. I settle into a side chair. She continues to slowly thumb through the album, anguish etched in the hollows of her face. I wonder if she's seen any of the images before.

I say nothing.

After carefully inspecting every page, Laura closes the album and places it gently on her lap. When she looks at me, her eyes bloom with pain, tears forming in their corners.

It's quiet in the room.

I immediately regret showing the album to Laura.

She looks stunned. As she transfers the album to the coffee table, her movements are mechanical, and her body seems poised, either to run or collapse. She appears to be looking at a spot somewhere on the wall behind me. I don't think she knows what to do or say.

I ask her if I can take the album with me to review. She isn't listening.

"Laura, it's probably best if I—"

"I didn't know," she interrupts, her voice cracking with grief. "I knew Amanda was hurting but...I mean, I knew they both were. Annie dealt with it in her own way, and still does, but Amanda's always been the expressive one. Now I see it. The way she revolted. It was her way of suppressing her pain, her loss."

The way Laura looks at me, I think she expects me to say something that will steady her, bring her back into balance. She tries to maintain eye contact, but her gaze keeps skating away.

"I was so wrapped up in my own suffering, I couldn't see how it affected them. How deeply they were both hurting. My pain was so big, I didn't have room for anyone else's. That was selfish."

Laura's gaze has gone back to the album, closed on the table in front of her. "This is my fault! I was angry with Amanda for leaving us. I accused *her* of being selfish, but I was the one."

Laura's honesty is an intimacy I hadn't expected. I want to go to her. Comfort her.

When her eyes come up to mine, she seems startled, as if she's just realized I'm in the room. The look on her face is heartbreaking, her pain almost palpable. I feel that if I wished to do such a thing, I might touch it.

118

"Laura," I say. "May I take the album with me? I'd like to read the articles more carefully."

"Of course," she says, standing.

Her tear-streaked face is so open, I feel I can see into her. When she hands me the album, I again feel the urge to embrace her, to comfort her. But something tells me she needs to move through this on her own.

As I navigate the darkening streets on my way back to *Paralus*, I think about guilt, the way it can scar one's life. Mothers always blame themselves when their children go missing. I saw it in Laura's face, well before she told me so.

And I'd seen something else. A longing to do something that, at some point in our lives, every one of us wants to do – turn back the clock.

I think about Laura and Annie Crow in their house, with the darkness of night descending, each longing for the missing pieces of their lives, and I wonder. What of Amanda? Where is she now? How is *she* coping with the dark?

21

Jane Mansfield

As Amanda Crow's journal suggests, Harry Crow's fatal crash spawned a fair amount of local news coverage.

I go up to my tugboat's high bridge – the former command station. It was from this small but lofty place – an abundance of windows provides a 360-degree view – that Captain Bullock piloted his tugboat for the better part of his life. Today, my computer sits on the mahogany platform where the tugboat's radios, compass and engine controls used to be.

I don't like computers. I use mine only when I'm flummoxed – when my gift has me running in circles and headlong into walls. I believe it unwise to become dependent on machines that think faster than I do.

I turn the infernal thing on and glare at it until it warms up. Using the date of the Harry Crow crash, I do searches in the *Providence Journal*, the *Boston Globe*, and four local newspapers. My first solid hit is in the *Journal*. As I read the article, I realize it's the same one Amanda pasted into her journal.

In the two weeks following that article, there were seventeen more that relate to the fatal accident. Interestingly, it's the *Kent County Courier* – a small, weekly paper – that provides the most complete list of individuals directly affected. Home addresses aren't provided, but hometowns are.

A number of these articles are human-interest stories: no one is injured when a minor fender bender occurs as passing motorists rubberneck the accident; a firefighter receives minor burns while attempting to rescue the family from the burning van; Cheryl Smythe, a newly certified EMT, throws up when the charred bodies are pulled from the smoldering wreckage – it was Cheryl's first day on the job.

After reading every article thoroughly, I do more searches using the names and towns mentioned. Three hours later, my names all have matching addresses. I even have a few phone numbers. I think I now have a list of pretty much everyone impacted by the accident, or its aftermath.

Using a magic marker, I make a rough diagram of Harry Crow's accident on a large piece of cardboard. I draw the three vehicles involved in the wreck. I draw in the fatalities as stick figures, each accompanied by its name. Four stick figures inside the van – the Creech family and their dog. One stick figure standing next to the van – Eldrick Creech. One figure inside the upside-down truck – Jonathan Tam. One inside the Cadillac – Harry Crow.

Lastly, I draw an ambulance and a few tow trucks.

At the top of the unsettling scene I write, "THE DEAD AND THE MISSING". I'll call this my D+M board.

After staring at the board for long time, I realize I have no idea why I created it. No idea how it's supposed to help.

What the hell am I doing?

Stupefied by the last three hours of seemingly senseless work, I decide to put the case out of my head for a while. After shutting the computer down, I lean back, put my feet up on the old helm and ponder the miraculous development of the World Wide Web. I'm not sure how I feel about its possibilities, its intrusion into our lives. But I'm certain of one thing. As it grows, the Web's appetite for darkness will grow exponentially.

While rummaging about in the affairs of the dead, I missed the shift in the weather. It's gotten dark outside and the temperature has fallen ten degrees. Rain sprinkles down through the fog.

When the weather threatens, there's no place I'd rather be than here, on the high bridge. I reposition my chair and rest the back of my head against a window. It isn't long before I drift off.

Time passes.

On the stage inside the theater of my mind, actors are rehearsing a sad, tragic play called *Jayne Mansfield – The Original Blond Bombshell.*

It's the final scene.

A country road at night. Heavy fog. Ms Mansfield and several others are motoring along in a luxury sedan, not unlike Harry Crow's Caddy. The chauffeur is distracted. As he stares at Ms Mansfield in the rearview mirror, the car slams into the back of a stopped truck. The actress is killed instantly.

I'm the director of the play. I don't approve of the actor's performances. I keep calling for the scene to be redone. Again, and again. As the rehearsals continue, more actresses die.

It's not easy to find replacements for actresses who can play

Mansfield – we're running out of lookalikes. If that happens, the play will never open.

Jayne Mansfield. Who better to convey the tale of a promising life cut short?

As the director, I ask myself. Who better indeed?

When I wake, I write down the details of my dream. I'm disturbed that it mimicked a real event. If there's a secret imbedded within the Jayne Mansfield dream, I have a feeling it will be an extraordinary one.

I replay the horrific, defining moment. My stomach begins to sour as I become aware of something. It's not the horror of the repeated deaths that makes the vision significant – it's the willingness of everyone involved in the production (myself included) to repeatedly instruct actors to perform until they die in the name of someone long dead.

As I ponder the puzzle, a bizarre idea floats up out of the black.

My God! My gift has just presented me with something so crazy, so completely insane, I'm afraid to let it linger.

22

Snow at the Tam House

A raised ranch sheathed in outdated shakes painted flat gray; Rosalie Tam's house is unremarkable. There are no shutters. The yard has few bushes. Not landscaped. Paved driveway left of the house. No garage.

The house sits in a plat occupied by a bunch of equally unremarkable houses. The only thing that sets Rosalie Tam's apart is its location – nine o'clock in the circle of a cul-de-sac.

The homestead seems to reflect the tragedy that has befallen its family. Flower beds overgrown with weeds. Green mold on the cement foundation. Mailbox dented and crooked.

I park on the street out front. When I step out of my rusty pickup, I immediately feel the grief – it attaches itself to me, like closed-up basement funk.

For the second time in a week, I'm looking at yellow police tape; a short ribbon of it stretches across the front door; another length curls around the left corner of the house, blocking access to a side door that opens onto the driveway.

I didn't come here to breach the tape or break into the house. My plan is to merely walk around, be open to whatever may come.

For now, I get out, go around the back of my truck, face the house and lean back against the side of the pickup bed. I tilt my head back. Welcome the warmth of sun on skin. Winter has overstayed its welcome, and I'm ready for the invigorating uplift of spring.

Focusing on it, I try to imagine what the house might have looked like, what its energy might have felt like, before Jonathan died and Rosalie disappeared.

I get nothing.

Then I notice a spot on the roof where a shingle hangs loose. This lone shingle becomes my focus point as I count backward from 100, inhaling and exhaling with each number, my body relaxing, intention displacing tension. As I approach the number sixty, my eyelids begin to feel as if there are little lead weights attached to them.

No longer able to keep my eyes open, I accept the gift of peace that always comes first with trance. My body becomes lighter. I imagine my burdens dispersing, like ashes flitting upward from a dying fire.

The feelings of grief and sadness drift away. I'm now ready to feel, hear, *see*, anything.

Time passes.

Nothing happens.

I'm close to reaching a meditative state Buddhists call *no thought*, when a voice speaks to me. Is it God?

"Is there something I can help you with?"

The voice is clear. Close.

"Excuse me. Is there something I can help you with?"

My eyes pop open. I push away from my truck.

"Excuse me!"

I turn. Face a woman who appears to be both scared and angry.

"You've been standing in front of this house for almost a half hour! Before I call the police, *do you want to tell me exactly what it is you think you're doing?"*

Tall. Sandy blond hair. Frank brown eyes. Maybe forty. Jeans, sweatshirt. The woman grips a large, cylindrical flashlight in her right hand like a weapon.

"My name is William Snow," I say. "Who are you?"

"I'm Sarah Kingsley. Rosalie's neighbor. Over there," she points to a brown and white tri-level, directly across from the Tam house. Three o'clock in the cul-de-sac.

I do my best to explain my presence, referencing Harry Crow's accident, pointing out the razor-thin connection between Amanda Crow's disappearance and Rosalie Tam's. For now – knowing it turns off most people anyway – I say nothing about psychic possibilities.

Although the woman continues to eye me suspiciously, her concern seems to soften.

I make a decision. This is the perfect time to lie. "Because I know Amanda Crow, and because I'm responsible for uncovering a possible link between the two missing women, I've been asked to assist the police in the investigation of Mrs Tam's disappearance."

This seems to upset Ms Kingsley. "Oh, no! Is Rosalie…?"

I raise my hand. "I'm not implying that Rosalie is dead. As far as I know, there's still no official determination as to what's happened to her."

Sarah seems only marginally relieved. "I've known Rosalie for six years. She's a wonderful person. Are you some kind of investigator or something, because you don't look…"

"I'm not." Hoping to ease her fear, I take a step back and deepen the lie. "There are a number of reasons why we think these disappearances might be connected, but I'm afraid we're not at liberty to discuss them."

We.

Concern draws Sarah's face tight. It's clear she's not done appraising.

I take a different tack. "I'm not working in an official capacity with the police. I was hired by Laura Crow, the mother of the missing girl. Her name is Amanda."

Sarah seems to struggle with my explanations, wavering in and out of a desire to trust. Then the gap between us widens as she takes her own step back. "Why would the disappearance of this Amanda person have anything to do with Rosalie? I don't understand. What could a car accident have to do with either of them going missing?"

"I don't know. I'm not aware of anything that links them, other than the accident. The accident seems to be the only thread."

By the look in Sarah's eyes, I may have lost what little credibility I gained. "I just don't understand any of this."

I switch gears. "Are you and Rosalie close? What I mean is, did she talk to you about Jon's accident?"

Sarah considers this. "We've been close but... Losing Jonathan was devastating for her. She has no one else. She never talked about it. Never went there with me. Rosalie was an only child. Her parents are gone, and she has no other family. Jonathan was her world."

"Did you know him?" I ask.

"Charlie – Charlie's my husband – he and Jonathan got along pretty well. They'd watch a football game together, give each other a hand with a project. Like when they built the shed out behind the house."

Sarah smiles at me. Her first sign of warmth.

"The four of us weren't so close that we went on vacations together or anything like that. I mean, we've got children and they don't. You know how that is. But we were both hit pretty hard when Jonathan was killed. I like Rosalie a lot. Now that she's missing, I think we were closer than I realized." Sarah looks at the Tam house wistfully. "What could have happened to her?"

"Mrs Kingsley. I'm not sure you understand what I'm getting at here. The missing girl I told you about from Rhode Island. Amanda Crow? She's Harry Crow's daughter."

Sarah shakes her head. "Am I supposed to know who that is?"

I tell her about Amanda and Annie's birthday party. Harry drinking too much. The argument. Harry driving off angry, drunk. The chain-reaction accident. The fire. The dead. When I tell her, it was Jonathan Tam's pickup truck that killed Harry Crow – that *this* is the link between Rosalie Tam and Amanda Crow – Sarah's head jerks back.

"*What!* What are you *saying*? What are you *talking about?*"

128

Sarah backs away from me. "I don't understand what you're *saying*."

I do my best to sound reassuring. "Amanda disappeared two weeks ago. At first it was thought she might have gone off with her boyfriend."

I wonder if I should tell her about Vinnie Ianucci's death. I don't want to scare her away, but it just comes out. "The boyfriend was murdered a few days ago."

Sarah Kingsley clasps a hand to her chest. She seems to wither as she stares at Rosalie Tam's house. "*Murder!* Oh, my God." Sarah shakes her head. "I wonder if this has anything to do with the phone calls."

I have no idea what calls she's talking about and I tell her so.

Sarah glances around quickly, as if she thinks someone might be listening. "I've heard a rumor that the police aren't acknowledging them. But who knows? Maybe if something really has happened to Rosalie this time, they're afraid they'll get sued."

"This time?" I say. "What are you talking about?"

"Right after Jonathan was killed, Rosalie began getting these strange phone calls from some nutcase with a blocked number. The guy would say all kinds of awful things to her and then hang up. She called the police, but they treated her like she was just some fragile *woman* going to pieces after her husband died."

I can feel my blood rising. "What did she tell you about the calls?"

"She said the guy sounded creepy. In the first two years after Jonathan was killed, the guy called about twenty times. He'd say stuff like, 'You deserved to lose your husband.' Or, 'I'm gonna see to it you meet your husband in hell.' Crazy stuff like that. And

Rosalie said he used Jonathan's name as if he knew him. The police never did a thing about it. No phone taps. Nothing."

"So, what happened?"

"Rosalie was very upset. Other than for work, she wouldn't leave the house unless she had to. She changed her phone number a couple times, but the guy always managed to find the new one. Then one day the calls just stopped."

I close my eyes, try to imagine how this could have anything to do with Amanda. Does adding a crank caller to the equation increase the odds that Rosalie Tam's disappearance is due to foul play? If the crank caller is one of the pieces of the puzzle, then this would suggest that both Amanda Crow and Rosalie Tam were abducted for the same reason. But how could that be? Why would anyone kidnap two people whose only linkage was a car wreck?

"Excuse me, Mr...?"

"William Snow," I say.

"Mr Snow? What do you think you're gonna learn by standing in front of Rosalie's house?" Sarah inches toward me, yielding some of the distance she'd gained.

"I don't know," I say. "I just had a feeling I should come here. Have a look at her house."

I tell Sarah I learned of Rosalie Tam's disappearance by reading an article in a newspaper.

Sarah looks lost. It's clear her concern for Rosalie Tam is genuine. I wish I could give her something hopeful regarding her friend. As I'm thinking this, another little puzzle-piece snaps into place. With this piece, the crazy idea that came to me after the Jayne Mansfield dream gets crazier.

Sarah Kingsley is staring at me. I give her a vague smile.

"Sarah, I want to thank you. You've given me a direction in which to look."

"I have?"

I nod.

Sarah's smile is equally vague. "A direction? Where will you be looking?"

"Inward," I say. "Always inward."

Sarah's smile collapses into a frown.

"It was a pleasure to meet you," I say.

I leave Rosalie Tam's friend and neighbor standing on the sidewalk with her confusion. I step under the yellow tape and circle the house slowly. Twice. As I'm doing this, Sarah Kingsley walks back across the cul-de-sac, turning her head every so often to look back at me.

Sarah's house sits at the crest of a small rise. She walks halfway up her inclined driveway. Stops. Turns. Watches me.

I make mental notes about certain aspects of Rosalie's house. The backyard. The padlocked tool shed in the back corner. Stepping inside the perimeter of the yellow tape once again, I inspect the windows on the lower level of the house. They'd be easy to break into, but they appear not to have been touched.

I feel an impulse. *The driveway.*

I go to the driveway and stand on the blacktop adjacent to the side door. I have a vague sense that I *should* feel something about this spot. I feel nothing.

Is *feeling nothing* really *nothing*?

Then it occurs to me. Where's Rosalie's car? Surely, she has one. That her car is not here suggests she drove somewhere. So, she ran into trouble *there*, not *here*.

131

See? I'm not feeling *nothing*.

But something about my premise (*there*, not *here*) is lacking. Is this my impulse talking? Or is it intuition?

Feeling Sarah's eyes on me, I climb into my pickup, start the engine, slide the floor shifter into first and ease the clutch out. I drive – very slowly – halfway around the cul-de-sac, my tires crunching and stuttering on the loose stones. When I get to the foot of Sarah's driveway, I stop. Sarah walks down to meet me, eyebrows raised.

"Rosalie," I say. "She had a car, yes?"

Sarah nods. "It was one of those little Mini Coopers. Dark blue."

"Does she always park it in her driveway?"

Sarah nods. "Always."

"When was the last time you saw it?"

She thinks for two beats. "I'm not sure." Then she tells me something I already know – that Rosalie has worked for six years as a waitress at the Newport Creamery in Sudbury.

"I'm used to seeing her car parked in the same spot. Since Jonathan passed away it's been there every night. Rosalie doesn't go anywhere that she doesn't have to. I'm sorry, I don't remember when I last saw it. I'm drawing a blank."

I scribble my name and number on a slip of paper and hand it to her. "If it comes to you – the last time you remember seeing her car in the driveway? Would you let me know?"

"I'll be happy to." Sarah gives me her first real smile; maybe her way of telling me we're now on the same side.

"Have the police spoken to you?"

"Twice."

"Maybe we'll speak again," I say. "Thanks for your help."

She nods. "I hope I *have* helped."

I pull away.

As my truck labors up the hill, Sarah Kingsley gets smaller and smaller in my rearview mirror. Then she's gone.

23

Gary

8:15 A.M.

Sitting on the afterdeck in my favorite teak chair, coffee mug in hand. The sky is overcast. The cool air is heavy with moisture.

Fascinated, I watch as a fog bank slips silently from across the bay and into our little cove, curling over the water like wind-driven smoke. In less than ten minutes, it rolls over everything. Docks. Boats. Marina. All the buildings. Bullock's house.

The fog is so thick, I can't even see my tugboat's bow. I go inside. As I settle into the couch, my cordless phone rings.

"This is all *your* fault," Ray says. "You know that, don't you." It's not a question.

"How do you figure?" I say, even though I already know how he figures.

"A small percentage of criminal investigations go smoothly, and the rest fight you till the end. After twenty-five years of wading through shit, nothing surprises anymore."

"Brilliantly put," I say. "And you're telling me this because…?"

"Keep cracking wise, Snowman. You'll get my meaning soon enough."

I project my sarcasm by elongating a sigh.

"Each crime has a unique life all its own." Ray sounds like a thespian, trolling for effect. "Certain crimes are compelling. They draw you in. But even the most straightforward investigations can get kinks in them. Like in a garden hose, you know? You get a kink, the flow stops? The next thing you know, the pressure builds up and the whole thing blows out in a direction you wouldn't have guessed."

"You saying you've got yourself a kinky crime, Ray?"

"Investigation," Ray corrects me.

"Okay. It's a kinky investigation," I say. "I got it. After the kinks are worked out, you think this thing is going to wind up somewhere no one would have imagined."

"You're quick, Snowman. No. I don't think that's exactly what I'm saying. But you're on the right track."

Ray and I had a similar conversation about my impact on a case a few years back, so I decide to save us some time. "Ray. My man. You're saying that any and all weirdness that may occur in this case will have occurred because of my involvement in it. You're saying that when I get involved in an investigation, it's destined to go kinky on you. Is that what you're saying?"

Hiss of empty space along the line.

"Yeah, that's about it. I guess you do have some of that psychic shit working for you after all. You're waaaaay out ahead of me on this one."

"Mine is not to reason why," I say.

135

"Sit on it, Snowman. You can't deny the facts. Every time you stick your unwanted ass into an investigation, things start getting strange. I mean, come on. In the history of law enforcement, there's never been a wreck resulting in multiple fatalities that, four years later, somehow morphs into a missing persons case. A *multiple* missing persons case."

"And you honestly believe my involvement has something to do with this?"

More silence. I imagine Ray on the other end of the line, nodding his head. Gravely. Yes, this is *exactly* what he thinks.

I give Ray another sigh. "Okay. For the sake of argument, let's say, *crazy as this may sound*, that you're right. When I'm around, things get weird. What are we supposed to do with that? You think I should back off?"

"No. It's too late. The investigation is already cursed. Things are just gonna get weird and there isn't anything anyone can do about it." Now Ray sighs.

I hold the phone in front of my face and give it a fierce look.

"All right," I say. "Given that you agree there's nothing to be done, can we just get back to the business of trying to find these people?"

"Well, of course." I hear a faint chuckle, Ray's cue that we're done fencing.

"Check this out. First thing this morning, there's an alert in my system. Gary Sawicki. White male. Twenty-six. Residence in Weymouth, MA. Looks like somebody dragged him out of his apartment. And that's an accomplishment, because the guy's a load."

"Okay," I say.

"He lives in a three-decker. About two-thirty in the morning, a neighbor across the street from Sawicki, name of Edwin Quirk, has trouble sleeping. Hears a commotion outside. Looks out his window, just in time to see Sawicki being rolled into the back of a big white van. Quirk says it looked so strange, he thought maybe he was dreaming."

"It was dark," I say. "How'd Quirk know who it was?"

"Sawicki," Rays says, "weighs almost three hundred pounds and has one of those mohawk haircuts with orange spikes on top. You know, like a plume? You think you'd recognize him?"

"It was dark," I repeat.

"Streetlight," Ray says.

"Okay," I say. "But *rolled* him? Into a *van*?"

"So?" Ray says.

"You said the guy weighs three hundred."

"I said, *almost* three hundred."

"*More* than three hundred. *Less* than three hundred. Jesus, Ray. Who rolls a guy that big into *anything*?"

"One strong son of a bitch. Anyway, Quirk goes back to bed. After a while, he realizes he couldn't have been dreaming because he knows he's awake because he can't get back to sleep so he calls nine one one."

"I'm awake so I can't be asleep," I say. "Cannot argue with that."

Ray grunts. "Weymouth cops been all over Sawicki's apartment. Lock on a back door jimmied. Signs of a struggle."

"Okay," I say.

"They're calling it an abduction. Gary Sawicki is officially missing."

Sawicki. Hearing the name for the fifth time starts a nerve twitching.

I ask Ray to hold on. I go to the high bridge. Get my D+M board. Bring it back to the salon. I go through the names of everyone at Harry Crow's accident. Gary Sawicki isn't one of them. But the nerve is still twitching.

"I'm not getting the connection, Ray. What does this have to do with Amanda Crow?"

"I wouldn't have gotten the connection either if it hadn't been for the orange hair."

"Orange," I say.

"About six months ago, a Providence cop goes to this fundraiser for the wife of a friend of his, dropped dead of a heart attack. Poor bastard was only forty-seven. Left a wife and two little kids. Can you imagine?"

"I cannot," I say.

"So, the community is raising money for the family with this fundraiser, and at the event there's this guy, mid-twenties, obese, orange hair, stands out like a bastard at a family reunion."

"Orange," I say.

"Exactly. Fat guy didn't have a Mohawk, but still, his hair was orange. Could've gotten the mohawk later."

"I'm with you so far," I say.

"Anyway, the guy who had the heart attack worked for a company called ESC, Emergency Serv-Co. ESC had been hired to clean up this wall-collapse inside of a—"

"Whoa. Wait a minute, Ray. What does this have to do with—"

"I'm getting there, Snowman. Remember, patience is its own reward."

"So said the sloth," I say.

"So, there was this wall collapse in a warehouse that'd been gutted by fire. Both the heart-attack guy, *and* the orange-hair guy, were working on the clean-up. Both of them were ESC employees."

"Ray. Come on."

"For fuck's sake, Snow. I'm almost there. ESC is this huge corporation with all these different divisions, one of which owns ambulance companies. Gary Sawicki, with the orange hair? He has a sister that works for an ESC owned ambulance company. She's an EMT."

Not only is the nerve still twitching, the skin on the back of my neck is beginning to buzz. "Ray, hold it right there."

I look at the upper right-hand corner of my Dead and Missing board. My stick-figure ambulance. I'd drawn a little rectangle with circles for tires. Next to this icon is my notation that an ambulance arrived after the fire in the Creech van had been extinguished.

The nerve twitches like an overheated wire.

"What was the sister's name?" I say.

"Cheryl Lyndell."

Next to the little ambulance, scrawled in my nearly illegible handwriting, are three names. Michael Grello. Anthony Boyce. Cheryl Lyndell.

"Holy crap," I say. "She was there."

"Yeah," Ray says.

The twitching stops. The buzzing goes away. "But Ray. How did you...?"

"It just happened that she was one of the people I spoke with that night. It's just a coincidence."

"I'll say. You gotta see what's happening here, Ray. We've got another abduction of a person connected to someone that was at the scene of the accident that night. We've now got *three* people missing in *two* different states, and all three of them are connected, in some way or another, to Harry Crow's accident."

"Not to mention the dead guy," Ray says. "Vinnie Ianucci. He's connected, too. He was hanging with Harry Crow's daughter."

"And what are the cops going to do about this?" I say.

"We're gonna continue to do what we're already doing. Look, you have your problem, which is Amanda Crow. She also happens to be part of our problem. We'll be looking for her, not for the reason you will, but because her boyfriend was murdered, and she's missing. Can you say, *witness*? Or, how about, *suspect*? Gary Sawicki is Weymouth's problem. It's not our jurisdiction. You never know about local cops when it comes to jurisdictional ownership. Sometimes they can be protective of their turf."

"But they *have* to cooperate, Ray. They have to see that this whole thing is turning into something incredible."

"Yeah, well…we'll see just how incredible it gets. In the meantime, keep this to yourself. I'm not supposed to be sharing anything with you. You know how to play it."

"You don't have to worry about me," I say.

"I always have to worry about you. But I'm not worried about your mouth. I'll give you that much. Just stay out of trouble."

I thank Ray and we hang up.

I stare again at my D+M board. I threw the thing together quickly, fashioned it inexpertly, but not so poorly that I can't see how bizarre some of the things on it are beginning to look.

As I look at the board, Salvador Dalí comes to mind. Recognizable figures with deformed features, twisted into disturbingly warped metaphor. A clock melting into the desert. A warrior exploding off his horse into pieces. Familiar objects and figures deconstructed into unfamiliar bits of whirling colors and light.

Why are so many people going missing? How could these disappearances have anything to do with an automobile accident?

I'm frustrated with my inability to see a link that, by the nature of its oddity, should stand out in bold relief. Whatever it is, at some point it will have to become obvious. It is, after all, the elephant in the room. Then why can't I see it?

Again, I think of Salvador Dalí, the way he deconstructed things. Melting clocks. Exploding warriors. Time and space warped by invisible forces. Reality bent grotesque. As I see it, Dalí was bringing death to life, and life to death.

Lazarus, called forth from behind the stone.

This is driving me crazy – liquid bits and pieces, warped and exploding clues. Yeah sure, this is some *gift* I have. Will it ever, just once, give me a puzzle piece that's solid and real – a piece I don't have to go mad trying to interpret?

Instantly I get an answer. The words are far away, yet moving closer, as if approaching from the other side of a hill: *And like no man before, death will reform his life.*

24

Rosalie and Amanda

"Oh, my God!"

The girl reaches for Rosalie.

"Where am I?"

Rosalie grabs the girl's arms and helps her up.

"What's your name?"

The young woman shivers. "Amanda."

"We've got to get you out of this water, Amanda!"

"I'm so cold!"

Rosalie rubs the girl's shoulders, then links arms with her. The two shuffle to the cot. Their movements leave a small wake in the filthy, shallow water.

Rosalie grits her teeth. *Where is this water coming from?*

They help each other onto the metal bed, struggle into sitting positions, knees pulled up to chests.

"I'm so *cold*." Amanda's whole body quivers.

"We need to stay close. Keep warm." Rosalie rubs Amanda's shoulders vigorously. "I'm Rosalie. Your clothes are soaked,

Amanda. Take off that blouse. You'll freeze in it."

Amanda looks confused, but quickly begins removing the blouse, her fingers shaking as she works the buttons. She shrugs the blouse off.

Rosalie removes her cardigan and helps put it on the young woman. She drapes the wet blouse on the far edge of the cot, praying it will dry somehow in the dank place.

"I was afraid you were never going to wake up," Rosalie says. "I'm worried about that water." She gestures toward the door. "It seems to have stopped, but we've got to get out of here."

Amanda looks dazed as she slowly scans the room. "Where are we?"

"Do you remember how you got here?" Rosalie asks.

"I just want to go home."

Rosalie sees that Amanda is in some kind of shock.

"He's going to come back!" Rosalie says. "We've got to do something! We can't just sit here. He's going to *kill* us!"

Amanda begins to whimper. "I watched him kill…" She shakes her head. "Oh, God! Did that really happen?"

"What?" Rosalie says.

Tears streaming, Amanda turns to face Rosalie. "He killed Vinnie. Mom couldn't stand Vinnie, but he's…" She chokes back a sob. "Last night we… No, it couldn't have been last night." Amanda shakes her head again. "I don't know. We went into this building to smoke some weed. What day is this?"

"It doesn't matter!" Rosalie says. "All that matters is…"

"Is it even *day*?"

"Jesus Christ, Amanda. *I don't know!*"

"Oh, *God*." Amanda sighs. "We were shooting nine-ball. Afterwards, we went next door to this empty building. It was dark, so Vinnie started a fire in this oil drum."

"Amanda! We don't have time for this!"

"This big guy comes in," Amanda says, ignoring Rosalie. "He says he's looking for his wallet."

"Shh! Listen!" Rosalie says, eyes fixed on the door. "Did you hear that?"

Amanda isn't listening. "The guy comes over to us and I'm pulling on Vinnie's arm like, *Let's get out of here!* but Vinnie doesn't get it…and the guy just walks up and…"

The horror in Amanda's eyes stops Rosalie cold.

"He slit his throat! It happened so fast! Oh God! Vinnie had this look, like he was just…surprised." Amanda drops her head into her hands and sobs. "His blood was everywhere! It was all over me!"

Both women look at the same moment. There is no blood on Amanda.

"Oh my God! *These aren't my clothes!* That creep must have…"

"He could be here any second!" Rosalie looks again to the door.

Amanda wipes her face with the sleeve of Rosalie's sweater. "He stabbed him so fast. Vinnie just dropped to the floor like the air went out of him."

"I'm sorry," Rosalie whispers.

"After that is a blur. I think I was in a boat, but… Where are we? What are we doing here?"

"I don't know any more than—"

Amanda jerks upright.

"What?" Rosalie asks.

Amanda points. The water all around them is rising.

25

The Driver

"You... Miserable... Mother... *Fucker!*" The Driver glares down at the fat man with the Mohawk, spiked and dyed orange, for Christ sakes. The guy is revolting.

Taking 'Spikes' down hadn't been easy.

Stuffing the big fat load into a box half the size of a coffin had been its own kind of bitch. To make matters worse, Spikes woke up right in the middle of it. Took another shot to knock him out again. Now, The Driver doesn't know if there's enough Fentanyl left for the others. He's not even sure he has enough to keep Spikes down for the whole trip.

At least he got him in there without breaking his bones.

The Driver has to face it. Spikes doesn't look so good. Crammed in there on his side, knees jammed against his chest, head bent so far forward it's almost touching his shins.

The Driver marvels at the way Spikes is bent. A man-sized fetus in a plywood womb.

Oh shit. Spikes' breathing is starting to go sideways.

His mouth opens wide. A big gulp of air goes in, but nothing comes back out. Spikes looks like a fish out of fucking water.

Oh-oh. Now he's not breathing at all.

He's dead. *Shit!*

The Driver waits.

And waits.

And just when The Driver thinks Spikes is definitely gone, the guy's mouth opens and he starts fish-breathing again.

"*Fuck me!*" The Driver screams as he slams the lid onto the compartment. Using his portable drill, he zips the screws back into place.

The Driver hesitates. What if Spikes croaks in there? How would he get him out? Just thinking about it makes The Driver angry. Then he thinks, Okay, what if Spikes doesn't die, but he doesn't wake up either? The Driver knows he won't be able to get him out of the box if he doesn't wake up.

Fuck! What to do if that happens? Does he cut up the box, or the guy? He doesn't want to cut up that box.

The Driver pulls the overhead door down with the loud bang he's come to despise. (No matter how carefully he does it, the son-of-a-bitch always *bangs*). He slides the bar into place, locks the padlock, climbs into his cab.

The Driver points the truck north. Heads for the coast, the boat, the island. He readies himself for the six-hour drive, a few stops factored in, so he can check on Spikes. See if he's still breathing like a goddamned son-of-a-bitching fish.

The Driver slides a CD into the stereo. Hits Play. The frenzy of Metallica assaults his senses and rattles the cab.

As The Driver settles in to a steady sixty-five, he thinks about his current situation. How drastically his life has changed.

He's been an independent trucker for almost thirty years in what he thinks of as *Biz One.* Owner-operator. Contracts with a bunch of companies. Good relationships with their dispatchers.

There's also a *Biz Two*, which is not now, nor ever has been, related to *Biz One.* Still, The Driver has combined the disparate endeavors, whenever possible. He accomplished this by accepting hauls specifically because their routes went through cities where certain individuals (on his hit-list in *Biz Two*) resided. These unfortunate individuals were the focus of verbal contracts The Driver had accepted within the realm of *Biz Two.*

This is how it works – how it *worked,* up until the day the bottom fell out of The Driver's life. In *Biz Two*, if The Driver was hired to neutralize an individual who lived in, let's say, Baltimore, MD, then (in *Biz One*) he would seek out shipments going to, or through, Baltimore. Putting two contracts side-by-side like this, The Driver often got to kill two birds with one stone. So to speak.

In *Biz Two*, The Driver was also an independent contractor. He was well known among members of organized crime in the northeast. None of them knew his real name, or where he lived. They knew nothing else about him, and they never would. The only actual fact they had about The Driver was that he'd never missed a target.

The Driver dispensed with his targets in whatever manner the contractor dictated.

He once accepted a hit from a mob boss in Lawrence,

Massachusetts. A guy The Driver had always been wary of. More than a psychopath, this boss was an unwashed pig. The Driver didn't trust him. But the man paid exceptionally well and… money is money.

As per the boss's orders, The Driver followed the target home one night, whacked him over the head, then tied him to a chair in his basement. Using his Ka-Bar tactical knife, he removed the target's genitals and placed them in his mouth. Only then did The Driver kill the target.

He never asked the boss why he'd wanted the target done like that. He was pretty sure it had something to do with a woman.

The Driver was proud of the fact that he'd never been on an FBI Most Wanted list and had never come close to being caught. As with the mob guys, the authorities – though fully aware of both his existence and his exemplary record – had no idea who he was.

When he wasn't working at *Biz Two*, The Driver was a family man with a wife and two children. Fortunately for his family, The Driver was a man of rules, and his number one rule has always been, *Work is work. Family is family.* End of story.

The Driver has never had a friend. Never needed one.

He is huge, powerful and fit – a well-coordinated physical giant. In another life, he could have been a defensive end. He is proficient with a wide variety of weapons: pistols, shotguns, knives, hammers, ice picks (thrust through the eye, jammed into the ear, slipped under the back of the skull). His favorite weapon is cyanide. If The Driver could love a thing, he would love cyanide, a compound so unique, it allows him to do creative kills. He has poured it into drinks. Sprayed it into faces. It kills within minutes. And, unless a coroner is specifically looking for it, it's undetectable.

The Driver considers himself to be a moral person. He has lived by his own code of ethics. Never kill a woman. Never kill a child. Never kill a civilian not in the mob.

The Driver takes contracts on mobbed-up guys only. They all deserve to die anyway.

Throughout the entirety of his career, The Driver only refused a legit contract once. A dozen years ago, a young boss from Scranton – smarmy little fuck named Mario Grasso – offered The Driver a contract. Grasso had inherited almost half the loan-sharking business in PA after his father, a well-respected syndicate boss, died mysteriously of an 'undiagnosed illness'.

Grasso wanted The Driver to kill the boss's right-hand man, a lieutenant and lifelong friend of his father's named Aldo. Aldo had refused an order to assassinate Grasso's ex-girlfriend. Grasso wanted the woman killed because she'd gotten pregnant by some other guy. He openly admitted this to The Driver, brandishing his cold-bloodedness as if it were an acquired asset.

When The Driver explained his code – *no women, no children* – and quietly made to leave, Grasso raged at the refusal, at what he called 'blatant disrespect'. He told The Driver, "From now on, you might want to sleep with one eye open."

The Driver said nothing and walked out.

Two weeks later, Grasso awoke at three in the morning to find The Driver standing over his bed.

The killing was slow and methodical, meant to send the message: *No women. No children.*

He went on with his day-to-day life, delivering containers, capital equipment, machinery, to shipping terminals and warehouses across fifteen states. Whenever he could squeeze it in, he ended lives.

The Driver's wife knew about *Biz One*. She knew nothing of *Biz Two*.

When he wasn't working, he spent every free minute at home. He was a devoted husband. He often told his wife he loved her, although he had never experienced the feeling and did not understand it. He drove his children to school. He played with them. The family went to the beach. Took driving trips to the Adirondacks.

Once, they went to Disneyworld.

The Driver never considered that death might visit *his* family. He gave no weight to such a possibility. Because he was independent – because he allowed no one into his life and kept the location of his home secret – he believed his family was safe from harm. They were untouchable.

But there came that day when his untouchable world was shattered. For the man who delivered capital equipment and death, death returned to him in spades.

After the tragedy, he went into a dark place, during which time he considered suicide. After that, having balked at ending his life and not knowing what else to do, The Driver went back to work. *Biz One* only.

Mob bosses still sought out his lethality, but he killed no one. When offered contracts, he thought about his dead wife and pondered the notion of turning wives into widows. It seemed, at least in the present, that the act of snuffing out life was a devastation he could no longer visit upon others. His relationship with death had shifted.

He became plagued by questions he'd never asked of himself. The most persistent of these was: *Why are they gone, and why I am still here?*

The Driver thought long and hard about that.

Not killing presented him with a philosophical dilemma. He no longer had a family. Period. He had more money than he could spend. Period. Given that he no longer had a *reason* to kill, then what possible justification could there be for his existence? These were hard questions, but The Driver was not only a disciplined man, he was a patient one. He regularly considered the philosophical dilemma, and he waited for the answers to come.

While he waited, his festering hatred of circumstance gradually coalesced into a fine point, like a needle of glass.

One day, God poked through the surface of his bubbling insanity with the answer. In that moment, he saw the MasterPlan in its entirety. The Driver was both stunned and relieved. He now had the only reason-to-live he would ever need.

The Driver rolls down the highway in his truck, violent music blasting, hate-filled lyrics injecting rocket fuel into his rage.

Here now is the essential mechanism of his survival, the fusion of what he was, and what he has become. This is not The Driver's salvation. This is his *completion*.

The Driver is no longer a truck driver.

He's not a mass murderer.

The Driver is a god.

26

The Missing and the Dead

For the past two days I've spent a lot of time looking at my M+D board, poring over it, trying to see either the elephant in the room or the melting clock. I'd settle for the truth.

I'm fed up. The visions, feelings and intuitions I'm getting have been mostly incomprehensible. Right now, my ability to intuit doesn't feel like a gift at all – it feels more like an encumbrance. I haven't had a single conventional idea that might help explain why three people have been abducted and one person has been murdered. And if pressed, I couldn't even fabricate a fantasy that could explain why the missing persons seem to have only one thing in common: an automobile accident.

In my frustration, I consider locking myself inside *Paralus* and not coming out until I come up with a useful idea, or at least a direction to move in. It's all I can think to do. It's something.

I shut off the phone. I lock the doors.

I head for the high bridge, muttering to myself that I'm not going anywhere, not budging until I'm either struck with a clear psychic inspiration, or my head explodes.

I stare at the M+D board. I make some notes. I sleep, go to the bathroom, walk to the convenience store for a newspaper. I speak to no one. I drink coffee. I go to the bathroom. I do my yoga. I sweat my way through karate katas.

I do these things for twelve hours of the first day. No phone, no TV, no visitors. The second day is no different. The only break is my daily walk to the store for the paper.

Early afternoon on the third day, it happens. I'm sitting on the floor asleep, my back against the couch, my legs stretched out in front of me.

I awake like an explosive bolt and smack my hands on the floor and yell out loud, "Holy crap!"

The newspaper.

It's lying open across my lap. Before falling asleep, I'd read it through. I don't think I missed a relevant article.

But in this case, what is relevant?

I take a deep breath, snap the paper open and flip through the pages like a crazy man.

I come to the *Rhode Island Living* section. Read through carefully.

There.

I see it again – a little quarter column article, down at the bottom of the section's last page on the inside corner:

"Neighbors Witness Dog Stolen From Front Yard"

In broad daylight, in front of two witnesses, a family pet was stolen out of a front yard in a heavily populated section of West Warwick. Just before noon, two neighbors chatting on a front porch noticed a dark sedan pull up in front of Walter Duran's house, next door. Leaving the engine running, a large man got out of the car and walked casually over to the chain-link fence that enclosed Duran's front yard.

Inside the fence, 'Inky', a small black poodle, looked up at the big man. Happy eyes. Wagging tail.

The man easily leaned over the five-foot fence, picked Inky up and nestled the little poodle against his chest as he calmly walked back to his car. As if all were normal, he nodded to the two neighbors, got back into his car and drove away.

The dognapping had been performed with such nonchalance, the neighbors didn't think to take down the license plate number.

Walter Duran, a local tow-truck operator, told a reporter that he didn't know why anyone would steal his little buddy Inky.

Not more than an hour ago, I'd read through the whole paper, seen the article about the dog. It hadn't registered. Now, as I see Duran's name again, three things pop into my head. 1) Duran Duran was a pop band. 2) Roberto Duran was one of the greatest boxers of all time. 3) *Walter Duran is the tow-truck driver that put a hook into Harry Crow's Cadillac and towed it away.*

This can't be happening.

A man has been murdered. Three people and a dog are missing. All of that is linked to Harry Crow.

I go to my M+D board and read aloud the names that,

out of the fifty-two, have meaning, so far: *Harry Crow. Amanda Crow. Jonathan Tam. Rosalie Tam. Gary Sawicki. Walter Duran.* I add another. *Inky.*

Saying the names aloud sounds powerfully *odd*, so I keep talking out loud. "What the hell is going on? Why three people and a dog?"

Given how crazy all this sounds, what kind of crazy might be coming next?

27

Snow Asks for Help

I stare at my D+M board. Read again the fifty-two names, searching for some kind of pattern. As I'm reminding myself that not seeing a pattern doesn't mean there isn't one, it hits me – if there's no pattern, *every one of these people on this list could be in danger.*

Someone has to tell them.

For each of the fifty-two, I have either an email address, a street address, or a phone number. I'm going to contact them all. I'll lay out the details of the case as I know them – people are either dying or being abducted because of a car crash four years ago.

They'll all think I'm nuts.

I construct the following message:

Hello,

This is not a hoax. <u>Your life may be in danger. As well, your response to this message could mean the difference</u>

between life and death for three people already abducted.
A fourth person has been murdered.

My name is William Snow. I live in East Greenwich, RI.
This message is not only a warning, it's a request for help.
Four years ago, at 5:30, the evening of 6 June 2002,
three vehicles were involved in an automobile accident
on the northbound side of Route 95 in Cranston, RI.
Five people were killed. If you have knowledge of this
accident, your life may be in danger.

I need help finding the killer of Vinnie Ianucci, and the
abductors of Amanda Crow, Rosalie Tam, Gary Sawicki
and a black poodle named Inky.

If you have any information related to the above crimes,
or if you know what links them to the 2002 accident,
please get in touch with me. I'm open to suggestions,
ideas, even theories.

My contact info is listed below.

Thank you in advance for your help,

William Snow

I send twenty-seven emails containing the message. I make six
hard copies to mail. I have nineteen phone numbers and will
begin calling later.

Just as I lean over to take the copies out of the printer tray, I sense something behind me.

Bradley must have padded up the steel staircase, quiet as a ghost. She's now snuggled in a corner. Her body is curled in a U, her head almost touching her tail. I find it amazing that, big as she is, she can sneak up on me like that.

I go to the corner and kneel beside my friend. Holding the copies in one hand, I stroke her crumpled skull with the other.

"What do you think of this madness, Brad?" I wave the copies to get Bradley's attention. She remains still, her seeing eye unblinking.

"How could that accident have anything to do with what's happening to these people today?" I waggle the papers again. "What do you say, girl?"

She says nothing.

"Okay, fine."

I sit on the floor next to her with my back against the wall. Bradley seems to be looking off into space, as if I'm not here.

I wonder what's going on inside her head. I wonder if she thinks I'm lost, that I've pulled free of my moorings, that I've drifted off to that point toward which she now stares – *out there*. I think she thinks I don't know how to get back.

Bradley is the smartest dog on the planet.

28

Things get Worse

The water has risen almost halfway to the cot!

Rosalie reaches down, scoops some into her palm and brings it to her nose. "This is seawater!"

Drugged. Kidnapped. Now we're going to drown?

"Amanda," Rosalie says.

"What?"

"Do you believe in God?"

"I…I don't know. I used to. Before my dad died."

"Some people believe in prayer even if they don't believe in God."

Amanda's face goes blank.

"Pray with me. Even if you have doubt. Please pray with me."

Rosalie reaches out. Just as their hands touch, a loud sound shakes the room. Somewhere, a combustion engine has been fired into life! The banging and wheezing sounds primitive, the cylinders pounding up and down, jarring the room, vibrating the metal cot beneath them. Dust falls from the ceiling.

Amanda shouts, "What *is* that?"

"I know that sound," Rosalie yells. "Maybe there is a God after all."

"What?" Amanda leans closer. "What did you say?"

"It's a generator and a pump!" Rosalie smiles. "When I was a kid, we had one in our cellar. It's going to pump the water out. We're going to be okay."

Then Rosalie's smile fades.

"What's wrong?" Amanda asks.

Rosalie looks at Amanda.

"It means someone's here."

29

An Unsettling Answer

Later in the day, I go back to my computer. There are seven emails in my Inbox. Four are junk mail. The other three have sender's addresses I'm not familiar with.

The first one reads:

Hi,

Someone forward your email to me. Very wierd. Sorry, but I got nothing for you. I was there that night. I seen it. It was so bad that I been driving more careful ever since. I hope you find what your looking for.

Pete.

There's no Pete on my list.

The second email has no name, and no misspells:

Get a life!

I wonder how angry a person must be, how groundless they'd have to feel, for them to waste even a minute writing something so pointless.

The sender's address on the last email is a local library. I open it and read:

> *MR SNOW. STOP WHAT YOU ARE DOING. FIND ANOTHER GAME TO PLAY. YOU WILL LIVE LONGER. YOURS TRULY, THE DRIVER.*

The Driver.

I get that creepy feeling again, like I'm being watched. I know it's just my imagination, but I turn around and look anyway, peer into the murky windows. I see only my reflection. And the dark.

My heart pounds.

Then the buzzing starts. It begins in my chest, moves outward, spreads through my whole body.

Read it again!

I turn back to the computer. Read the threatening email a second time.

Slowly.

Word by word.

As I stare at the message, it goes out of focus and becomes a blur – but the signature in the lower left corner remains clear. *The Driver.* Is he (or she) enticing me with a clue? Was The Driver somehow involved in Harry Crow's accident? But two of the three drivers were killed. Maybe there was a hit and run. Could The Driver have been the cause of the accident? *Not* Harry Crow? Did he hit Harry's Caddy, forcing it into the van? *Had Harry Crow been a target?*

My head pounds.

I decide to let it go. Perhaps I need to open a space between *it* and *me* – a space within which puzzle pieces might appear.

I turn off the computer. Head down to the Pit to feed Bradley. As I descend the steel stairs toward the main deck, those two words come into my mind, pulsing in time with my heart.

I see them out there in the dark…

like a crackling neon sign…

The Driver.

30

The Driver

It seems to take hours for the water to recede. The last of it swirls and gurgles down the hole in the corner, leaving a slurry of mud and grit on the floor, and little puddles of brown water.

Rosalie and Amanda sit on the cold metal cot, shivering. Now that the rattling engine has shut down, the silence seems even more unnerving. They hear each other's breathing, each drop of water as it plops into the muck.

Rosalie slowly uncurls her legs and slides off the cot. She intends to stretch – instead, she cocks her head and holds her breath.

"What?" Amanda says, her voice rising. "Jesus, *what is it?*"

Amanda stands, steps behind Rosalie and grabs her arm. Flinching at the girl's touch, Rosalie raises a finger to her pursed lips. "Shhh!"

When the scratching noise comes again, Rosalie knows what it is – a key being inserted into the lock. The sounds continue, as if the holder of the key is having trouble finding the sweet spot in the old tumblers.

The scratching noise stops. Then comes the sound of the bolt being thrown. The doorframe thumps, dust tumbles from the old wood casings, and the door slowly swings inward.

"*Fuck, fuck, fuck,*" Amanda whispers.

"It's all right," Rosalie says, even though she knows it is not.

As the door opens, Rosalie instinctively reaches behind to protect Amanda.

Hinges groan like they've not been used in a hundred years. As the door opens wide, coming from a high point out in the hall, a round beam of light cuts a burning swath out of the darkness. When the beam sways, the room seems to sway with it.

Amanda slides her arms around Rosalie's waist and holds tight.

Rosalie's heart pounds. Her eyes shocked by the light, she sees shapes. Then the beam of light swings over to Amanda's old blankets on the floor. For the moment, it remains fixed there.

When Rosalie's eyes adjust, she sees a huge shape, like a giant robot emitting a beam of light from its forehead! The monstrous thing steps into the room, its head and shoulders brushing against the doorframe, its boots make squishing sounds in the mud as it advances slowly on the women.

It stops.

Standing before them is a giant of a man, wearing a head-lamp. A large duffel bag hangs from his right hand, a suitcase-like box from his left. Whenever the man moves his head, the head-lamp's beam reflects off the puddles of water, causing eerie slivers of light to dance across his face. The slivers create both shadow and ghastly sheen.

In this moment, a powerful feeling of energy floods through Rosalie. She's a survivor! She has survived the deaths of her parents, the heartbreaking loss of four pregnancies and the death of her best friend and husband, Jonathan. Now, standing between Amanda and a monster of a man, she feels that survivor surging within her. With this feeling comes pure clarity. Rosalie is a warrior. She will not die without a fight! *Let's get on with this.*

"Ladies." Within the musty, earthen space, the man's voice is like a rumbling in the earth.

My God, it's him!

The man who'd called himself Chester Ramsey smiles. "Welcome home."

Rosalie suppresses a gasp. Her recognition of Ramsey horrifies her. In her kitchen, she'd thought him well over six feet tall, but in the confines of their darkened cell, the man seems even more immense. His shoulders are cement blocks. His face is carved bone.

"I hope you're both feeling well. I apologize for the after-effects. To be truthful, I didn't like giving you those drugs. I've never used that particular one before, but I was careful."

When Amanda moves next to Rosalie, Rosalie puts an arm around the girl's shoulders. "You almost killed her! When I woke, she was still unconscious. Whatever you gave her, it was too much."

The man reaches up and switches off the light. His cold gaze sweeps back and forth, ratchets from one woman to the other.

Rosalie is confounded. The man's matter-of-factness is baffling.

167

He speaks again, almost gently. "Well. I'm really sorry to hear that." He addresses Amanda directly. "Is there anything I can do to make up for my error?"

Amanda looks at him defiantly. "Sure. You can let us the fuck out of here!"

Amanda's anger makes Rosalie's blood surge – it's exhilarating.

"*Yes! You can let us go!*"

"Why did you drug us and bring us here?" Amanda asks. "Why did you kill Vinnie?"

The man nods decisively. "I drugged you because it was easier than letting you put up a fuss. And, besides, you wouldn't have enjoyed your confinement if you were awake. As for your friend…Vinnie, was his name? Well, he was simply in the way. You see, ladies? Reasonable questions get reasonable answers. Are we all good now?"

"No, we are not *all good!*" Amanda screams. "You *killed* him! *You cut his throat!*"

The man seems unaffected. "Trust me. I take no pleasure in killing anyone. I never have. I only do what's necessary to get the job done."

He looks around the room. "I am definitely not happy with the conditions here," he says, as if to himself. "This whole project has taken more time and work than I'd expected. But I'll be getting these things squared away soon."

Rosalie wonders how much damage she'd do if she just said fuck it and kicked him in the balls.

"I apologize for the flooding. That's on me. I forgot to switch over the fuel tanks. You see, I forgot because of the stress.

You have to watch out for stress. It can kill you."

The Driver laughs at his own joke.

Rosalie can't believe how relaxed he is. His casual demeanor makes him seem even crazier.

"When it's high tide – twice each day, ladies, pay attention – the water comes into the machinery room first. That's where the floats are."

His diction is perfect.

"When the floats rise, the generator automatically comes on. Yes, I know it's loud, but it drives the pumps, and the pumps pump the water out. Of course, when the fuel runs out, the generator doesn't kick in, and with no genny to run the pumps... Well, no one knows better than you what can happen then."

The man's smile is ghastly.

"All of you should be thankful that I remembered to come back. Because if I hadn't," he makes a swirling motion with his fingers, "you'd all be circling the drains right now."

Rosalie's heart jumps. *All of you?*

The man lifts the duffel and the box for emphasis. "I've brought some essentials for you. And some dry blankets." He looks to the mound of sodden blankets in the mud. "I know the ones I left for you got wet."

The man's face goes blank, his mannerisms robotic. "Okay," he says, like a cruise director. "You two should get out of those clothes. You must be freezing."

Rosalie shivers. *Does he want to watch?*

The man walks past them and places the duffel and the box on the cot. He doesn't seem at all concerned that his back is to them, nor that they both have a clear path to the open door.

Rosalie wonders, is he taunting them? *Should we run now?* She holds her breath.

The man turns to face them. "Please. For your own sake. Don't try to escape. You'll only get hurt."

Rosalie breathes out.

"It would not please me to see you hurt. It's a long way to the nearest medical facility and we're surrounded by water. The ferry…" He looks away, as if distracted.

Rosalie wonders if there's something wrong with the man, something more than just crazy.

"Well, let's put this to rest," he says. "The Portland-to-Boston ferry is not an option."

Portland? Are they in Maine?

"So!" The man claps his hands. "Let's have no trouble out of you two. Because if either of you give me any trouble, I won't hurt you, I'll kill you."

Rosalie feels dizzy. "We won't make trouble. But please, tell us why we're here."

He ignores her. Pointing at the cot. "Sit," he says.

They sit.

He opens the duffel and pulls out two wool blankets. When he takes one and moves toward Rosalie, she jerks back.

"I told you I'm not going to hurt you. These are to keep you warm." He drapes the blankets – one around Rosalie's shoulders, the other around Amanda's. Rosalie is surprised by how gently he does this.

"There are sealed containers of food in here." He lifts the lid on the box. From it, he takes a smaller metal box and places it on the cot. "There's a flashlight, a gallon of water and a large thermos filled with hot soup. Get some of that soup into you. You'll feel better."

For a second, he looks derailed, as if his mind has skipped a track. Looking at the women, he seems startled by their presence.

"Again, I apologize for the conditions. Once I'm back on schedule, I'll be able to make some improvements. Then, you won't have to spend the nights cold and wet."

"Can you just tell us where we are?" Rosalie asks.

"You're in Maine. Off the coast, so to speak."

He spreads his hands out in front of him, like a man about to tell an amazing tale.

"Don't worry, ladies," he says. "Soon you'll meet the others. Then we can get started."

There are others!

He makes as if to go, then turns back. "Perhaps I'll bring some books down here for you. Keep you busy until everything is in place." He nods, then heads for the door.

"Wait!" Rosalie hears the panic in her voice.

The man half-turns. Gives them his left profile. Closes his eyes as if to seal in his annoyance. Waits.

"This isn't fair," Rosalie says. "You have us at a disadvantage."

The man's eyes remain closed. He doesn't move.

Rosalie fears he's about to explode.

"Mrs Tam," he says. "You have just made the understatement of the century."

Hearing the man say her name makes Rosalie feel weak. "What I mean is, you know *our* names, but we don't know *yours*. At least tell us what we should call you. You're not an insurance adjuster. I'm sure your name isn't Chester Ramsey. It would be easier if we knew how to address you."

His eyes open slowly. He doesn't look at them. He just stares into the murk. His words come like a low growl. "You want to know…how to *address* me?" A muscle twitches at the corner of his mouth, like a worm trapped under the skin.

"Yes. Who are you?"

Two beats…

…three.

The silence is terrifying.

The man swivels his head and glares at Rosalie.

"I am your…"

The word that follows is a glowing iron pressed against her skin.

"…husband."

31

Ray and Snow on the Bridge

Ray and I are sitting out on the small steel deck, just aft of *Paralus'* high bridge.

Two days ago, I called Ray and told him about the connections – that Harry Crow's accident was the common denominator in the murder, the abductions and the dognapping. Ray didn't buy it.

He called me back this morning. Told me it was his day off and he was coming to visit. With beer. Interesting. In the five years we've known each other, he's been on *Paralus* only a few times, and always in an official capacity. Never on his day off.

We're enjoying our beers, and evaluating manly things – the life expectancy of my rusty pickup (short); the guy that owns the boat that's loud, goes too fast and is painted like an American flag (jerk); Susan, the marina's general manager (hot).

One spring day. Two beers. Two friends. One killer view. All normal.

Until Ray brings up Amanda Crow. He makes it clear that

my findings and my theories are of no interest to the Providence cops. They won't be switching gears in Slo-Mo's murder case based on anything I've come up with.

"Jesus, Ray. What the hell is their problem? The odds against all these links being coincidental are off the chart!" Right away I regret my tone. Ray doesn't make policy and he doesn't deserve my ire.

Because I'm frustrated with the cops and their closed minds, I'm tempted to up the ante, to tell Ray my theory about what might be going on. But I hold back. Ray is used to hearing my wild ideas, but this one is so far out there, he'll think I've gone completely off the rails.

"Ah, you gotta love it," Ray says, with a hint of sarcasm. "When I laid it all out for the captain, he raised his eyebrows, said his *Hmms,* and his *Ah-hahs,* and then said, *Bullshit.* He says to me, 'How could a murder, two kidnappings, and the theft of a dog – a dog for Chrissakes! – have anything to do with a ten-fifty from a few years ago?"

"Four years ago," I say.

Ray stares at me. I have a fair idea what's coming next.

"Look. I gotta tell you this straight up, Snowman. If it was anyone else but you throwing me these bones? Like, if I didn't know from personal experience that you were the second coming of Harry Houdini? I'd tell you…"

I cut him off. "Houdini was a magician. I'm psychic. I may not be particularly good at it, but no matter; your analogy is faulty. Try, the second coming of Edgar Cayce."

Ray gives me a look that's supposed to be threatening. "Edgar Cayce. Houdini. Who gives a shit? If I didn't know you,

174

I'd tell you to take a hike. Probably what I should do anyway."

"I didn't throw you *bones*," I say. "I gave you *facts*."

"Granted, they're facts. But just because certain unrelated *facts* may give the *appearance* of being related does *not* mean that they really *are* related."

Easy for him to say.

I take a moment to think about whether or not I want to put any more energy into trying to convince the Providence Police to buy into my findings and theories. I lean back against the wall, feel the steel rivets press into my back like brass knuckles. Up here, almost twenty feet above the cove, we can see the buildings of Providence to the north, the Newport and Jamestown bridges to the south. From here, I can watch the sun come up over Riverside.

I'm a lucky man.

"Snowman?"

"Hold on a sec." I look up at the powder-blue sky. There's not a cloud in sight.

"Hey, I got a life to live over here," Ray says, tapping his watch.

"What is your problem, Ray? You just got here."

"Yeah, but I didn't come here to watch you watch clouds." Ray sneaks a glance upward.

"There *are* no clouds," I say.

"Fuck," Ray says to himself. "Here we go."

"Just another sec," I say, holding up one finger. I am, in fact, not gazing at anything. I am trying to decide whether or not I should tell Ray my theory.

I look at Ray. "With your seniority, your pull, you'd think you could get..."

"I've gone too far already!" Ray says. "It's not going to happen. Just let it go. You're not going to get any help on this one, not until you get something concrete, something at least halfway believable. And even then I don't…"

"Stop!" I hold out my closed fist. "Can you count? The boyfriend of *Harry Crow's* daughter is dead." I unfold my thumb. "Then *Harry Crow's daughter* vanishes." I unfold my index finger. "The wife of the guy that ran into *Harry Crow* vanishes." Another finger. "An EMT at the scene of *Harry Crow's accident* vanishes." And another. "A dog – and I know it sounds silly – but a *dog* owned by the tow-truck driver who *hauled Harry Crow's car away* vanishes." I unfold my pinkie finger. "Five coincidences? You getting this? *Five!* And you want *believable*?"

"It's not me that wants it. Look man, I'm sorry. I agree with you. That's a hell of a string of coincidences. There's just nothing I can do right now."

My frustration is obvious. "Yeah, I got that. But if you—"

"No." Ray holds up his hand.

"Okay," I say. "I appreciate that you tried."

Ray springs to his feet. For a big man, he accomplishes this rather well. He shakes my hand. Turns. Leaves the bridge.

I feel empty.

I get up and go to the railing, watch Ray as he walks down my boarding ramp and heads for his car. It's so quiet, I can hear each step crunching in the gravel.

Ray gets to his car. Pulls the door open. Glances up.

We briefly make eye contact. Without so much as a nod, Ray folds himself into his car and drives away.

I'm on my own.

32

The Driver

The Driver has a tattoo on his left bicep.

He doesn't like tattoos.

All the gangsters in the joint, covering their bodies in ink. Elaborate displays of prison art meant to announce not only their gang affiliations, but what badass motherfuckers they are. To The Driver, they look like fools.

The Driver can kill a man with tattoos, easy as one without.

Ten years ago, The Driver took a contract on a half-white, half-black guy name of Leroy Gunnerson. Guy's skin was an ugly blanket of tats. Even had his head shaved so you could read the ink on his ugly skull. Gunnerson was a hard-case, just released from jail after doing a dime for robbery and aggravated assault.

They said Gunnerson was a hard-timer. To The Driver, he was just a skin-bag held upright by a bunch of bones.

Gunnerson belonged to a biker gang, called themselves The Huns. A group of tattooed assholes if ever there were. Gunnerson was easy to find. Late one night, after a Hun's meet at a local bar, The Driver followed the fool as he cruised home on his Harley. The guy was clueless.

When Gunnerson parked his all-chrome, custom hardtail inside his garage, The Driver came out of the shadows with a lead pipe.

The Driver could have just shot Gunnerson in the head and been done with it. But because of all those stupid tats, he decided he wanted to make a statement about ink. Even though he knew no one would understand what his statement meant.

The Driver eased up behind the biker. Quietly watched as the fool unzipped his leathers, then smashed his left leg with the pipe. The tibia is a heavy bone, but The Driver's swing was epic. He heard the snap, like a 22-caliber pistol shot.

When Gunnerson dropped to the concrete floor, screaming like a little girl, The Driver looked down at him and said, "Why'd you have to ink yourself up like that, you stupid fuck? You guys kill me. You think ink makes you look badass. It doesn't. It makes you look dumb."

Gunnerson wasn't screaming any more. He was lying on his back, hands gripping his grotesquely bent leg, pain twisting his face out of shape, staring up in disbelief at the giant hovering above him.

The Driver could see death in the man's eyes – they had that empty "Oh no" look, like the man fully understood that his karma had finally caught up with him.

His voice was feeble, quavering. *"What the fuck?"*

The Driver smiled. "You think your tats make you look bad, motherfucker?"

Gunnerson grimaced.

Then The Driver took an even mightier swing than the first and caved in Gunnerson's skull.

What a mess *that* had made.

The Driver thinks about the tattoo on his bicep – it has no lofty purpose like the hundreds on Gunnerson. The Driver had it etched into his skin merely to commemorate his life's work. A bone-white skull with a black dagger clenched between its teeth. Under that, the words, "Born to Kill".

It's morning, and the diesel generator is running again in the mechanicals shed behind the house, pistons banging up and down, the whole thing sounding like it's about to explode.

Sometime over the past few days the pilot went out in the gas water heater. *Again.* Drafty damn house. In the airy, first-floor bathroom, The Driver had to take his second cold shower in as many days. Woke him the hell up, that's for sure.

As he dresses, The Driver's thoughts fall to the orange-haired freak. Fat bastard went and died on him. So, it hadn't mattered. All the trouble The Driver went to. The fucker died anyway.

Which means, of course, that he has to get back in his truck, head south, get a replacement. *Shit.*

Well, there is *one* consolation. At least Spikes didn't die inside the box. He died earlier that morning, when The Driver was bringing his guests their breakfast. He found Spikes sitting on his cot with his back against the wall, staring up at the ceiling like he was looking for something. His chubby hands were clutched at his chest, his tongue sticking out of his mouth like a hunk of gray meat.

Something about the look frozen on Spikes' face bothered The Driver. Maybe it was that the kid had obviously been wanting attention so bad.

Well, he'd gotten attention all right.

The Driver is getting a little worn down. He's trying to pull off the most difficult and complex operation the world has ever seen. The underground network of gravel and mud rooms and constantly dripping tunnels and all the other nasty shit? Taking care of that stuff alone is a full-time job. Plus, he has to juggle the time schedules. And he has to track his targets. And he has to make his grabs. And throughout all of this work, he has to keep everyone alive, right? It's almost too much, even for him, a man of such phenomenal drive, such maniacal will.

The Driver needs a nap.

33

Snow, Ray, and the Rain

"What do you expect me to do with this theory of yours?" Ray says.

"You're kidding," I say. "You're making a joke, right?"

"No point in that. You *have* no sense of humor." Ray grins and looks away.

It's quiet inside the marina restaurant. Outside, the rain slams against the windows and the wind whistles through the rigging on the boats. In front of the marina office, ropes and pulleys clang and bang against the wooden flagpole.

Ray stares at me. "Seriously. I mention your theory and I'll be laughed out of the station."

"C'mon, Ray. I'm just asking you to be a little open-minded."

Watching the rain, Ray pretends to ignore me.

"My theory is backed by so many facts, it can no longer be called a theory."

Ray gives me his death stare again, but I sense an invitation to proceed.

"Why is it so hard to imagine? A few years ago you would have called me crazy if I told you a bunch of Saudi Arabian guys were going to steal planes and fly them…"

Ray makes a pushing motion toward me. "Back it up! In 2000, if you'd asked me which was more believable? 9/11? Or this whacked-out theory of yours? I'd have taken 9/11."

"Do you have a better explanation for why people are being taken?" I ask.

"You say 'taken' as if that's a fact," Ray says. "The only one we know for sure was 'taken' is Sawicki. Right now, Amanda Crow and Rosalie Tam are only missing."

"What about the dog?" I say.

Ray sighs. "Give me a break."

"Two neighbors witnessed Inky's abduction. We know he was taken, too."

Ray looks down and shakes his head.

"There's a link between the dog and the accident," I say.

Ray looks up. I think he wants to kill me.

"I'm not going to stop asking that question," I say. "Do *you* have a better explanation?"

"Don't ask me to prove a negative, and then tell me I have to use the unprovable result as a rational explanation for…" Ray sighs. "For anything."

"Damn it, Ray! Use your imagination! Imagine that you and your wife and your kids are headed for…"

Ray chuckles. "Ask me to imagine something I can imagine."

I can't tell if it's his intention, but his stubbornness is getting to me. "*You*, the wife and the kids are headed for a much-needed vacation in the mountains. You've got your dog in the back of the

182

van along with your tent and your sleeping ba—"

"Stop!" Ray huffs. "I been working my ass off, haven't had a vacation in ten years, and I'm gonna sleep on the ground? In the boonies? With the rug-rats, the old lady *and the dog?*"

"Okay," I say. "You're *not* headed for the mountains. You're going to the beach in South Jersey. You're planning to spend the week sitting in your beach chair with your feet in the sand and a cooler of cold beer by your side. You're thinking about that one day in the middle of the week when the wife and the kids are going to drive up to the Palisades to visit Aunt Gertrude, and you'll be left alone to watch the girls in their bikinis. How's that?"

"Okay. Now you're talking." Ray closes his eyes and starts bobbing his head. "Now I'm there. I'm using my imagination."

"You've been driving for hours," I say. "You're tired, so you pull over to switch places with your wife. She gets behind the wheel, and you're about to open the passenger door when, BAM!, someone smashes into the back of your van! Thirty seconds later, you're watching your family burning to death."

Ray's not staring anymore. He's looking at me.

"Something like that could break your mind. Make you crazy enough to do crazy things."

Ray says nothing.

"Out of a hundred people, something that horrible happens? Most of them would probably need therapy, a few would start taking drugs, and maybe *one* would have some warped idea of revenge."

The restaurant is empty but for Ray, myself and the waiter. It's deathly still. Beyond the windows, the weather's getting worse.

"Your theory about what's happening here?" Ray says. "I wouldn't call it revenge. This is revenge multiplied by a zillion. I can't even see Hannibal Lecter doing something like this."

"That's because you're sane. That and the fact that you have no children and no family. You can't imagine the nightmares you'd have, or the relief you might seek from them."

Ray blinks.

"The human mind is capable of anything. Look at Jeffrey Dahmer. If I'm right about our guy, maybe what he's doing seems like justice to him."

"I'm not buying it," Ray says. "It's not just crazy. It's complex and complicated, not to mention risky and dangerous. I don't even see how the thing could be doable. He could never pull it off. Even if he was a perfectly sane *genius*."

"No?"

Ray shakes his head. "Jesus, Snow. Think about what it takes to kidnap *one* person and get away with it."

"I already have," I say.

"What does he do with them all? No, I can't… Look, I can see maybe a guy going off the rails and shooting someone. Even shooting a bunch of someones."

"But who would he shoot?" I say. "The guy who caused the accident is already dead."

Ray sighs. "This wouldn't be the first guy to go postal. Just for a different reason. But snatching random people for no reason? What's he gonna do with them? Have some kind of ritualistic dinner together, *then* kill them?"

I shake my head. "This is the part of my theory that turns everything inside-out." I pause, then decide to go for it. "Just listen to this, Ray. He's not just kidnapping people at random, there's consistency. He's only taking people related to people who were at the scene of the accident."

I stop, because my theory is starting to sound even more ridiculous to me, and because Ray's eyes are closed, and his face has gone blank. I imagine that, in his mind, he's already gotten up from the table and gone home.

He opens his eyes and gives me a soulful smile. "I gotta tell you, my friend. I like your intensity. I like your focus. And I really like your determination. You find a cause? You're a bulldog with a piece of rawhide."

I nod.

"You're a lot like me in that regard," he says.

"So…" I say.

"Yeah, well…" Ray pushes his chair back and stands up. "I guess it doesn't matter, because this is all wrong."

"That's it?" I say.

"That's it," Ray says. And leaves.

I stay in my chair and watch him go. When he opens the door, the wind almost pulls it out of his hand.

"You'll come around," I mutter to myself.

Nothing's changed. I'm still on my own.

But something *has* changed. There's a new feeling in my gut, and it's telling me, *You're right. But you're also wrong.*

34

The Driver

The Driver sits down at the kitchen table in the drafty house and pulls out his maps and his yellow-lined pad. On the pad is a list of his potential candidates, as well as each brilliant idea he's had so far, all written down the instant it popped into his head.

Poring over the info, he searches for the next one.

The selection is critical. Snatching a random civilian would be pointless. It has to be someone with a direct connection to the accident. He must create maximum pain. Only in this way, like the self-cutter, will his suffering be relieved.

The Driver flips through the pages of the pad. No, not that guy – he has no predictable schedule. Flip the page. Flip the page. No, not her – she lives in a section-8 dump. Too many witnesses hanging around the place.

The Driver flips again. *There he is!* The newest member of the family! James R. French. 134 Bowlen Avenue, Scituate, Rhode Island. Twenty-three. Mechanic at Warren's Auto Clinic in Cumberland. A fair commute from Scituate to Cumberland, which is why The Driver is choosing French. A nice long drive home from work ends at his house in the woods. Alone.

What sours his choice just a little is the other reason The Driver decides on James R. James R is the son of Richard A French. The Driver had originally chosen Richard A, owner of French's Towing. Richard A would have been easy. Workaholic. Out on the road a lot, often at night. Problem is, Richard A just had himself an on-the-job accident. Main cable snapped and fractured his leg, and now he's wearing a big cast. No way that thing will fit into the box.

While it's true that taking the son represents a shift in the plan, The Driver reasons that destroying the son will make the father suffer even more than if he, the father, had been taken.

The Driver could have just killed them all.

In the first few weeks after the tragedy, he'd certainly thought about it. He'd imagined driving under the cover of darkness, house to house, placing incendiary devices, blocking exits, encircling the homes with moats of gasoline. He could see the roaring infernos, hear the screams as they tried to escape, as they slowly, agonizingly burned to death.

But The Driver isn't ready for it to be over.

35

Carmella DeLong

A cloud of paint dust hangs in the air. When I cough, the cloud scatters. I should be wearing a particle mask, but in this heat, the thing makes me gag.

The chattering of the heavy-duty sander is starting to grate at my nerves. When I shut it off, the sudden quiet is stunning. Numb from the vibrating machine, my hands and fingers immediately buzz with blood.

For the past two hours I've been sanding the exterior wall of *Paralus'* wheelhouse, grinding through layers of heavy lead paint. In that time, I've managed to expose just a four-foot square of bare metal. *Paralus* is 100 feet long and sixteen feet wide. Her main superstructure rises almost twenty feet above the waterline. Doing some quick math, I calculate that at four square feet every two hours, I'll be done in 200 years.

Why am I doing this?

To hell with it. I take my tools down to the lazarette, stow them, grab the wet-vac, go back to the wheelhouse and carefully vacuum all the paint chips and dust. Can't have all those chemicals blowing into the cove.

I go up one level to the high bridge, my office. Without thinking, I swat at my clothes. Now I have a cloud of dust *inside* the boat. Nice move, genius.

Of the five emails in my Inbox, four are junk. The fifth is from someone named Carmella DeLong.

I say the name out aloud, "Carmella DeLong." It rolls warmly off my tongue. Just hearing it evokes the image of a Mediterranean woman. Eyes like warm chocolate. Caramel-colored skin. Lots of long, auburn hair tumbling softly over elegant, bare shoulders.

Ms DeLong's email is somewhat cryptic. She writes that a friend of hers showed her one of my emails. As it turns out, not only does Ms DeLong know something about the accident, she has information she believes will interest me. She says she's a physical therapist, that her most memorable client is a man who burned his hands in a car fire. His name is Chester William Ramsey.

The name isn't on my list and I know I've never heard it before.

The email closes with a provocative line: "I have no doubt you will want to hear what I've learned about Mr Ramsey." Carmella DeLong includes her cell number.

I grab the phone and dial.

Three rings.

"Hello?"

"Is this Carmella DeLong?"

There's a pause, then, "Who wants to know?" The woman's

voice is grating, acerbic, heavily weighted by an ungainly Rhode Island accent. Not at all the Carmella of my fantasy.

I tell her my name.

"Mr Snow?" Her volume is almost at shout-level; "Oh, my Gawd! That was so *fast!* I didn't know if you'd ever call me. I mean, maybe you'd think I was just another nutjob or somethin'."

Carmella DeLong goes on to tell me that one of her patients has burns on his hands, and she thinks he may have gotten them in 'my' accident.

My first thought is, the victims of the accident all died, except Eldrick Creech. Creech survived, but he wasn't injured. I recall writing on my M+D board, five fatalities, *no injuries.*

When I glance at my board, my eyes immediately fall upon Creech's name. I close my eyes and imagine him standing in the breakdown lane with his hand on the passenger door, just as his van is bulldozed by Harry Crow's Cadillac.

"I'd rather not talk about this on the phone," I say. "This isn't a secure line. I'm worried someone might be listening."

I'm lying. The truth is, I want to be able to look Ms DeLong in the eye when she tells me about Mr Ramsey.

Despite my bogus warning, Carmella begins gushing about the first time Ramsey came to her office. I gently cut her off and ask if we can meet tomorrow.

She suggests a local coffee shop. Three o'clock.

After we hang up, I wonder, is Ramsey actually Creech? If so, then why haven't I heard anything about him being burned? Creech was the only survivor. (Wasn't he?) And why does it just now occur to me that, throughout the investigation, I haven't heard any accounts of Eldrick Creech attempting to rescue his family? However, there *was* someone injured while trying to rescue them – a fireman. I make a mental note to add him to my board.

What am I missing? As I ponder these questions, I hear a familiar sound – it's another puzzle piece, clicking into its place.

36

The Plan

The women are huddled together on the cold metal cot, drinking water, wearing their new, dry clothes. Gray sweatpants. Gray sweatshirts with the hoods pulled over their heads. Dry blankets wrapped around their legs. They're no longer shivering.

Amanda sniffs, coughs, then leans over and lifts the lid on the metal box. True to his word, The Driver left a thermos of chicken soup, a gallon of water, a roll of paper towels, a roll of toilet paper, four cans of Spam with the roll-tops and sliced bread in a ziplock bag.

Next to the box, the women's discarded garments lie in the mud.

Amanda tears off a tissue and blows her nose. She looks at the door, drops her head and begins to cry again. "This is a nightmare."

Rosalie rubs Amanda's back. "Come on. I know this is hard, but if we're going to survive this, we *must* stay focused."

Once again, Rosalie feels something heavy inside. The weight is a hardness, a pressure that makes her want to *do something now!* Take some kind of action that will give them a chance at survival. She feels it. A distant, indefinable strength gathering.

The instinct for survival exists in all living things. But this strange feeling is more than that. This is white-hot anger. Who does The Driver think he is? *What gives this bastard the right?*

The more Rosalie thinks about him, the hotter her anger gets. It's becoming a fury. Like stones, grinding themselves into knives. Although Rosalie has never hurt a living thing, she's certain that if she had a gun, she would kill him.

"There are two of us," Rosalie says, quietly.

Amanda raises her head.

"Two are better than one. We have to find something to hit him with." Rosalie reaches out and stabs the air with her hand. "Maybe jam something into his eyes."

Amanda leans away from Rosalie. "I'm with you, but did you see the *size* of that freak? He killed Vinnie like he was an insect. Whatever we decide to do, it better be good."

"We have nothing to lose," Rosalie says. "He's going to kill us. Then he's going to bury us in this mud hole under the ground and no one is ever going to find us."

Amanda stares at Rosalie.

Rosalie jumps to her feet, hikes the blanket onto her shoulders and begins to pace. "We've got to come up with something. Otherwise, we might as well just lie down and die."

Amanda nods her head. "What can we do?"

As Rosalie looks around the room, something in the far corner catches her eye. She puts her lips close to Amanda's ear.

"Don't make it obvious, but look up in the corner."

Amanda squints, looks slowly around the room, then whispers, "That looks like…" She glances at the door, then lowers her head again. "Air vent?"

Rosalie whispers, "There could be a camera or a microphone in there." Rosalie leans forward and puts her elbows on her knees. She holds her face in her hands to cover her mouth. "We have to assume he can see and hear us. Maybe we can use that to our advantage."

Amanda looks at Rosalie, wrinkles her brow into a question, then leans forward and puts her head in her hands, too.

Rosalie figures they must look like two helpless women. Dejected. Resigned to their fate. But she knows they are much more than that.

In a whisper, Rosalie outlines her plan.

37

Carmella DeLong

It's 3:23. Carmella DeLong is almost a half hour late. The way people are going missing, I wonder if I should be concerned.

A popular meeting place in the West Bay area, Mia's Cafe is not for me. There are too many types of coffee to choose from, and a hysterically small piece of lemon poppyseed crumb cake goes for $6.95. Enough said.

Mia's is long and narrow, with lots of couches and overstuffed lounge chairs, fieldstone fireplace with faux fire, faux walnut book case with faux books. The couches and chairs are arranged into a dozen or so little alcoves, each with its own immense, leafy palm plant hovering above like an umbrella, which helps create the illusion of privacy. Wide-planked wood floors covered with imitation Persian rugs complete the theme. Mia's Cafe has all the warmth of a feng shui'ed bowling alley.

Today, the cafe has a full house, with the exception of one small table sharing a corner with a giant palm; I'm parked next to the plant, much too far from the fire to enjoy its "warmth". Even more disheartening, I have no *Wall Street Journal* to read.

Most of the people sitting under their big leaves are leaning toward each other in conspiratorial earnest, whispering as if in church. What secrets are being shared, what friendships betrayed, what gossip fabricated, consumed, regurgitated?

Carmella DeLong is now twenty-seven minutes late. Just as I'm about to give up, I notice a woman speaking to the cashier. Her head is covered in a scarf and she's wearing large, dark sunglasses. The cashier points toward me and my plant. The woman wearing the sunglasses nods to me. I nod back.

Carmella threads her way toward me, navigating furtively past the customers and the plants, nervously glancing behind her as she goes. When she arrives, she sits abruptly, removes her sunglasses, then her scarf, revealing an impressive mane of chestnut hair. I'm guessing Carmella, who is wearing a coffee-colored silk blouse and sand-colored shorts, is mid-to-late thirties. Her almond skin looks so tight, you could bounce a quarter off its flawless surface.

While I would not call Ms DeLong pretty, she is a handsome woman. Her facial structure and her moderately dark skin hint at a Hispanic heritage. Her brown eyes radiate both curiosity and fear.

"Mr Snow?" *Mistah.*

I nod.

"I'm late," she says without apology. "On top a that, I only got a few minutes before my next appointment."

I quickly learn that what I'd assumed to be her Rhode Island accent is more a vernacular that leans toward ghetto-speak.

"All right," I say. "Then let's get to it. Please tell me about Mr Ramsey."

Carmella folds her hands on the table. They're shaking. "Like I said, I'm a physical therapist. *Hand* therapist. I do hands. That's all. I been working at York County Rehab almost ten years now.

"Four years ago, Ramseys gets referred to me by a surgeon at Rhode Island Hospital. Doc actually calls me, which docs *never* do. That was just the beginning of all the weird shit."

Surprised by her openness regarding her patient, I say, "What about privacy issues?"

"That's more for doctors. My people are clients. At York we have them sign a waiver saying privilege is implied. But the bottom line is, I'm not gonna share any medical info about Ramseys you couldn't research on your own."

"Got it," I say, ignoring her mispronunciation.

"Okay, so…" Carmella glances around the room. "Ramseys' hands were cooked pretty good. Second- and third-degree burns. After he had his skin grafts, I worked with him for more than a year to get his hands more flexible."

"Were you successful?" I say.

"Yeah, we did okay," Carmella says.

"Tell me again how you found out about what I'm doing?"

Carmella shifts in her chair. She looks around, eyes jittery. "Well, this good friend a mine, he drives ambulance. Diesel – I call him D – tells me he got this email a yours, the one where you was sayin' you needed help, or somethin' like that. Some stuff about a bad accident." *Ax-ee-dent.*

I nod.

"D tells me this weird stuff. Like, that some people who were there have been disappearin'? And when D says, like, eight

197

or ten people were killed in that accident, and some burned to death? Didn't take me long to put two and two together. I figure, whoever sent that email to Diesel, they'll wanna hear about this. That would be you," Carmella points a trembling finger at me.

"And you were right," I say.

Carmella nods. Again, her eyes dart around the room. "Like I was sayin', me and Ramseys was doin' the rehab. Workin' workin' workin'. During that time, he's tellin' me these pieces of his story, 'bout how he got his hands burned up and all. I mean, at first I felt bad for the guy."

Carmella hesitates, then her expression flattens as she gives me the story Ramsey gave her: that he was injured trying to rescue people from a burning van; that he heard the people screaming inside.

"He was traumatized," Carmella says. "I understand that. But it doesn't give him the right to act like a crazy man. It scared me."

Carmella briefly makes eye contact, then looks away.

"What scared you?" I say.

"I'm getting a little ahead of myself." Carmella takes a breath, then raises her hands, using her own fingers to instruct me. "When skin burns, it shrinks. Then when it heals, it loses flexibility. It hurts to move your fingers. If skin is grafted from other parts of the body onto the burned area, it can get even tighter." Carmella pauses, as if to get her thoughts clear.

I say nothing.

"When Ramseys' doc called me, he said his patient was a difficult one." Carmella gives me a quick, humorless chuckle. "Shit. He wasn't tellin' me the half of it. The doc says that after the operations, Ramseys used his hands before they were healed. Tore some of the grafts open and suffered a longer recovery than he had to. A stubborn guy.

"Anyway, I accepted him as a client. I know the exercises were wicked painful, so I did my best to ignore the guy's crazy behavior."

Still avoiding my gaze, she pauses, giving me space to ask. "What things?" I say.

"There was a lot of swearing. Hey, I'm no prude, but that man said things would make a hooker blush. Still..." Carmella leans forward and lowers her voice to a near whisper. "I seen a lot of people sufferin' with the most terrible pain, and what that man had to go through was right up there. I'm not talking about the physical. But him listening to them people bein' burned to death? And not bein' able to help?"

"It's hard to imagine," I say.

She nods. "Because of that, I did my best to give the man a pass. But looking back on it now, I realize that the other things he said were..." Still staring at the table, Carmella stops. Three or four beats pass. She blinks, then goes on. "We'd been workin' for twelve, thirteen months, when he started saying stuff about how he was gonna fry the bastard that caused the accident. Let me ask you somethin'. The accident your email was about? What was the guy's name, the driver of the car that started it?"

"Crow," I say. "Harry Crow."

Carmella's eyes come up to mine. "I don't know. Are we talking the same accident?"

"I don't know yet. In the accident I'm dealing with, Harry Crow crashed his Cadillac into the back of a van," I say. "The van had a family inside. Mom, two kids and a dog."

Carmella's face tightens. "Right."

"Let's say it's the same accident," I say. "Harry Crow died. Why would your patient say he wanted to kill someone who's already dead?"

Carmella looks even more frightened. "I can only tell you what he told me. By this time, everyone at York knew about Ramseys' accident. When I told him I'd heard about it?" Carmella leans forward. "As long as I live I'll never forget what he said. We were doing these finger stretches, and he was hurtin' big time. He just looks up at me, grits his teeth, and says in this growly kind of whisper, *The guy who killed my family is in the ground. But I'm going to dig him up and kill him again.*"

Carmella leans back and shakes her head. "That is *the* most fucked-up thing I've ever heard. And I've heard some pretty fucked-up shit."

"I imagine you have."

"I can tell you one thing," she says. "That guy means what he says." Again, Carmella glances around the room.

"Ramsey frightened you," I say. "That's clear. But as you just said, people say crazy things when they're in pain. Ramsey probably has some form of PTSD. Hearing people screaming while they're on fire would make anyone a little crazy."

Carmella's eyes flash. "I *know* that! I *know* he was tormented! I *know* about his physical pain! But I'm telling you, I've worked with other people been through horrible things. People torn up in car crashes. Kids busted up by their own *parents*. But I never heard anyone say anything like that. That they was gonna kill somebody who's already *dead?*" Carmella raises her voice. "That's fuckin' *sick!*"

When Carmella closes her eyes, I can see them rolling around underneath the thin skin of her lids. Something awful is happening in there.

Carmella opens her eyes. "Sure, he was a little crazy with it. But I think toward the end he got *real* crazy. I think something snapped inside. But, there was *other* things that he said." She holds up her hands to indicate something big. "Sayin' stuff about *dogs*, for Christ's sake."

Carmella's hands go to her throat. Her eyebrows are bunched, her lips pursed. Her eyes begin scanning the room like a machine.

"Dogs?" I say. "What about dogs?"

Carmella lowers her voice again, as if she fears Ramsey might be lurking behind a palm. "He said he was gonna kill their dogs."

"I don't get it," I say.

"You think *I* do? It was before he said the thing about digging up the dead guy. This one day we was workin' on his left hand. Workin' workin'. Suddenly he pulled away, stares at me and says he's gonna kill them dogs. Can you believe this shit?"

I say nothing.

Carmella crosses her arms under her breasts and leans so far forward the table tilts. Her whispered words are barely audible. "He wasn't looking at me. He wasn't even *talkin'* to me. He just says, *Every one that has a dog. Every one that didn't help.*"

Carmella's fear is getting to me. "Go on," I say.

"So, I say something to him about how I'm sure everyone did everything they could to help, and he says, *They killed mine. I'm gonna kill theirs.'* Then he just walked out of the session."

Carmella's face sags. She appears to age with every word. "What the fuck was that?"

"Did he come back?" I say.

Carmella nods her head affirmatively. "The next week he walks in for his appointment like nothin' ever happened. And this is the day he says that shit about digging' up the dead guy. So when he says that, I say I'm done." Carmella's hands go up.

"I imagine you were," I say.

Carmella glares at me. "Look, like I told you, people with serious injuries in terrible pain? When you work on them you never know what you're gonna get. Releasing the tissues can release emotions the client's kept locked inside for years, maybe their whole lives. A lot of stuff comes up that's not even related to the injuries. I thought I heard it all, but what that freak said was the creepiest. For a while after, I didn't sleep so good."

"Scary," I say.

"You got that right." Carmella looks me in the eye. "The dog thing. I'm thinking it had something to do with the dog that died in the fire."

"Inky," I say.

Carmella blinks, as if unable to process this specific piece of information. My awareness of the dog's name confirms we're talking the same dog, same accident.

"How did it turn out?" I say.

"He was creeping me out so bad, I told him I couldn't help him anymore. He gets off the table, kind of stumbles around and yells at me, like '*You! You're just like everybody else!*' Mr Snow, I am freaking out! This man is huge! I start prayin', Dear God, please don't let this crazy man kill me."

"What happened then?" I say.

"Ramseys left my office, cursing and screaming at everyone on his way out of the building. I wanted my manager to call the cops but he wouldn't cuz Ramseys hadn't touched anybody." Carmella slaps her hand on the table. "I was officially *freaked out!*"

Certain now that Chester Ramsey and Eldrick Creech are one and the same, I feel a pang of sympathy for the man. The horror he endured is unimaginable.

"I gotta go," Carmella says, putting her sunglasses and scarf back on. She looks terrified. Getting up, she puts her hand on my shoulder and brings her lips close to my ear. "If you find that Ramseys? You didn't hear any a this from me, okay?" The hand on my shoulder is shaking. "*Please?*"

I stand and take her quivering hands in mine. "You don't have to worry. He'll get nothing out of me. I appreciate your help, Carmella. Thank you."

Carmella takes a few quick steps, then stops and turns back to me. "Mr Snow? I'm afraid that when you find that nutcase, you're not gonna be thankin' me for anything."

38

Mooney

My bunk is under two open portholes. It's past midnight and I'm only half-asleep, which is why I hear the vehicle when it pulls into the gravel parking lot.

Tires crunch to a stop. An engine shuts down.

It's quiet again.

A door slams.

I get out of my bunk. Through one of the portholes, I see Mooney's Blazer parked, lights out, and Mooney, headed for the docks. Last time we talked, he was off to Key West for a race.

I watch him as he walks along the seawall. His powerful upper body leans forward, countering the weight of a large duffel slung over his shoulder. His movements are deliberate. Autonomous.

I'm perfectly comfortable living here alone, even though I've made a few enemies over the years and there's been the occasional threat. A growling voice on my answering machine. A threatening note in the mail, written in a manic scrawl. There's no question,

I feel a little safer when Mooney's in his shack, not far from my boat.

There's irony in my relationship with this man. A few years ago, he saved my life. Yet being in his company might one day get me killed. Collateral damage.

Mooney's thinking is uncluttered. He knows what matters and has no doubt about what's right or wrong. It's 'right' to protect children at all cost – anything counter to that is wrong.

Losing sight of him, I cross to the other side of my cabin to another porthole. There he is again, gliding toward his shack. I see his boots make contact with the dock yet hear no sound. As he takes his long, silent strides, his wavering reflection tracks him in the water. I'm struck by how lonely he looks. Maybe I'm projecting. What do I know about how Mooney feels?

Nothing.

While he believes in his country, he eschews government. He thinks everyone in the community, no matter how meager their contribution, shares a responsibility in maintaining order. He believes the collective should put what's 'right' first, and that they should show no mercy to the wrongdoers.

Mooney is a throwback to the Wild West, a modern-day gunslinger. He's gonna make the abusers pay.

I feel an affinity with him. Maybe because we both survived childhood violence. Maybe because he thrives while operating out on the edge. Whatever my fascination with Mooney, I believe I'm a better man for knowing him.

In three minutes I'm dressed and standing in front of his shack. Through a small window I see the shadow-dance of a candle.

I rap on his door.

The candle is snuffed. A moment later, I hear a slide being racked.

Mooney's voice is strong yet soft. The same way he walks – like the big cats.

"What."

"It's Snow."

Beyond the glass, a match flares and the candle's flickering light returns. Sounds of multiple bolts and locks being undone. The door swings inward. Mooney stands in silhouette, a black shadow framed by quavering light.

Hands by his sides. A small 'package' stuffed into his belt. *Handgun.*

"Is that necessary?" I point.

"It is," Mooney says, in a voice smooth as tumbled stone.

His head tilts and his long hair falls. I can't see his face. Can't read his expression.

"You could be someone, come to do me harm."

Ah, you mean a fool.

Mooney steps aside. As I slip past him, he leans close and whispers, "Never underestimate the other guy's capacity for *stupid*."

Because of the torture he suffered at the hands of his father, Mooney sees every man as a potential threat.

Sitting across from him at his tiny kitchen table, candlelight bending the shadows, I tell him about Harry Crow's accident, as well as the little I know about Eldrick Creech. I tell him I need help finding the man. I don't mention the murder of Vinnie Ianucci, or the kidnappings. I've learned it's best to give

Mooney the dark stuff in small doses.

Mooney's brow is iron plate. His eyes are unblinking holes in his ravaged flesh. When he responds, his scars writhe in the flickering light.

"Creech?" he says.

I nod.

"I don't like him already." Mooney's eyes blaze. "What'd this character do?"

I tell him the rest. The death of Ianucci. The kidnappings. And I give him my theory – why I think Creech is carrying out his one-of-a-kind act of revenge. Unlike Ray, Mooney doesn't question my ideas.

He does something feral with his mouth. "I'll find him."

For Mooney, *find* does not mean *locate*.

"You can't do that," I say.

One eyebrow lifts.

"You can't put a glove on this guy. I'm asking you to help me find him. Actually *locate* him."

The other eyebrow twitches.

"I have no proof that Creech killed Iannucci or that he had anything to do with the kidnappings. My theory is all from my gut."

"Your gut's money." Mooney's voice is like the patter of the candle's flame. "You can take your gut to the bank."

"If you're going to act on my intuition only," I say, "then forget I asked." I move to get up.

Mooney's hand shoots out and grabs my wrist – a snake strike.

"*Find* only," I say.

207

A few beats pass. Mooney lets go.

"Done," he says, and gets up.

"I have your word?"

"My word," he says, voice firm, eyes liquid lead. "Just as good as yours."

I'm not sure what that means, and I'm not about to ask. I'm just hoping he won't kill Creech when he finds him. And Mooney *will* find him.

I still can't sleep. Toss and turn in my bunk.

I think about Mooney's unearthly influence. His is a compelling tale. Acts of mayhem visited upon a child. The child grows into a crucible of a man who will move heaven and earth to save the next child – who will burn heaven and earth down if he has to.

I used to wonder how Mooney gets private info on people. Then, when I finally questioned him about it, he gave me the old, "I'll tell you, but then I'll have to kill you" answer. I probably won't ask again.

Still, lying here, staring blankly at the ceiling, I can't help but wonder about all of him.

I close my eyes.

I drift, but the questions won't leave.

Maybe Mooney has stainless-steel tools. The kind used to pry information from the unwilling.

I breathe. Tell myself to tone down the drama.

Then, just as I'm about to drop into the bottomless chasm of sleep, Mooney lunges at me from out of the dark! I roll off my bunk and stumble to the light switch.

There's no one here – of course there isn't.
I'm a little *freaked*.
Sleep won't come easy tonight.

39

Who Are You, Eldrick Creech?

Three days later, Mooney marches up my boarding ramp. Hammers on my steel door like a landlord with an eviction notice.

He hustles me into the salon, telling me as we go that he has no time for chit-chat. Chit chat? Him? As if.

I do my best to keep up, scribbling notes while Mooney reads from a dirty, tattered notebook.

"I got lucky," Mooney says. "I met this lady named Louise. She's a clerk at the Chepachet Town Hall. She liked me." Mooney pauses, as if this fact has just dawned on him. "She knows pretty much everyone in Chepachet, including Eldrick Creech."

"Okay," I say.

Mooney looks away. "Creech was born in Red Bank, New Jersey. Graduated from the local high school. Didn't go to college. Married his high school girlfriend when he was twenty. Within three years they had two kids. Boy and a girl."

Mooney looks out at the parking and says, so softly I strain to hear, "In 1981, Creech moved his family to Millville, Rhode Island. They rented a house out in the woods. Eight years later they moved again, to a big stone house on thirty acres at the top of a hill. Louise says eighteen Huckin's Hill Road has the finest view in the county."

"The finest view," I say.

"Yes." Mooney's eyes dart back to me for a second, then return to the window. "Creech's landlord was, and still is, a Delaware corporation."

"A Delaware corporation," I say.

Mooney's head swings around and his dark eyes flash. This time the effect is chilling. "Just *listen!* The corporation, Grand Hill Properties, purchased the stone house just a month before Creech moved his family in. Grand Hill paid one-point-three for the place. Cash. No mortgage recorded."

"Cash?" I say.

Mooney looks at me. I think I should just listen.

"Questions were raised at town meetings. Who's this stranger that can afford to rent such a large piece of property? There were rumors. One piece of gossip hinted at the possibility that Creech was a straw buyer, that he's actually the owner of Grand Hill. That would make him his own landlord."

I can't help myself. "It would," I say.

Mooney says nothing.

"Go on."

"Between Louise, the Internet and some tax records, I learned a lot about your man. She says Creech is big, fierce and unfriendly."

"So I've heard," I say.

Mooney continues. "I talked to a couple guys. Connected. Up until a few years ago, Creech was known in the mob. Had ties to different organizations. Rumor was, he might have even run his own crew. Might have been a button man, but nobody knows for sure. Which is not a good sign."

"No?" I say.

"No," he says, softly. "There's been this contractor out there for years. A ghost. Running independent contracts under different names. If that contractor *is* Creech? And if he's managed to keep his identity hidden all these years? Means he's very good."

Mooney looks at his notebook. He has more. Excise tax records indicate that in 1981 – the year Creech first moved his family to RI – he purchased a used tractor-trailer rig. Listing himself as sole proprietor and driver, Creech subcontracted the rig out to BlueLine Vans, a furniture and electronics transport company with a dispatch office in Weymouth, Massachusetts.

Mooney located Creech's accountant and paid him a visit. Managed to come away with confidential information about Creech's finances.

How did he accomplish this?

Creech operated his truck under the BlueLine Electronics Division label, hauling computers and printers back and forth across the country. When Eldrick Creech signed on with BlueLine, he named his one-man operation Indie-Haulers. As a contract carrier, Creech paid his own expenses – fuel, food, pretty much everything. Over a ten-year period, his average net per year was $75,000.

I'm further intrigued by the fact that Mooney was able to verify a parting of the ways in 1996 between BlueLine and

Indie-Haulers. Calling in a marker from 'a friend' at the Department of Transportation, Mooney also learned that Creech's license, fuel permits and logbooks all expired in the same year that Indie-Haulers broke off from BlueLine – 1996. Since then, no applications for the re-issuance of licenses or permits have been made in either Creech's name or the name of Indie-Haulers.

It appears that Creech has no criminal record. Never even got a parking ticket.

Thanks to Mooney, I now know that, beyond the oddity of Creech's name, there are three elements to his life that are out of the ordinary: 1) the fact that he could afford to live in a million-dollar piece of property, or that he may have actually owned it and, for appearances, rented it back from himself. 2) the accident that took the lives of his entire family. 3) the curious, disparate information Mooney was able to unearth relating to Creech's business.

Even more hard to believe, Mooney claims he was given access to several ledgers containing Indie-Hauler's records. One ledger, neatly recorded by hand, indicated that the operation began on June 1, 1981 and ended on April 24, 1984. At that point the ledger entries abruptly ended. Nothing was resolved, no figures totaled. It's as if Creech lost all interest in the business. The second ledger began with the same starting date, June 1, 1981. Its figures were entered in handwriting that had now become almost illegible. These recordings continued until they, too, ended. The final entry was dated May 21, 2002.

It was only two weeks after this last entry that Harry Crow's car smashed into the back of Eldrick Creech's van, incinerating Creech's family.

Even though this data supports my theory, the whole thing is still too insane to believe.

I tell Mooney I have much to think about, that I'll call him when I figure out what the next move is.

As Mooney leaves, he tells me to "think fast" because he has "other fish to fry".

Pity the fish.

I drive my rattling truck west on Route 44, through Greenville and Foster, and finally into Chepachet. I'm so captivated by the fields, ponds and woods of western Rhode Island, I almost miss the turn.

The Huckin's Hill Road sign is just beyond an empty, one-bay fire station that looks like an abandoned outpost. Turning right, my pickup labors up a narrow incline. Stone walls border both sides of the road.

There isn't a house in sight. I'm no more than a thirty-minute drive from Providence, yet it feels like I'm passing through the woods of 400 years ago, when Roger Williams founded Providence Plantations.

The road continues for another two miles, up and down through woods and fields. I come upon a dilapidated tin mailbox on the right. Nearly miss this turn as well. There's no name on the box. Above, the number eighteen, carved into a small wooden plank, nailed to a tree.

I find myself on a deeply rutted driveway. The suspension squeaks and groans. The drive ascends. I follow it deeper into the woods for about a half mile. Here and there, gaps in the foliage offer snapshots of green fields and more stone walls. But most of the time the thick bushes and tall, old-growth trees block the view of the magnificent property.

Rounding a sharp curve, I come upon a structure made of stone blocks. I brake to a stop just under an overhanging portico that juts out from the side. A cloud of dust drifts past me. I look around, see no signs that anyone's here. I chug forward slowly, under the portico and out, and continue toward the back of the house.

I stop in the middle of a grassy area and shut the engine down. It's perfectly quiet. When I step out of my truck, the slam of the door sounds like an insult.

Near the edge of the woods, a long steel building. Next to it, an old tractor-trailer rig, paint faded by time and the elements.

In all other directions, vast expanses of green and gold fields, edged by forests of grey and green trees. To the east, I see the black spires of the Providence skyline. To the southeast, Narragansett Bay.

The breeze brings with it the rich scent of evergreen. I'm moved by the beauty of the place. If the man I seek is as twisted as I think, what's he doing here? Do only good men settle in places of beauty like this, come to be fully present with their families? To sink their roots into the soil? Lunatics don't care about such aesthetics. Or do they?

Do I have Creech all wrong? Would someone who is both killer and madman choose to live upon such a hilltop, while he plots to commit atrocities upon those who live below?

Who are you, Eldrick Creech?

40

Lair

Three stories high, with great granite walls and an immense wraparound porch, Creech's house is massive. The warm, dark wood of the window frames, portico and porch stand in stark contrast to the cold stone.

The long metal building behind the house is a more recent addition to the property. The rusting Kenworth cab that sits next to it is at least a half-century old. Its once-black paint faded to gray, all ten of its tires gone flat. The cab stands alone without a trailer – a frail, elderly horse with no wagon to pull.

There are no windows in the garage. The front doors are at least fifteen feet high and wide enough to back two trucks through. Sliding on steel rails, the doors are secured by a hefty padlock that looks bulletproof.

Glancing again across the property, I wonder how a truck driver could afford a spread like this – rent *or* own.

I go to the house, climb the wide steps to the wraparound porch. A half dozen green wicker chairs are spread around. One dilapidated Adirondack chair is pushed into a corner. In the middle, hanging from giant hooks in the ceiling, is the biggest couch-swing I've ever seen. Wide enough to accommodate four adults, the swing creaks in the breeze, inviting me to ride.

I try to get a look inside through a big window, but the drapes are tightly drawn. As I approach the wide, front door I notice a tiny security camera tucked up into a corner. When I press the doorbell, I hear its muffled buzz inside.

I wait.

Silence – save the creaking of the porch swing.

I wait some more.

Nothing.

I dismount the porch. Go around the house to the expansive side lawn. With the house at my back, I walk about a hundred feet away and turn. Now I can see, every window has its blinds drawn. This hints at what I'd already suspected. The last time Creech left, he didn't expect to return for some time. If ever.

I think about jimmying the bulkhead door at the back of the house but decide it's a bad idea – an invitation to get shot.

I walk back to the garage, this time on the lookout for security cameras. I find another one, up in the eave of the corrugated roof.

I feel a kind of dread, knowing my image has already been recorded – that it may be seen one day by Eldrick Creech.

I absentmindedly wiggle the industrial-sized padlock. It's as heavy as the sledge it would take to break it.

Why would an independent trucker need this kind of lock on a garage in the middle of nowhere? Why the cameras?

Because something of atypical value or interest lies within. What I wouldn't give for an industrial-sized bolt-cutter.

Now what?

My eyes follow the dirt driveway as it meanders past the garage, curves off in a northerly direction and disappears into the woods. I glance over at my truck. I decide to walk.

I follow the drive for several hundred yards as it curves through the field. Follow it into the woods. The ruts are filled with muddy rainwater. I switch over to one side, pushing aside branches and tree limbs as I go.

In every direction, the woods are a chaos of old-growth trees, hanging vines, encroaching bushes and blow-down. The air is heavy with the aroma of moss and lichen, rotting wood and decaying bark. The forest is so dense, sunlight barely reaches the ground.

The road eventually brings me to a break in the woods and an old farmhouse, its roofline sagging, its shakes badly faded. A few windows in the upper floors have been broken by the torque of the collapsing frame, jagged pieces of glass still in place. At some point, plastic sheets were stapled to all the windows. The sheets that have come loose snap noisily in the breeze.

There's a barn behind the house, its right-half collapsed into a pile of kindling. In the middle of a cleared area beyond the barn, a relatively new ranch house, freshly painted white with green shutters.

As I draw nearer, I hear loud, hollow banging coming from somewhere behind the old house. Like someone is thumping an empty oil drum with a ball-peen hammer.

Walking past the old house toward the sounds, I feel

vulnerable, as if someone above is watching me from behind the flapping plastic.

Rounding the corner at the back of the house, I almost walk into a black man beating the crap out of an old truck. He spins to face me, long-handled sledgehammer held high off his right shoulder. His face is rigid with purpose. His eyes are as wide as brass coins.

"Hello," I say.

Maybe a decade older, and a full four inches shorter than me, the man has the lean, wiry frame of a gymnast. He's so close, I can see the roots of his close-cut hair, the twitch of his flared nostrils, the scarred head of his raised hammer.

I take a step back. "My name is William Snow," I say. "I was just paying a visit to your neighbor. Mr Creech? But he's not home."

The man seems carved from a solid slab of onyx. His face is stamped with a horseshoe-shaped birthmark. The mark goes up his left check, curves over his left eye and travels down in front of his ear. He looks like he was kicked in the face by a Clydesdale.

Holding the heavy sledge in the air seems effortless for him – it floats above his shoulder like a balloon. "Why'd you walk up on me like that?" he says.

"Sorry." I gesture behind me. "When I found that Creech wasn't home, I thought I'd take a walk. See where the road goes."

The man isn't buying it. I can see it in his eyes.

"I thought his was the only house up here." Again, I gesture in the direction of the muddy road. "Will this take me back down to Huckin's Hill Street?"

He considers my question, then says, "It will. But then your car would still be at Creech's, wouldn't it."

I'm an idiot.

Considering his size, the man does something amazing. He merely twitches his shoulder, and the ten-pound sledge rockets behind him and lands inside the truck-bed with a crash. The truck shudders.

"Road," he says.

"Excuse me?" I say.

"Huckin's Hill Road. It's not a street."

"Is it always this quiet up here?" I ask.

He narrows his eyes. "Tell me again why you're at the Creech place?"

"I'm assisting the police. We're looking into the disappearance of a girl."

Hearing this, he seems to relax. "I used to tell Lydia. The police will come one day."

I assume Lydia is his wife.

"If you're no friend to Eldrick Creech, then you're a friend to me." He lowers his voice. "What's that man got to do with a missing girl?"

I extend my hand.

"Clovis Baughm. B-A-U-G-H-M." His handshake is firm. "Now, who is she?"

"I'm not at liberty to say. Why have you been so sure the police would show up at Creech's place?"

Avoiding my question, Clovis Baughm proceeds to tell me he was born here, in the crumbling old house. Brokers have always been keen to buy the house and its acres. They want to develop it, but the Baughms have never been interested.

"We don't need any more people on this hill. Got one too

many already." Clovis points in the direction of the Creech place.

"When he first moved in, he stopped me from using the south entrance to this drive. It comes in from Huckin's Hill Road, goes past Creech's house, past here, then down the hill to meet with Huckin's Hill Road again. Makes a kind of half-circle. You can use the south entrance or the north. What's the difference?"

"First time I came in from the south and drove past his house, he was coming out of his garage. I stopped to introduce myself, and what does he do? Pulls a gun and tells me never to come this way again!"

"What did you do?"

Baughm gives me a sideways glance, like he's not sure if I'm being a smartass. "What did I *do?* I said, 'All right, Sir.' What else you say to a man holding a gun? I told him, even though we both have a legal right to use either end of the road, I'd be happy to use only the north entrance, if he feels that strongly about it. There's no need to stick a gun in my face."

"There is not," I say.

"And what does he say to that? He says, if I drive by his house again, he'll shoot me."

"Nice guy," I say.

Clovis gives me an indecipherable look. "I hired a lawyer. Turns out this isn't a town road after all, even though the town's been maintaining it for as long as anybody can remember. It's a legal right of way, registered in both deeds. The town sent a letter to Creech, saying so."

"Did that put an end to it?" I say.

It's clear Clovis Baughm wants to share his story. "Not by

221

a long shot," he says. "Even though I never used the south entrance again."

"You still haven't told me why you wouldn't be surprised if the cops showed up here."

Clovis leans against the battered truck and tells me about his family. He has two grown children. His daughter, Mary, lives in Georgia with her husband and two of his grandkids. His son, Proud, is serving in the army in South Korea. His wife, Lydia, passed away seven years ago.

Clovis points toward the road. "After our first encounter, that man drove by here hundreds of times. Never gave us so much as a look. First three or four years, he was either in the truck, or in a white van." Baughm points again toward the road. "Then one day he rolls by in a green Buick. Never saw the truck again. Figured he must have gotten out of the business."

"Why would Creech keep driving by your house? Looks to me like his side of the hill is the shorter route."

Baughm's face tightens. "The man was showing me, he was the man. He was marking his territory. Like a dog pissin' on a fence.

"Creech's kids used to go to the same school with Pride's." Baughm looks away for a moment. "Then there was the accident. Wife and kids died. You're investigating Creech, you must know about it. I didn't have any use for that man, but I wouldn't wish that kind of loss on my worst enemy."

A breeze rustles the loose plastic above our heads. Clovis glances up, then looks at me. "The whole town was shook. Teachers said the Creech children were good kids. By all accounts, Creech brought them up right."

"Did you ever meet his wife?" I ask.

"No. But over the years, I'd see her here and there. Shopping at the supermarket. Gassing up at the convenience store. She looked like she was living the life. Like it couldn't have gotten much better. I always wondered if she knew what her husband was really like. At his core. From my dealings with him, I knew Creech was evil. You ever get in the same room with him, you'll know, too."

"Was?" I say. "You think he's gone?"

Clovis Baughm furrows his brow and gazes again in the direction of the Creech place.

"What is it?" I ask.

"I haven't seen him in a long time. I'd be lying if I didn't say I was glad as hell about that. Considering what finally happened between him and me."

"You two had another run-in?"

Baughm nods and sets his jaw. "One day he comes down the road in his truck and pulls into my yard and gets out. This was five, six years ago, before he lost his family. It was in September, just after school started. Hot as hell. Mary was living here with her two kids from her first marriage. My grandchildren were in school, Mary and my sister were off somewhere, and I was here by myself. Working outside."

"Your sister?"

Clovis Baughm shuffles his feet, then glances down at them. "For a short while after Lydia passed, Rita came to help Mary with the kids. It was a bad time."

It's been easy to see Clovis Baughm's strength. Now I see his pain, bleeding through his purple-stained skin.

"Creech had the gall to drive in here, just so he could tell me that my grandchildren, my *blood*, weren't good enough to share the same classroom with his children." Baughm looks at me hard. "I don't take kindly to insults from any man. He'd got out of the car. I took a step toward him, and something happened. I still don't know what."

"What do you mean?"

Baughm looks confused. "That's the hell of it. I don't *know* what I mean. All I remember is taking that step toward him. Next thing, I'm on my back, my body buzzing like I'd been electrocuted.

"I don't know what that son-of-a-bitch did to me, but he did it so fast, I never saw. Knocked me cold. Near paralyzed me."

"That's not good," I say, more to myself.

"No, it's not," Baughm says. "When I was finally able to lift my head, Creech was still there, standing over me, looking calm as a man waiting for a bus.

"I felt helpless. Him just standing there, eyeing me like I was a bug. It took a while to get my wits back."

I shake my head.

"I managed to get myself onto my hands and knees, just trying to get my breath back. Creech leans down and puts his mouth next to my ear and says, calm as a preacher, 'You keep your crumb-grabbers away from my kids. If you don't, I'll come down here some night and kill your whole family'."

"Jesus."

"You can say that again. The look in his eyes put the fear into my bones."

I may already know the answer, but I have to ask. "Did you report this to the police?"

Clovis Baughm looks at me as if I have one eye in the middle of my forehead. "Mister, you are not *hearing* me. If I'd gone to the police, I have no doubt he would've put us in the ground."

I nod at him. "I guess I've got someone special in my sights."

Clovis makes a clucking sound with his tongue. "If you're looking for that man, you've got the devil in your sights all right, brother. You ever get up on him, you either drop the hammer, or get the hell out."

"Let's hope it doesn't come to that," I say.

Clovis makes the clucking sound again. "You better be armed to the teeth. He's got guns, you know. Lots of 'em."

"You know this, how?"

"Because I heard them. He used to shoot inside that garage of his. Must have a firing range inside."

I have one last question. "Clovis, why are you killing your truck with a sledgehammer?"

Clovis frowns. "I bought that old truck about five years ago. Got a hell of a deal, and now I know why. I've had nothing but trouble with the damned thing. Spent good money trying to get it right, but it didn't do any good. About half the time, that son of a bitch won't start. This afternoon I needed to haul some junk to the dump, but the truck wasn't havin' it. So, I did what I should've done a while ago. Took the sledge to it." He pauses and looks at the wreckage. "I think I've killed it for sure."

Clovis shakes his head. Then with his boot, he delivers a mighty kick to the truck's side. Without another word, he wheels and heads off in the direction of the fallen barn.

I guess we're done.

41

The Break-In

As Clovis Baughm walks away from me, I shout two words. He raises his hand above his head and waves, changes direction, goes to the bulkhead at the back of his newly painted house, pulls the doors open and disappears into his cellar.

He returns a minute later with a pair of heavy-duty bolt-cutters. I assure him I'll return them shortly. We shake hands and say goodbye.

I return to the road and hoof it back to Creech's garage. Standing in front of the padlocked doors, I look, listen.

Nothing. The emptiness is still here.

I look up at the security camera, smile and slam home the powerful jaws of the cutter.

It takes several attempts, but the padlock finally falls away. I put my shoulder to one of the big doors and walk it open. I flip a switch, and two banks of work-lights bathe the interior with fluorescent light.

Big as a gymnasium. Everything set up for maximum utilization of space.

The garage consists of two long bays, separated by a half wall. The right bay is empty, its wall mostly pegboard, from which hang all manner of tools. Underneath the pegboard is a work bench. Under the work bench are hydraulic jacks, air cylinders, an acetylene torch rig, various other heavy-equipment tools. This is where Creech maintained his trucks.

This garage feels like Creech's most private space. Everything here is *his*. The man's ownership and presence is unsettling. As I wonder what would happen if he walked in, I also wonder why the prospect of a face-to-face with someone I believe to be insane excites rather than frightens me. Does my apparent absence of risk-aversion suggest a kind of madness? If so, who am I to call another man crazy?

I feel something rumbling inside. My deepest feeling toward those who abuse isn't anger, it's *rage*, and I'm itching for a fight. My feelings toward Creech are not rational, they're *animal*. I want to hurt him.

The left bay of the garage is divided into three separate areas. The one at the front has been set up as a gym. Workout mat. Punching bag. Large, multipurpose Nautilus machine. An ample set of free weights.

Taking another deep breath for good measure, I move toward the back of the garage, passing through the workout area into an open office. Computer and printer on a gray metal desk. Metal filing cabinet. Large map of New England tacked to the wall. On the map, three red circles have been drawn just off the northern coast of Maine – where there's nothing but ocean.

Beyond the office, against the back wall of the garage, there's a firing range. A gun rack on the wall holds various rifles and shotguns. It's locked. Cardboard cutouts of human figures have been nailed to the foam-insulated back wall. The cutouts are riddled with various-sized bullet holes. No shell casings on the floor.

I'm learning a lot about Creech. He's a neat freak. He's serious about his physical skills. I have no doubt he hones other skills.

I go back to the office area. Sit behind the desk. Its three drawers are unlocked. One is empty. Another holds empty file folders, packages of copy paper, pens, markers, other office supplies. In the third drawer, I find more maps of New England, neatly folded, stacked into a package, and held together with a rubber band. Tucked into the rubber band, on the underside of the package, is a business card.

In large, bold type, the card says, "Crumpler Sells Real Estate". The card says that Cecil Crumpler, licensed in the state of Maine, has many fine property listings along the northern coastline. It provides Crumpler's home address and phone number. I slip the card into my pocket.

The filing cabinet next to the desk has four drawers. All have file folders filled with trucking manifests, going back many years.

I look again at the map on the wall. What's with those three red circles over open water? Upon closer inspection, I see that the circles have been drawn around clusters of small islands.

I look at the business card again. *Crumpler Sells Real Estate.* I wonder if he sells islands.

I walk slowly through the garage again. Give everything a second look. Finding nothing more of interest, I exit the garage.

I glance up at the camera. I don't smile this time. Walking away, I leave the sliding doors wide open.

Fuck you, Eldrick Creech.

42

Into The Twilight Zone

"What are we doing here?" Rosalie asks.

Amanda stares blankly at the wall.

"*Why you? Why me?*" Rosalie jumps off the cot and throws her hands into the air. "I've lived a quiet life. I've never hurt *anyone!*"

Rosalie turns to face the girl. "Do you have any idea why we're here?"

Amanda continues to stare.

Rosalie puts her hands on Amanda's shoulders and shouts, "*Amanda!*"

The girl looks up, eyes vacant.

Feeling badly, Rosalie softens. "Where are you from?"

Amanda says nothing.

"Amanda, please. We need to talk about this. We're all we have."

Amanda looks into the dirt, sighs, then says, "I'm here."

Rosalie smiles, sits next to Amanda, and puts an arm around

her shoulder. Hoping to ground the girl, she says, "Tell me about your life."

Lifting her head, Amanda responds in a monotone. "Annie and my mom and I live in West Greenwich. Kind of in the boonies."

"Annie's your sister?" Rosalie asks.

Amanda nods. "Yeah. She's my twin."

"Are you identical?"

"Yeah."

"How's life been treating you out in the boonies?" Rosalie says.

"It's been pretty good. At least it was, until four years ago when everything turned to shit."

"What happened?"

"My dad died."

"Oh. I'm so sorry."

Amanda nods.

"How did he die?"

"It was our birthday. We were having a party with some of our friends and my parents got into a fight. I think it was because Dad got a little drunk. They were yelling at each other in front of everyone. It was pretty embarrassing." Amanda looks away.

Rosalie rubs Amanda's shoulder. "Go on."

Amanda closes her eyes. "Well... My mom kicked my dad out. He got into his car and tore off down the street. After that, everyone went home. It kinda ruined the day. A couple hours later the police came to our house and told us Dad had been in an accident." Amanda slowly shakes her head. "He was dead and it was all *her* fault."

What a strange coincidence, Rosalie thinks. My husband, Jon, Amanda's father. Both killed in car accidents.

Both, four years ago?

Rosalie feels something, like an insect creeping up her spine. "And you think that if your mom hadn't kicked your father out…"

"Yes. He'd still be alive."

"But it wasn't your mom's fault, Amanda. It was an accident."

Amanda lifts her head. "But it wouldn't have happened at all if…"

"Amanda," Rosalie says. "Do you think your mom would have let your father leave the party if she knew what was going to happen?"

"That's not fair," Amanda says.

"What's not fair about it?"

"It didn't happen that way."

"Tell me this. If your mother knew he was going to crash his car, what would she have done differently? I want you to say it."

Amanda's eyes fill with tears. "She would have taken his keys."

Amanda bows her head. Her hair hides her face as she cries.

Rosalie rubs Amanda's back. "I know it hurts. My husband died in a car accident, too. Once I got past the shock, all I could feel was anger. At myself, at the guy who cut him off and with God for not watching over him. But eventually I realized my anger was pointless. Jon's death was an *accident*."

"I'm sorry about your husband," Amanda says.

"I lost my husband," Rosalie says. "But your mother lost her husband and the father of her children. She must be feeling pretty lonely, too, don't you think?"

Amanda again nods. "Yes."

"How old are you?" Rosalie asks.

"Eighteen."

"When's your birthday?"

"June sixth."

Rosalie gasps.

"What's wrong?" Amanda says, looking frightened.

An icy cold rushes through Rosalie's body. "I can't believe this! *What is going on?*"

"What is it?" Amanda says. "You're scaring me."

Rosalie's voice trembles. "Your birthday is June sixth?"

"Yes!"

"Are you saying that your father was killed on June 6, 2002?"

"Yes," Amanda says. "What does…?"

"June 6, 2002 was the day my husband Jon was killed."

"What?" Amanda's eyes go wide. "*What are you talking about?*"

"Where was your father's accident?" Rosalie asks.

"What do you mean where?"

"What road?"

"Road?"

Rosalie's on the verge of panic. "*Where did it happen, Amanda?*"

"It was…on the highway. Over by the airport. On Route 95."

Am I losing my mind? "What kind of car was your father driving?" Rosalie whispers, "Was it a Cadillac?"

233

Amanda stiffens. "How do you know that?"

Rosalie can't breathe. This is insane! *This is impossible!* "Oh, my God, Amanda!" Rosalie claps her hands in front of her, as if praying. "*That's* why!"

Amanda's face goes white. "That's why, *what?*"

"My husband. Your father. They died in the same accident! *They're why we're here!*"

43

Cecil Crumpler

B ack home, onboard *Paralus*.

A shot in the dark, I call the number on Cecil Crumpler's business card. On the fourth ring a man answers. "A-yuh," he says, in his unmistakable accent.

"I'm looking for Cecil Crumpler," I say.

"That'd be me. What can I do ya for?" Crumpler sounds like a typical old-Mainer.

I introduce myself. Explain that a friend recently spent some time on an island off the coast of northern Maine and told me how magnificent it is up there. I tell Crumpler I'm a writer, that I'm interested in renting an island for the upcoming summer. Something private, where I'll be able to work without interruption. I tell Cecil that I may also be in the market to buy.

There's a pause, then Crumpler says, "Well, if that don't beat all. Just goes to show you that things come in bunches." He tells me he has listings for several islands that can be rented or purchased. "Thing is, you don't sell an island every day. In fact, no one's called about any of my island listings in quite some time. Till recently.

"You're the second person to ask in as many months," Crumpler goes on. "Would your friend be Mr Creech?"

I get a jolt. "No," I say.

Crumpler tells me about an island called Grayson's Cliff that rents by the season. It's also for sale. He goes on to say something about the old man who last owned it, his death, the probate court, etc., but I'm not listening. Grayson's Cliff isn't one of the islands circled on Creech's map.

"Did this Creech gentleman rent or buy?" I ask.

"Ah, he purchased Little Harbour Island. There's a dock *and* a full-size house. Maybe you don't need no big house, but you pretty much got to have yourself a dock. Can't get on or off most of these rocks without no dock. Now, given what it sounds to me you're looking for, I suppose you'd want to have yourself at least a cottage. Or are you a rough-it-in-a-tent kinda fella?"

"No, no tents," I say, forcing a chuckle. "Even though I'll be up there by myself most of the time, I have a big family. There'll be times we'll all be there, so yes, a good-sized house, maybe even with a guest house, or a cottage, as well."

"Uh-huh. Okay then. What price range we talking here?" Crumpler says.

"Well," I pause. "I'm comfortable with mid-six figures. But let's take it one step at a time."

"I hear you. As far as privacy is concerned, distance from the mainland will be a factor. The farther out you go, the less likely you'll get yourself any unwanted visitors. But no matter, you sometimes do have your touristy-type folks. Not to say you wouldn't be startin' out as a bit of a tourist yourself. But they come up here in the summer, imagining themselves as grand fishermen, and they sometimes drive their boats up onto private property, God only knows why."

"Stuff happens," I say.

"There you go," Crumpler says. "Course, when – or should I say *if* – you decide to buy, the farther out you go, usually means a lower price. Still, you go too far out in your boat, you'll pay the price the first time a good Nor'easter drops the hammer on you. Handy with a boat, are you?"

"I own a hundred-footer," I say, as if it means something.

"All right then," Crumpler says affirmatively, as if he now has what he needs to get started. But he hesitates. "I know it ain't my business, but before we go on here, I feel I should remind you of something. All these islands are surrounded by pure Atlantic Ocean. Some folks come up here with these grand notions, wind up biting off more than they can chew. About fifteen years ago, this fella come up in the middle of the damned winter all the way from New Jersey. Said he was on some kinda vision quest or something. Just paddled out there in a canoe and took to squattin' on Little Harker. No one even knew he was out there. Month later, a local fisherman found him sittin' on the shore, stiff as a frozen moose hide."

"I'm a careful man, Mr Crumpler," I say. "But I appreciate the concern."

I give Crumpler my contact info. He tells me he'll send his listings.

We're about to end our conversation when the old man throws a curveball. "What you just said you're looking for? That's pretty much what that Creech fella was looking for. Pretty much what he wound up with, matter of fact."

"Really," I say, wondering if Crumpler might have sensed my interest in Creech.

"Yup," Crumpler says. "The both of you. Wantin' to be a fair distance offshore. Wantin' enough shelter that you can take care of a handful a folks, if the need arises. And the both of you wantin' to be left alone."

I say nothing.

"One big difference, though."

"And that would be?"

"*You*," Crumpler says, "sound like you're a might more levelheaded."

I pack an overnight bag. When I ask Bradley if she wants to go see Paula, she almost knocks me over going down the ramp.

All the way to Morningstar Kennels, Bradley alternates between licking my face and thrusting herself halfway out the window, head facing forward. Maybe she thinks she's going to have both Paula and me. Like a two-for-one. Like she's just hit the jackpot.

44

What Lies Beneath

It's almost noon when I pass a sign saying I've entered Foghead Bay, Pop. 324. Following the directions, I turn left at the bright red farmhouse, climb Simmon's Hill Road to the top of a hill, turn left onto Bay Top Road, which is mostly dirt, and follow it 1.2 miles to Cecil Crumpler's house.

Crumpler's is an old farmhouse, big as two houses together, with lots of intersecting eaves and oddly angled rooflines. Cupolas, turrets and bay windows abound. They don't build grand old houses like this anymore.

The house is weather-worn but appears to be solid. To keep winter's cold out, thick sheeting has been affixed around the entire foundation, giving the house a plastic 'skirt'.

There are no other houses in sight. Out back, stretching for several hundred yards to the edge of a dense forest, a wide field of hay trembles in the wind.

Before mounting the front porch, I turn, look across Bay Top Road, and take in Cecil's view. From here, one can see Foghead

Bay and the dozen or so islands beyond – the farthest out being the largest. Beyond the islands, the Atlantic stretches all the way to the horizon.

The front steps creak. There's no doorbell, so I knock. I wait a few beats and knock again. A minute or so goes by. I pace back and forth. Steal quick glances into windows. Catch reflected views of the ocean.

I'm about to dismount the porch when the door opens. An old man appears, cut from a Norman Rockwell painting. He's about my height, lean, with a full head of white hair. Old, scuffed, blue coveralls over red plaid shirt. Jawline softened by a two- or three-day growth of white. A hint of grin on his wrinkled face.

"Mr Snow," Cecil Crumpler says, extending a weathered, wrinkled hand. In his seventies, Crumpler is strong, sturdy, and direct – a no-nonsense man. I like him instantly.

"Mr Crumpler," I say, smiling. I follow his gesture and step into the house.

We're in a foyer, heavily built with shining wood. Hallways lead off in different directions. Double-wide stairs with large ornate banisters ascend into the upper realms. It's hushed and warm, like a reading room in an old library.

"This way," he says.

I follow Crumpler down a corridor to the left, studying him. His back is straight, his steps sure, his gait as steady and purposeful as mine.

We enter a grand room at the front of the house. Light pours in through a large bay window – a padded stool and an old brass telescope are positioned in front of it.

"That's some view," I say. "Do you mind if I call you Cecil?"

"Be my guest." Cecil holds his wrinkled smile.

Stone fireplace opposite the bay window. Large wooden desk along the far wall. Four plush, wingback chairs. A thick Oriental rug covers much of the worn wood floor. The walls are lined with bookcases crammed with hundreds of books. The welcoming smell of roasted wood hangs in the air.

"Have a seat," Cecil says. He takes his place behind the desk, in an old swivel chair.

"If you don't mind, I'll stand," I say. "I've been sitting behind the wheel of my truck for hours." I put a hand on the back of a chair and look out the window. "You can see halfway to England."

Crumpler gestures toward the water. "We bought this place for the view. Evenings, Cecilia and I would sit on the porch." He chuckles. "Talk. No talk. Didn't matter."

Seeing my smile, he nods and says, "That's right. Cecil and Cecilia. First time we met, soon as we heard the other's name, we knew right then we was made for each other. She was a talker, Ceelie was, which I never minded. Every night, right out there on that porch we'd sit, weather permittin'. And on Sunday mornings, we was out there with our coffee. Those Sundays, our agreement was, neither says a word till the sun come up."

I nod.

"It was like that more than a half-century. Ceelie's been gone three months now. The sun don't shine quite so bright these days, if you know what I mean. Which ain't to say I'm not still grateful for it. A man be a fool not to be grateful for the sun."

"I'm sorry for your loss," I say.

Cecil nods. "Happens to us all. Can I get you anything? Coffee? Water?" Crumpler's eyes beam both sea and sky.

"No, thanks," I say. "I'm all set. It must be difficult for you, after all those years."

Crumpler nods. "We was high school sweethearts. The first time I seen her, I couldn't believe my eyes. And when she tells me her name is Cecilia, I figured God brought us together. We was Cecil and Ceelie for more than fifty years."

Cecil looks around the room. I follow his gaze as he takes in the furniture, the knick-knacks on the windows and shelves, the pictures on the tables and the walls.

I make a decision. Cecil Crumpler deserves the truth.

"Cecil," I say. "I feel compelled to tell you exactly why I'm here."

The old man frowns.

I take a seat in one of the soft wingback chairs. Tell Cecil about Amanda Crow, the twins' birthday party, their father's deadly accident, the tragedy of the fire, the death of Creech's family in the van. Then I tell him about the four-year time span, and the recent murder and subsequent disappearances. I carefully explain how each missing person is connected to the death of Harry Crow.

Cecil Crumpler is no longer frowning. He's staring at me with a look that suggests I'm about to be tossed out on my ear.

"That's some tale," he says, choosing his words with care. "In fact, that has got to be one of the damndest things I ever heard. And you know, I been sitting here listening hard, trying to imagine why anyone might spin such a yarn, and I come

242

to the conclusion you got no cause to. There's no reason I can think of to do such a thing, other than to tell the truth of it all." Crumpler's smile returns.

I smile back.

"I think you're doing what you believe is the right thing," he says. "And on top a that, knowing how I've felt every time I been anywheres near to that Creech character, I suppose there's somethin' I should be tellin' *you*."

Cecil tells me.

Creech made his purchase three years ago. Little Harbour Island has a dock protected by a little cove, and a sturdy old house perched away out on the east-facing bluffs.

He tells me that when Creech first bought Little Harbour, local fishermen saw the big man going out to the island a few times in a rented boat, poking around a bit, they supposed. He never stayed past the day.

After a few initial forays, word was he went home to New Jersey and didn't come back. At least not till around the time Cecil's wife died.

A few days before his Ceelie passed away, Creech showed up in Foghead Bay in a big commercial-size van, hauling an eighteen-foot center console boat behind, on a trailer. It was rumored that Creech bought enough supplies at several local stores to feed a small army for a year.

Using the boat, Creech began ferrying supplies out to Little Harbour. For three days he tore in and out of the bay, back and forth between the town dock and his dock, which was nestled inside the cove at the southeastern tip of his island.

On the fourth day the show was over. No one saw Creech

again; at least not in the light of day.

I ask Cecil if he recalls exact dates. He says, yes. The first time Creech showed up was two days before Ceelie died. The day Creech made his last run in daylight was the day after Ceelie's funeral.

I ask him why he makes the distinction, 'daylight'. Cecil says, the first time he saw the lights was at around one o'clock in the morning, two nights after Ceelie's funeral. Cecil couldn't sleep. How's a man supposed to sleep when he's alone and in a bed he's been sharing with his wife for half a century?

That night, he came downstairs and dug out an old book. He'd never been one to read a tear-jerker, but it was the last book Ceelie had read, and Cecil felt holding it in his hands might make him feel closer to her.

Cecil couldn't get past the first few pages. Kept thinking of Ceelie's hands holding it. Kept losing his place. He was on his third try when he saw the light.

The moon was almost full that night, and Cecil could easily see the dark shapes of the offshore islands, out yonder through the big bay window. The light was bobbing across the water, and it was all he could see of the vessel it was attached to. Most likely a small boat, following the shoreline up from the south. He watched the light for ten minutes, till it made the number-eight bell just outside the mouth of Foghead Bay. The light abruptly turned ninety degrees and headed straight out to sea.

Cecil knew that if the captain of the boat held that course, before it got to England it would run smack into Little Harbour Island.

Curious, Cecil went to his padded stool and looked through his old brass telescope. He located the boat, a center console, maybe eighteen to twenty feet, one person driving.

Cecil watched.

The further out into the deep water the boat got, the higher the sheets of water that sprayed off the bow.

I asked Cecil if he was sure it was a man. Well, he told me, he pretty much knew it had to be a man. There were some local women could handle a boat like that, but they wasn't crazy. Every one of them had more sense than to go out into the open water in the middle of the night like that.

Sure enough, the boat went straight to Little Harbour Island, where Cecil lost sight of it.

I ask Cecil if he's sure about his details. After all, it was the middle of the night, and Little Harbour Island is quite a distance away. And after all, I could add that Cecil is old. I don't.

Cecil reminds me that he's been looking at the same bay, the same ocean, from this same spot, for fifty years. He knows where each of those islands are, which one is which, just as sure as he knows where his old outhouse is out back, even though he hasn't never used the thing. And, Cecil says, in all those years, he ain't never seen a boat go out to Little Harbour at night.

"That boat," Cecil says, "had to've been driven by Creech."

"You seem pretty sure of that," I say.

"I am," he says. "And I'll tell you something else. There's been a rumor going around lately that a boat's been runnin' out to Little Harbour at night again." Cecil's face crinkles into another frown. "Given your story and your concerns, what do you suppose that means?"

"I don't know," I say. "But I intend to find out." I get up. "Thank you, Cecil. You've been a big help. But I have one more question."

"Fire away," he says, his smile easing back.

"What was the date, the first night you saw that boat going out there?"

"Like I said, it was two nights after the funeral. The third of March."

My heart pounds. It was one day after Amanda Crow disappeared.

Cecil walks me to the door and we shake hands. "Thank you for telling me everything."

Cecil snaps his fingers. His smile widens, and his eyes gleam. "Here's something you're gonna want to know about. I told you about Little Harbour Island. Told you about the cove. About the house settin' out there on the bluff."

"You did," I say.

"Yessir, I did. But what I didn't tell you was what the previous owner of Little Harbour went and done to her."

Cecil reaches out and taps my arm.

"More to the point, what he done *underneath* that wind-blasted place."

45

Rosalie

Standing in front of the cot, Rosalie watches in dismay as Amanda throws herself against the door, hitting it with her shoulders, then her back. When the girl tires, she bangs her palms against the heavy wood planks. Each cry is accompanied by a hand slammed against wood.

"Let.

"Us.

"*OUT!*"

Rosalie is about to scream when Amanda puts her back against the door and slides to the floor. She sits in the mud, clutching her hands to her chest.

"Save your strength," Rosalie says.

"If I had a gun," Amanda says. "I'd shoot that motherfucker."

Rosalie doesn't know if it's day or night. Time isn't the only thing distorted by their captivity. The fear of death forces Rosalie to think about life as a pinpoint of reality – each second precious.

Her ability to hear feels like a curse. The drip of water. The scratching of rodents in the dark. Those shuffling noises outside the room, like something heavy being dragged.

As Rosalie thinks this, she hears the jiggling of keys in the lock again. Hearing it, too, Amanda jumps to her feet and runs to Rosalie's side.

When Rosalie steps back against the cot, her hip catches on something. "Ow," she whispers, then notices the steel box on the cot – the sharp corner exposed by the opened lid. She closes the lid and slides the box away.

Again the bolt is shot. Again the hinges groan as the door swings inward and their captor steps into the room.

Rosalie sees no concern, anger, or pity on his face. There's nothing. She and Amanda could be bugs on a wall.

"We're going to die," Amanda says, under her breath.

The man stares at Amanda, his eyes empty.

Words just seem to fly from Rosalie's mouth. "I'm assuming, if you wanted us dead, we'd be dead. So you must want something. Let's get on with it. What do you want?"

The man's smile is cold.

"Did you hear what I said!" Rosalie shouts.

In two strides, the man stands before them.

Amanda gasps. Rosalie flinches, regretting her outburst.

"Sit."

Rosalie and Amanda sit on the edge of the cot, shoulders touching.

Rosalie forces herself to look up at the man. He's so close she can see a loose thread on his shirt, a patch of stubble where he missed shaving. If she wanted to, she could count the long brown lashes curling above his empty black eyes. She even sees them fluttering with his heartbeat. And his odor – like the funk of an overheated animal.

Rosalie welcomes her rage – as it gathers, she sees the man that dwarfs her in a different light. He's a worm, lower on the evolutionary scale than a tick. Like Amanda, there's no doubt – if she had a gun, she'd put a bullet in each of his eyes.

The sick bastard squats down on his haunches, putting himself at Rosalie's eye level. His words seem to slither out of his mouth. "What's going on inside that pretty little head of yours?"

Adrenaline screeches through Rosalie's body. In her amygdala, the ancient 'fight or flight' response has made its choice. She will fight, but she can't let him know. She needs to hide her strengths from him. Let his ego set its own trap.

"What are you thinking there, Missy?" His metallic smile glistens.

Rosalie *burns* with hatred. It's unlike anything she's felt before. Fuck the gun. If she had a pen, she'd jam it through his eye into his brain. When he went down, she'd stomp his balls, tear his ears off with her teeth. She'd inflict so much pain, the fucker would regret even *thinking* her name.

Rosalie breathes deep.

Again, words come to her lips unbidden. "I was just thinking how grateful I am for the clothes."

The man's smile is not conciliatory. It's not the ingratiating smirk of the politician, nor the calming grin of the savior. It's the sick sneer of a man who believes he owns her.

He says nothing.

She motions to the steel box behind her. "Thank you for the food and the blankets. I was wondering…" Rosalie plants her feet and pivots her upper body without moving hips or legs, "…if you could just help me with one thing." Rosalie taps Amanda's shoulder. "Excuse me." When the girl slides out of the way, Rosalie reaches behind her for the box. Watching her, the man's smile seems stitched to his face, as if he couldn't care less what Rosalie wants or doesn't want, does or doesn't do.

Rosalie places the fingers of her right hand under the lip of the lid and begins to lift. "If you could…" Bending slightly at the waist, she reaches around with her other hand. In her peripheral vision, she sees the man close his eyes – the same show of petty annoyance he displayed before.

"If you could just help me with this…umm…"

Rosalie grips the box in both hands. She makes a grunting sound, as if the box is still filled with its contents. *He's so arrogant, he can't imagine…* Then, without another thought, Rosalie swings the box as if blasting a 150-mph serve.

The man opens his eyes – but not soon enough. The pointed corner of the box slams into his left temple.

The impact jars Rosalie's shoulders.

The man's head quivers, and his eyes begin to roll.

The box is now above Rosalie's left shoulder. She slams a vicious backhand and drives the opposing corner of the box into the man's other temple. There's a flash of white bone and a dark spray of blood.

The box flies out of her hands and clatters to the floor.

The man topples over onto his back, legs splayed, hands gripping his head.

Eyes like moons, her mouth a perfect O, Amanda yells, "*Holy shit!*", then flies off the cot and stomps on the man's crotch.

"*FUCK!*" he screams.

"Oh my *God!*" Amanda screams, then stomps with the other foot.

Rosalie retrieves the box and scrambles back to the man. Blood streams from his wounds. As he opens and closes his mouth, blood bubbles at his lips.

Rosalie raises the box over her head. Howling like an animal, she slams the box downward and buries the corner into the man's forehead.

He stops moving.

When Rosalie raises the box over her head again, Amanda screams. "*Kill the motherfucker!*

"*KILL HIM!*"

46

Little Harbour Island

"They call it the Doomsday House."

We're back in Cecil's office. I've accepted his invitation to sit on his padded stool and have a look at Little Harbour Island through his brass telescope. I'm able to see the cliffs that make up the island's shoreline, and the little cove at its southeast end. But I can't see the Doomsday House.

"Uriah Harper had the house built. Uriah's grandfather started Harper Lumber Mills in the late 1800s. You probably heard of them."

"No," I say.

"Been livin' in a cave?" Cecil chuckles. "The Harper family owned half of The Pebbles back then. Owned half of everything around here."

"The Pebbles?"

Cecil points. "That group of islands you're lookin' at. At one time or another, Harpers has owned most of them. The grandfather built a house on Little Harbour. Out at the edge of the east cliffs, on top of solid granite. Sturdy, it was. Drove big lag bolts into the rock so's it could be screwed down."

"Is it still there?" I squint into the glass.

"Yessir. But it's Creech's house now."

I nod.

"The Harpers used the islands mostly for vacations. Eventually the family died out and the Mills was sold. Uriah was the last of 'em. Got a little hinky in his older age. Moved out to Little Harbour and become a hermit. It was sometime in the fifties when he got a bug up his ass about the end of the world." Cecil hooks finger quotes and deals heavy the sarcasm. "You know... the *apocalypse*?"

"Uriah was the one who did the excavations?" I ask.

"He sure was. The years went by. At some point Uriah Harper stopped comin' to town for supplies. Wasn't seen nor heard of for a while. Sheriff went out to have a look. Told folks later he wished he hadn't. Found Uriah down in one of them holes he had dug. Been dead a good while."

"Sad," I say. "Tell me about the excavations."

"Like I was sayin', the story goes that Uriah got to thinking on how the world was gonna end. Whenever he was in town for supplies, folks at SaveRite said he could be heard mumblin' about how the Russians was gonna send their nuclear missiles flyin'. It was the late fifties. Cold War, ya know.

"Anyways, Uriah hired hisself a crew. They stayed on the island, livin' in tents behind the house."

"But if the house was built on granite," I say. "How did they...?"

"Apparently it was a granite shelf," Cecil says, his blue eyes lighting up. "Blew a hole through the shelf with dynamite so's they could reach the soil. Then the crew went down and commenced to diggin'. After a while, Mr Harper had his shelter.

"Seems he got a little carried away with the diggin'. Wound up puttin' a half-dozen or more rooms down there, with tunnels connecting 'em and goin' here and there. Everywhere and nowhere. He run electric, put in some kind of air-exchange electric fans. Dug some channels for drainage. Some say if he hadn't 'a died, he woulda built hisself a damn hotel down there. The man flat lost his mind."

"Sounds like it," I say. "Have you seen the tunnels?"

"Went down there once while showing the property to a potential buyer. Won't never do it again."

"Because?"

"Because it's spooky as hell. At high tide, the place is almost underwater."

It's the middle of a pause, and I realize Cecil and I are staring at each other.

"What?" he says.

"Are you thinking what I'm thinking?" I say.

"I don't know about you," Cecil says, "but what I'm thinkin' is flat out crazy."

"How so?"

"If your man Creech is up to no good like I'm thinkin' he must be, it would explain something I've wondered about since he first showed up."

"What do you mean?"

"There's islands for sale all up and down this whole coast, and that man had his pick. But when I told him about Uriah

254

Harper's house and what was underneath it, took him about two seconds to go from 'I ain't in no rush' to 'Got to see that house today!'"

I smile at Cecil. "I'm starting to think you believe me, Cecil."

Cecil smiles back. "If Creech is doin' what you say, then he's makin' Uriah Harper look sane. And that island is the perfect place for the whole of it."

"Sounds like it is," I say.

"You been to the police about this?" Cecil asks.

I explain to him why I'm on my own, then I look through his glass again at Little Harbour.

"Well, I guess I don't have much more to say about all this," Cecil says. "Except for one thing."

"What's that?"

"If even half this stuff about Creech turns out to be true? Someone's gonna have to come up with a whole new word for *that* kinda crazy."

47

The Boathouse

Turner's Point Way gets you to Foghead Bay by cutting directly through a vast, swampy bog. Marred by potholes and uplifted frost heaves, the poorly maintained road is bordered on both sides by acres of brownish still-water, clogged with vegetation and brush. Cecil says the moose that hang out here will look you in the eye as they step directly in front of your car.

Four miles out, the paved road turns into a hard-packed dirt lane that ends at a parking area and the ocean. Off to the right there's an old, sagging boathouse. No other structures in sight.

Massive boulders line the shore, and long sea grass grows between them. I park close to the water, get out of my truck and look out across the southernmost end of Foghead Bay. It's warm here, with a steady offshore wind. I hear the soft brush of waves against stone, the soft rustle of the sea grass.

Perpendicular to the shore, the boathouse is long and narrow. Built on stilts, the back of it hangs over the water. From the back, a badly weathered dock juts out into the bay. Plywood patches dot the exterior walls. The edges of each patch has been slathered with black tar.

Something is wrong.

Cecil said there'd be holes in the walls. "Fixin' to fall down" was how he put it. It is indeed old and sagging, but it looks like it may stand for some time.

I check my cell. 3:30. No service.

I look across the water. The Pebbles are smudges of green on the horizon.

Standing in this beautiful, peaceful place, I have an odd thought: in a medical emergency, there'd be no help for hours.

I look at my cell again. Still no bars.

Even though the dirt here has been hammered flat by the elements, there are several sets of tracks. A vehicle has recently backed up and turned around. The wide tires of a truck. One set of tracks leads around the corner of the boathouse and disappears on its far-right side. Cecil said it rained a few days ago. Based on the depth of the tracks, it appears the truck may have been here shortly after the rain, when the ground was soft.

As I walk closer to the boathouse, I see that the repairs were hasty. Sheets of rough plywood have been screwed onto the walls, then sealed with the black tar.

The boathouse roof is corrugated tin. There are no windows. There's one door, on the side nearest to me – when I pull on it, the wind blows the door out of my hand and slams it against the wall, causing the whole building to shake. Cecil was right. This place won't stand much longer.

I step inside. Where the dock juts out into the water, the rear wall has collapsed into the bay. A few old support pilings poke up from the water. Because the wall is no longer there, I again see The Pebbles, far across the water.

The Pebbles.

A few of the support joists in the remaining three walls have been strengthened by sister-joists. There's an empty workbench along one wall. Empty shelves above the bench.

Lots of patchwork done here, and recently. The work is shoddy. Clearly a quick fix.

The dock is in no better condition than the building. Many of the original pilings supporting the dock are still there, but more than a few have rotted and collapsed, and the dock sags in these places. Many of the planks on the floor of the dock are missing. I've seen safer tree houses.

Along one side of the dock, four cheap bumpers have been nailed in place to protect whatever boat may pull in here. But as for tying up, there isn't a line in sight.

The bumpers are brand new.

I climb a little ladder and walk carefully out of the boat-house, all the way to the end of the dock. The view is beautifully wild and thankfully free of man's influence. In both directions, fir trees grow to the shore – all along are the huge boulders, worn smooth by time.

I sit on the dock, hang my legs over the edge, listen to the water gently lap at the rotting pilings beneath. Yet again, my eyes are drawn to The Pebbles. I stare at the group of islands. Close my eyes. Breathe. Try to conjure what it's like out there.

I get nothing.

For a moment, the old doubts come rushing back. I feel like

a fraud. An unbalanced man suffering from delusions. A charlatan who thinks he can communicate with the world of spirit and travel to other dimensions.

I wish for something to prove me wrong. Or right.

A sign. An inspiration.

But nothing comes.

I stand and sigh. As I turn around to go back to the boathouse, I get a shock. Parked tight against the far-right side of the building is a white van. How could I have missed it?

Avoiding the holes, I retrace my steps along the rotting dock. Go out the boathouse, around to the side.

It's a commercial van, about twenty feet long, diesel powered. There are drapes on the insides of the windows. The doors are locked.

The van has no logos. No front plate. At the back, I find a big padlock on the sliding door, a license plate affixed to the bumper underneath. Rhode Island. This has to be Creech.

He's out there right now, on the biggest of The Pebbles.

Time to go there.

48

Run

Rosalie drops the steel box into the mud. Her chest pounds as she gulps air. Her feet feel like rocks. "We have to get out of here!" she yells, her voice cracking. The power of her rage has both liberated and exhausted her.

"Jesus Christ!" Amanda shouts. "*What did we just do?*" Her eyes dart back and forth.

Lying on his back, the man looks like a fallen giant, his chest heaving as his body struggles to stay alive. His eyes are open but unseeing, as if his brain has been short-circuited. Copious amounts of blood flow across his face, down his neck, and collect in a puddle on the floor. His hair is drenched in blood. The gore is sickening.

"Oh, my God. I'm going to be sick." Amanda turns and vomits into the mud.

The man's right hand twitches, then goes still. It twitches again, violently. Rosalie freezes as the hand reaches out toward her, fingers spread.

"Jesus!" Rosalie shouts and jumps back.

The man's hand goes limp. Finally, he stops breathing.

Rosalie grabs Amanda's hand and pulls. As they're going through the door, Rosalie stops and looks back. "We did it, Amanda. The two of us."

Amanda squeezes Rosalie's hand. "We did. We killed that big fucker dead. Now let's get the hell out of here!"

49

The Madman at the Wheel

Walking back to my truck, I hear a scream! I spin to face the sea. There's only the sigh of wind, the soft brush of wave upon rock. It was a girl's voice, from far away. A cry for help.

I'm staring, transfixed, when I hear a second scream.

I dash into the boathouse, run to the end of the dock and stand still, all my senses attenuated to the girl's voice. I scan the coastline. North. South.

I don't move for at least a minute, but there is nothing. How could there be? The screams came from inside my head. Even though I think they might be real, and despite the fact that I have a fair guess as to where they might be coming from, I tell myself to calm down. Rushing without knowing will get me into trouble.

I drive back through the bogs to the coast road, turn right and head north. Five minutes later I'm rumbling past the turnoff for Cecil Crumpler's house. A few minutes more and I enter a small, pristine village. Foghead Bay does not cater to tourists.

Following Cecil's directions yet again, I take a right after Turner's General Store, drive a quarter mile to a jumble of old, clapboard covered buildings clustered at the edge of a deep-water cove. A fishery. Several rows of long docks supported by pilings the size of telephone poles. A handful of commercial fishing boats.

I shut down my truck. Go into one of the buildings through a door marked 'office'. Find myself in a huge open room. There's nautical stuff everywhere, crammed onto shelves, piled and stacked all over the place. Lobster traps, nets, fishing poles, immense fishing reels. Lights, horns, anchors and large coils of rope. Enough electronics to outfit a flotilla. Gear I've never seen before. Some new, some old, some ancient.

A sea of odors. Diesel oil, motor oil, gasoline. Brine-soaked wood and cigarettes. Creosote and rope. And the overwhelming smell of fish, so heavy it might contain the DNA of man's entire relationship with the sea.

Somewhere a radio is tuned to NOAA. The speaker is squawking today's weather forecast in a computer-generated voice. Like Stephen Hawking.

The wall to my right is all wire-mesh, reinforced glass. Through it I see the docks and the boats, the harbor and the ocean.

And yes. There. The Pebbles.

Across the expansive room are four large, wooden desks, so badly scarred they could well have been chain-dragged through a rock quarry. Thousands of cigarette burns at their edges.

There's a man behind one of the desks. Older, in his sixties, seventies. Maybe eighties? He has gray eyes, a long white beard and scraggly white hair that explodes from his scalp like he's taken a hell of a shock.

The man seems not to notice me as he chats on the phone. His voice and his accent are remarkably like Cecil's. If I closed my eyes, I'm not sure I could tell the difference.

I pace back and forth, glancing at the boats out at the docks as they rise and fall on the incoming tide. Long shadows slide across their bobbing hulls. Outside the cove, the ocean beckons.

Finally, the old guy puts the phone down and looks at me. Looks me up and down, as if comparing me to a description.

"I'm looking for Jeb," I say.

He stands up. "That would be me. And you look like a man who needs a boat," he says, his smile showing crooked teeth. "Cecil gave me the warm-up. Told me to take good care of ya." He waves me over.

We shake. Jeb sits. He motions me to do the same.

"Thanks," I say. "I'll stand. Don't mean to rush you, but I don't have a lot of time."

"Whatever you say," Jeb says. "Don't hear much from Cecil no more. Not since his wife, Ceelie, passed way, bless her soul. He tells me you're wantin' to have a look at The Pebbles."

I nod. "I just want to go for the afternoon."

Jeb's eyes twinkle. I get the sense he knows more about where I'm going than he's letting on. "Well, young fella. You'll be needin' the boat more than a few hours if you're fixin' to go out there." He points through the window toward the ocean and the islands. "Gonna fix you up with *Betsy's Due*. She's a good boat. Plenty deep. Which you'll be needin'. It's calm enough here inside the bay, but once you get past the number eight bell, it'll get windier'n hell. Have yourself three-to-five's most of the afternoon. Mostly rollers, and old *Betsy* got herself a nice flare to her so she'll keep you dry enough, long as you keep her bow quartered to the wind. Otherwise, you better bring along a slicker 'cause you're gonna get wet out there."

"Okay," I say.

"I'll feel a little better if you'd tell me you got some experience with boats. But, I suppose Cecil wouldn'ta sent you along if you didn't."

I decide not to tell the man I live on a hundred-foot tugboat that has no engine. "What's *Betsy's Due* got for power?" I ask.

Jeb shakes his head. "Ain't none of my boats got no outboards. Can't say as I ever had much faith in 'em. Inside the bay, that's one thing. Outboards is all right in here. But you'll never catch me out in the big water with one a them things hangin' off my transom. Anytime I'm fixin' to go out past the number eight, I'll take a V-8, thank you very much. *Betsy* got herself a small block Chevy. Those 305s, you take good care of 'em, they'll run forever. And it gets her up on plane slicker than you please. Never had a single problem with that motor. Not so much as an oil leak. You won't, neither." Jeb straightens his back.

I nod.

Jeb nods back. "We Americans know how to build our V-8s. Them Japs and Krauts, they can't hold a candle to 'em." The old man hesitates as if reconsidering something, then picks up a set of keys from the desktop and tosses them to me.

"You take care a yourself. It can get right nasty out there."

*

Idling away from the docks, I point *Betsy's Due* toward a narrow cut in a high seawall built with boulders. Halfway there, my cellphone rings. I flip it open.

"Ray!" I say.

"Snowman," Ray says. "I've got something that might interest you. Do you have a couple minu—" The signal is gone.

"Ray?"

Then he's back. "We got a bad cell."

"I don't think that's it," I say. "I'm in Maine. Way up, almost to the Canadian border. Service isn't too good here. I'm out on a boat, headed to some offshore islands. Whatever you got, give it to me fast. I'm afraid I'll lose you soon."

"Maine. *Maine?* Jesus Christ. Listen, I've been poking around. Talked to this detective, remembers something from four years ago. An informant of his, a made guy, comes to—"

The signal drops and the call goes dead again for a few seconds. Then Ray is back.

"...all cranked up. Seems he went to this funeral home to attend a service for a friend. The informant doesn't realize there's two funerals going on at the same place. He walks into the wrong one. Got the hell out of there in a hurry when he—"

The call drops for another second or two.

"...swears he knows—"

It drops again.

"Knows what?" I say. "Make it fast, Ray. I'm losing you."

"Not what. *Who.*" Ray says. "The wrong funeral the informant walked into was for Creech's family."

"And?"

"The informant *knew* Creech, but not by that name. Not

266

as Eldrick Creech, family man, but as *The Driver*. He's a button man. Contract killer. The most fear—"

More dead air for a few beats.

"...than he remembers. Says The Driver has over a hundred kills."

My mind flashes to Creech's garage. The gym. The shooting range. "You're sure about this, Ray."

"As sure as I can be. The informant's been dead over two years now. But back then he was considered one of the most reliable—"

Dead air. This time for five or six seconds.

Come on.

"...and that was that. *The Driver* was also known to use a variety of—"

"Ray!" I yell. I'm getting more frustrated with each break.

"...could kill thirty different ways."

Ray's gone again. I think for good. His information turns my skin cold. Eldrick Creech is a six-foot-six, 275-pound assassin. Terrific.

But Ray's back. "...so I had to get this to..." He sounds like he's at the bottom of a well. "...would be something..."

"Ray? *Ray!*"

"...in an ankle holster...backup weapon. If he...for the... you know he's..."

Ray is gone. I try his number again, but I think that's finally it.

When I reach open water, the wind blows directly into my face from out of the east. Coming from miles offshore, it blows steadily, piling the water into four-to-five-foot rollers. *Betsy's Due* does indeed handle well in this heavier stuff, but I have to lower my speed to keep from getting soaked.

The further out I go, the rougher it gets. *Betsy's Due* climbs, then topples over. Wave after wave. Her bow pounds, sending sheets of spray fanning into the wind. Each time the boat levels off I make sure my eyes are still pinned on the dark mass ahead – Little Harbour Island.

I imagine another boat out here on the open water, under the cover of darkness. Its cargo is hidden, perhaps under a tarp, a victim of the madman at the wheel.

50

A Thundering Absolution

"*Run!*" Rosalie screams.

"I can't believe what we just did!" Amanda yells.

As they're running together, Amanda glances over at Rosalie and immediately stumbles – Rosalie tries to catch her but misses. When Amanda hits the ground she cries out.

"Oh no," Rosalie thinks, as she watches the girl roll onto her back, grab her left wrist and grimace. Rosalie's heart sinks.

Rosalie kneels and inspects the wrist. It's already swelling. *Dislocated or broken.*

Rosalie looks back along the corridor. She half expects to see the huge man pounding toward them.

"This is going to hurt." Rosalie pulls her sweater over Amanda's head. The girl cries out when it passes over her wrist.

"Stand up." Rosalie helps Amanda to her feet. Amanda is silent, pale. Rosalie fashions a crude sling out of the sweater, ties it around the girl's neck and fits her left arm inside.

"Listen to me. Hold your arm in tight. Let's go!"

They follow the narrow earthen corridor another fifteen feet, where it turns and abruptly ends at a wall. To the left is an iron ladder, to the right a door like the one on their cell.

Rosalie points at the ladder. "You go first. I'm right behind you."

Amanda doesn't move. "I heard something," she says, pointing at the door. "Like a whimper."

Rosalie looks up the ladder and sees only darkness. Still, she wants to climb. Her whole being screams, *GO!* But what if there's someone in the room?

Rosalie turns away from the ladder and goes to the door. A skeleton key hangs on a hook. Rosalie inserts the key into the old lock and turns. She takes a breath and pushes the door inward.

The smell is horrendous. The stench coats Rosalie's throat. She turns her head back toward the hallway, takes a few breaths, pulls her shirt up over her face and steps inside.

The overhead bulb from the hallway casts both light and shadow into the room, a replica of theirs. Same cot hanging from the wall. Same disgusting toilet-hole in the corner. There's a small metal box on the cot, crumpled newspapers and food containers strewn about the floor.

What is that God-awful smell?

Then she sees a shape, down low against the right wall.

"Hello?" she says. "*Hello?*"

When Rosalie steps closer, her shadow falls on what she thinks is a man, sitting on the floor in the dark. Knees drawn to chest, arms clutching legs, chin on knees, eyes open.

Rosalie steps aside. Now the light shines on the man's face. He wears the expression of a stuffed animal on a shelf.

"Are you all right?" Rosalie asks softly.

He looks young. His body is bloated, his clothes are filthy, and he's covered with dirt and mud, head to toe. His head is shaved on the sides. The strip of hair in the middle is matted into clumps, tinged a muddy orange. His skin is dried leather.

His eyes are feral. He seems to be looking past Rosalie, right at Amanda.

Rosalie's first thought is, *Leave him!* She feels selfish, but if the man won't move, there's nothing she can do.

She glances back at the open door, her body ready to bolt for the ladder. Amanda is in the doorway, arm in the sling, slumped against the casing. Spent.

The wretched creature on the floor seems incapable of helping himself.

Still, Rosalie cannot bring herself to leave him.

She moves closer. The stench is tremendous.

"Can you get up?" Rosalie says. "Hey! Come on! You have to get up!"

Rosalie drops down on one knee, looks into the man's eyes, jerks back and almost falls into the muck.

"He's dead."

As Rosalie backs away from the corpse, Amanda enters the cell, goes to the opposite corner and leans into the shadows. "What *is* this?" she says. When she straightens, she's holding a small bundle.

Amanda speaks softly. "It's all right, Sweetie. It's gonna be okay."

Rosalie sees that the girl is holding a little dog. It has dark, tightly coiled ringlets of black hair. Its shivering, and its brown eyes are wide with fear.

271

"I've got you now," Amanda coos – at the sound of her voice, the dog tries to burrow deeper into Amanda's body. Amanda guides the dog carefully into her sling and begins stroking its head. "It's okay, honey."

"Let's go," Rosalie says, and steps sideways through the door.

"Well, would you look at that. A couple of good Samaritans."

Rosalie freezes. The man towers over her. She sees his blood all over and the glint of his gun. She feels his breath on her skin.

The barrel of the gun quivers.

The man's skin is sickly gray and sheened with sweat. His eyes gleam like madness dragged out of hell.

"Score ten points for the little women," he says. "That was quite the scare you gave me back there. Bravo, ladies." His voice sounds wet.

Rosalie closes her eyes.

"I must admit, your efforts were admirable. And now you have a little doggie for your reward." When he jams the gun against Rosalie's temple, she imagines the bullet screaming through her skull. To her surprise, instead of a gunshot, she hears a sound in the man's chest – the familiar moan of grief.

"You see?" He lowers the gun. "It's all been for nothing. There sits my son. Dead." The big man's eyes are as gray as dying coals.

His son? *What is he talking about?*

The man seems lost. His eyes track all over – the corridor, the ceiling, the floor. When he speaks again, it's as if he's talking to someone not there.

"The accident. My wife dead. My daughter dead. My son burned alive. I bring Richard back to me. But he dies again.

272

Everyone keeps dying." The man waves the gun wildly. "Now you steal my dog?"

He glares at Amanda. "Have you no shame?"

"But," Amanda stumbles, "you—"

"Stop," Rosalie says. "Don't talk."

The man points the gun at Rosalie again, then swings it back to Amanda.

Rosalie sighs. She took a chance. She lost, and there's nothing to be done about that now.

The man points the gun at Amanda's head. "Your father destroyed my life! *Like father like daughter!* I did everything a man could do, everything a *father* could do to bring us back together. And you ruined it."

The man's senseless words rip into Rosalie. She watches in disbelief as he stuffs the gun into the waistband of his pants, then withdraws from his pocket a small device like a TV remote. He holds the device up so they can see its red button.

"This place. I wanted to make it our home. Our final resting place. The only way out is *there*." He waves the device toward the ladder. "It's wired, too. Everything is wired with enough explosives to blow this island apart." Tears begin streaming down the man's blood-caked face. "No one will ever know what happened here."

Suddenly, the realization slams home. Chester Ramsey, alias Eldrick Creech, is the sole survivor of the accident. He's the man who watched his wife, daughter and son being burned alive. Now she gets it – the staggering depths of his madness.

Rosalie can't take her eyes off the device. She's horrified by the tremble in Creech's hand, by the twitching of the thumb that hovers over the red button.

A bold idea comes to her. She must join Creech in his madness!

"Eldrick!" Rosalie shouts. "After the horror we've been through, why are you giving up?"

Creech reels. "What are you talking about? No one could have tried harder. You know that!"

Rosalie commands herself to step forward. She wills herself to feel compassion for the lunatic who wants to kill her. She speaks softly, using a tone she prays will sound like love. "But I *do* know, Eldrick. How could I *not* know?"

Something wells up in Creech's eyes. His face relaxes as he looks intently at Rosalie. She knows, for the first time, he *sees* her.

"Rebecca?" he says. The grief and pain drain from his blood-stained face. His hand drops to his side, still gripping the remote.

Rosalie says gently, "It's been hard for me, Eldrick. I've been trying to get *through* to you."

"What...do you mean?" Creech says.

Rosalie looks down, assessing herself, then lifts her eyes to meet his. "This body. It's fighting me. It doesn't want to let me through. This *Rosalie* person is strong. But, when she's afraid she weakens, and then I can feel myself about to make it. It's exhausting. I can't...I can't remember it all. I only know...that I *miss* you."

Rosalie's heart pounds. Even as she's forcing herself to offer the man kindness, she wants to see him die.

Creech inches closer, his gaze searching. "Rebecca?... Is... Is that *you*?"

Though Rosalie has managed to drop into Creech's fantasy, she knows the illusion could shatter at any moment.

"Yes. It's me. Rebecca. I'm trying to get back to you."

Rosalie steps back and tries to imagine what she should look like while fighting for control.

"What was that?" Rosalie grabs her head. "*Who is Rebecca? And what is she doing in my head?*"

Behind her, Amanda whispers, "What the *fuck*?"

Creech inches closer still. "For four years I've wanted to die. Then one day, God showed me how to stop the pain. He told me that if I would exchange an eye for an eye, then we could be together again in heaven. He forgave me for all the lives I've taken."

Rosalie is incredulous. *He believes me!*

Creech's eyes turn to stone. "You're not Rebecca! *You can't be!*"

As Rosalie watches his thumb edge closer to the red button, she can't help but feel sympathy for the man, for the wretchedness of his soul.

"*Eldrick. Don't!*" she shouts. "We can be together. Here! Now!"

Creech takes a half-step toward Rosalie. "Rebecca, we…" But he doesn't finish. His knees collapse, and he tumbles forward. As Rosalie grabs for his hand, *for the remote*, his thumb comes down on the button.

51

The Quaking Cliffs

Closing in on the southeast tip of the island, I can see the waves crashing against the rocks at the base of the cliffs, but the engine, and the pounding of the hull, drown out all other sound.

A few hundred feet from shore, I pull back on the throttle and let *Betsy's Due* settle down into the water. The lapping of the waves against her hull is comforting.

The cliffs of Little Harbour are overgrown with pine trees. Some sprout from cracks in the rugged granite face and reach for the sun. Others lean precariously, as if longing for the sea. I look up, head tilted back, and the cliffs in *Deliverance* come to mind.

As I draw closer, I get the feeling I'm being watched.

I grab binoculars from the console and look behind me to the mainland. Within seconds I locate the thin black line of the road that climbs the hill to the ridge. I track left and locate Cecil Crumpler's farm, his house a tiny white dot in a field of gold and green.

I get the sense that Cecil is seated on the round stool, shoulders hunched as he peers at me through his brass telescope. It's both an odd and a comforting feeling.

I line up with the entrance to Little Harbour's cove and push the throttle a notch. *Betsy's Due* idles slowly forward. As I seek the protection of the tiny harbor, the thundering of the waves around the entrance is impressive.

Inside, it's quiet. The oval-shaped cove is small indeed, but there's room enough to turn my boat around.

Protected from the elements is a dock, bolted to the granite at the base of the cliffs. Tied to the dock is a boat, about twenty feet long with a center console. From the dock, iron stairs ascend the face of the cliff in switchbacks. At the top of the cliff, next to a landing, is a heavy-gauge tripod supporting a large pulley. I'm guessing a cable once ran through the pulley, so the furnace and other heavy gear could be hauled up when they were building Harper's house. Though old and rusty, the well-constructed dock and stairs appear to be in reasonably good shape.

The boat looks much like the center-console fishing boat Cecil described; the one Creech purchased from down the coast. Small cuddy-cabin forward, center console just aft of the cuddy. Above the console, a large, sturdy fiberglass hardtop supported by heavy aluminum piping. Behind the console, a large cockpit. In the middle of the cockpit, the hump of the inboard engine cover. On the back of the transom, the name, *KingFisher*.

I hold the wheel hard to port, allowing my boat to turn in lazy circles. There appears to be no one on board *KingFisher*. Unless they're in the cuddy, which seems unlikely.

I feel vulnerable, fully exposed to anyone up above. I have two options. Go up the stairs, or go home.

I tie up across from the fishing boat. Once I shut the motor off, the quiet is stark. I can still hear the waves outside the cove, but the sound is distant.

I climb aboard the fishing boat. It's a mess. The requisite safety equipment – life jackets, chart kit, portable horn, lines, anchor, etc – are strewn about the cockpit. It looks as if the operator of the boat left in a hurry.

Above the console are the electronics. Two VHF radios. Both mike cords hang in the air, swaying with the gentle motion of the boat. One of the radios is on, its volume low. I hear the crackle and chatter of far-off communications coming from its speaker.

A shiny new, heavy brass padlock secures the cuddy's hatch. Though smaller, the padlock is similar to the one I cut off Creech's garage doors.

I unsnap two latches and tilt the engine cover back. Leaning down, I put my hand on the motor. The boat has been sitting here for hours, long enough for the engine block to cool. I close and re-secure the covers, climb back onto the dock and take a breath.

You shouldn't be here.

Shut up.

If this is Creech's boat, if he is indeed somewhere up above, he could shoot me. Throw my body into the ocean and sink *Betsy's Due*. My body would never be found.

I look up the stairs. My fear of heights rears its irrational head. I begin climbing, hands gripping the railings, meticulous with my foot placement. Up I go, carefully negotiating the switchbacks, back and forth, higher and higher, my boots making hollow sounds on the iron grate.

As I approach the top, I'm more than winded, I'm scared. I have no weapon. Not so much as a knife.

What was I thinking, coming out here unarmed?

Just before I get to the top, I reach into a small alcove on the cliff face and dislodge a fist-sized rock.

When I step onto the upper landing, I let out a sigh of relief. There's no one here. Leaning over, hands on knees, I drag in lots of fresh, salty air.

The wind is coming directly at me, steady and strong. It whips my hair and balloons my shirt behind me. The fabric flaps against my skin. The views of the Atlantic and the coast of Maine are spectacular.

Spreading out before me, a wide plateau. Mostly rock. Some small trees. Sparse scrub brush. There are pine trees, but only a few here and there.

Looking like the backs of sounding whales, expanses of smooth, rounded granite rise and fall out of the plain. Tufts of grass poke out of small sections of hard-packed earth between the rounded granite humps. Boulders, stones and scree are scattered everywhere.

All this grandeur rises gradually up and away. I can see perhaps half the island from here. The other half is out of sight, beyond the rise.

The wind is coming from the east. Everything that grows on this open plateau – bushes, evergreen trees, even the sea grass – bends in my direction. The island is pointing at me. The intruder.

And there's the house. Perhaps a quarter mile away, sitting atop a flat granite shelf near the edge of the eastern cliffs, less than a hundred feet from their edge. Its front door faces a feast of nature – the rising sun, the Atlantic, the cosmos.

Standing alone on the cliffs, the house seems like a monument to a man's potential for both vanity and loneliness.

Shingles bleached gray by years of sun and relentless wind. Solitary clothesline out back, strung between steel poles anchored in stone. Beyond the line, two small outbuildings, sheathed in the same weathered-gray shingles.

To my surprise, almost every window in the house is open. Caught by the winds, lace curtains flutter madly. I can almost hear them flapping.

My feeling of vulnerability increases. Anyone in the house looking this way could easily see me.

A path winds its way across the plateau and ends at the house. The trail is well-worn. Wherever it crosses the whale-backs, there's a single white line painted on the rock. The paint is faded, nearly worn off in places. Along both sides of the trail, black iron posts, iron rings dangling from their tops, have been driven into the granite. At some point in time, a chain must have snaked through these rings, post to post, all the way across the plateau. For tens of thousands of years, this exposed granite has been polished smooth by erosion. I imagine it would be dangerous trying to walk across in a storm, without the aid of the chains. Anyone crossing the plateau today – its smooth stone lubricated by rain and flushed by the wind – risks being blown off the cliffs into the sea.

Setting off along the path, my heart races. As I make progress along the trail, I feel more exposed than ever.

Not thirty feet from the house, the nerves in my legs begin buzzing as if I've just entered an electrical field.

Now the stone beneath my feet begins to vibrate! I look down at the flat expanse of smooth granite, knowing that what I'm experiencing simply cannot be. It would take an act of God to make these cliffs quake.

I get the sensation that something bad is happening *beneath me*. If I could only see through stone.

Then I know. *He* is down there, and he's not alone.

52

Resurrection

In disbelief, the three stare at the remote, lying in the mud.

"Thank God," Rosalie says. "You would have killed us, and we wouldn't have—" She stops and watches Creech stiffen, his eyes as heavy and dull as beads of flattened lead. *He's not buying it.*

Refusing to give up hope, Rosalie continues. "I don't blame you, Eldrick."

Creech again appears confused by her familiarity.

Rosalie knows she has no choice but to go on playing the role of the resurrected wife. "I *can't* blame you. You watched us burn."

"What are you doing?" Creech's voice is scorched iron. He again looks at the detonator.

"*Wait!* I know, Eldrick. I understand. I'm sorry about him…" She gestures toward the room behind her.

"I didn't kill that boy," Creech says. "We fought, and he hit his head on the cot." Creech wears the shattered look of the recently condemned, certain they will soon bear witness to the ending of the world.

Rosalie can only hope she sounds something like Rebecca. "You wanted us to be a family again," she says, shivering fiercely.

Creech moans.

"I'm here, Eldrick. So is she."

Rosalie points at Amanda, leaning on the wall, clutching the dog with her wounded wrist.

"She can be your daughter. After all it took to create *this*, you can't just give up. Without you, we'll die all over again. You didn't push the button, Eldrick. Maybe that was God telling you to stop."

"*God?*" Creech says, his face bulging. "Don't talk to me about that son-of-a-bitch. Where was he when you were burning?"

Now, Rosalie thinks. *It's all or nothing.* "Eldrick," she whispers. "*I am here.*" She makes a sweeping motion with her hand as she looks down at herself. "This woman you see standing here. This body. She's trying to stop me from coming back to you. If you kill her, I'll have no way to come through."

Creech's eyes look like compressed balls of molten glass. "Those people stood by and watched you burn. They need to suffer, and their families need to suffer."

In the space between breaths, Creech's voice softens. His body trembles as he takes a faltering step toward Rosalie. "I've missed you," he says, offering his arms.

Rosalie stifles her fear and goes to Creech. As he slides his arms around her, she at once fears, loathes and pities him.

They embrace.

Sensing Amanda's approach, Rosalie worries the girl's

presence will break the spell. But when Amanda throws her arms around them, it only strengthens the charade.

"My girls," Creech says. He makes a pitiful sound and begins shuffling his feet. The three – clumsy, unstable – begin to slowly turn, round and round in the stinking murk.

53

The Fog

Feeling a chill, I look to the eastern sky. The weather is deteriorating. Banks of dark clouds are rolling toward the island. A powerful gust of wind almost knocks me back. Day is turning to night.

I look across the plateau to the mainland. It's gone. A massive fogbank has appeared out of nowhere, enshrouding everything west of the island.

I go around to the front of the house and step up onto the porch. Roaring across the cliffs, the wind pushes at my back, nudging me toward the front door. The curtains flap inside the open windows like gossamer flags.

The front door is open. Only a screen door separates me from the living room. Inside is all wood – walls, floors, ceilings – a true, old-style beach house. Braided rugs on the wood floors. Threadbare furniture. On the right wall, a stone fireplace.

I yell a greeting above the wind. "Hello!"

No answer.

I yell again.

The curtains snap back at me.

Sensing Eldrick Creech's presence, I open the screen door and step into his house.

54

Die!

"*He's got a knife!*" Amanda screams.

Rosalie slams her palms into Creech's body and pushes, sending her, and Amanda, tumbling backward.

Creech swings the knife, slicing through Rosalie's shirt and parting her flesh. "Do you remember *the smell?*" he screams.

Rosalie clutches her wound and shouts, "We weren't even *there!*"

Creech points the knife at Amanda. "You don't know why we're here, do you?"

Bewildered, Amanda shakes her head.

"*Do you!*" Creech yells.

"No," Amanda whimpers. "I don't."

Amanda grabs onto Rosalie.

"Just tell us what you want us to do!" Her fingers slick with Creech's blood, Rosalie pulls Amanda closer.

Creech seems to be collapsing in on himself. He lurches, and stumbles, slices the air with the knife.

Then suddenly, he stops, brings the knife to his head and begins thumping his skull with its handle.

"What's happening to him?" Amanda whispers.

Creech's body shudders, as if in seizure.

"Eldrick," Rosalie says, almost lovingly. Amanda gasps.

Creech regains his balance. His eyes dart, search up and down the hallway, come to rest on Rosalie.

Rosalie feels Amanda's breath on her neck.

Creech sways before them. When he speaks, his voice cracks. "You know what must happen now."

Amanda squeezes Rosalie tighter.

"This whole…" Creech points the knife down the tunnel. "This has to go. We have to make them pay. Only then can we be a family again."

Rosalie can't take her eyes off the madman.

Creech bends and snatches the detonator out of the mud. "I'm doing this for *us*."

Rosalie holds her breath. *Will I feel it?*

"We all… We need to be cleansed." Creech wobbles, then falls back against the wall. "We would have lived forever."

For a brief moment, Creech no longer seems mad. When he drops the detonator into his pocket, his eyes go clear and he looks peaceful. Then, back pressed against the wall to hold him up, he begins inching toward the women.

"We will receive the greatest gift." Creech's free hand shoots out and grabs Rosalie's elbow, so fast, it shocks her. "You must go before me."

"Please," she whimpers.

55

Down

I begin my search upstairs in the bedrooms. No clothes in the closets. No boxes. No suitcases. In the bathroom, two crumpled towels on a rack. Disposable razor on the sink. Toothpaste. Toothbrush. Sink and tub, stained with rust.

Downstairs. Living room. Dining room. Obviously unoccupied for years. At the back of the house, a pantry, its shelves lined with rusting cans of food and disintegrating boxes of staples. Kitchen, small table, bare essentials. The refrigerator door is open just a crack. Light on inside, compressor humming away. I open the door wider. Half-full quart of milk. Plastic bag containing a loaf of bread. Six-pack of beer with one can missing. That's it.

I take the cap off the milk carton. The milk is cold, fresh. I put the milk back. Leave the door open a crack, exactly as I found it.

What is powering this house? I listen for the sound of a generator. Hear only the wind.

I inch the back door open and peer outside. Then I hear

it. The rhythmic thump of an internal combustion engine. The generator. A wisp of smoke rises from a small exhaust pipe, cut through the side wall on the larger shack. The fumes instantly disperse on the wind.

When I first approached the house, the generator could not have been running. I would have heard it. As I'm thinking this, the engine shuts down. Either someone is in the shack, or the generator is on-demand.

The refrigerator.

Heart pounding, I slip back into the kitchen. Now the refrigerator door is shut. I press my back against the wall and listen.

All I hear is the wind, and the incessant flapping of those damn curtains. Maybe the wind closed the refrigerator door.

I'm sure there's no one in this house, yet there's something eerie about its emptiness. Maybe because it feels as if whoever was here has only just left.

Then I see something I'd missed. A narrow door at the end of a hallway next to the downstairs bathroom. I go to the door and open it slowly. A stairway. I can see halfway down, then darkness. I find a switch and flip it. A dim bulb above me comes on. Tightening my grip on the sharp-edged rock, I descend. As I go down, the smell of rotten eggs almost turns me around.

There's no basement. Only a small room carved out of solid rock, with a ceiling so low I have to bend over to move. In the near-dark, I can just make out several rows of reinforced shelves along the walls. Hunched over, I step further into the room. Now I understand the smell. The shelves are packed with huge batteries, each twice the size of a car battery. Thick cables connect them all together, forming a chain of power that winds up in a square electrical panel. There must be fifty batteries down here. All of them are leaking a whitish, flaky fluid, and every cable end is caked with calcified acid.

I pull my shirt over my mouth and run back up the stairs.

At the back door I suck in lungfuls of fresh air. Then I say a prayer and step into the yard. Out here, there is simply no place to hide.

On the granite shelf between the two outbuildings, a square concrete abutment with something on top. With the wind threatening to blow me off my feet, I walk across the open space toward the abutment, feeling like the target in a sniper's sights.

Atop the abutment, a round hatch with an old, rusty wheel, like an escape hatch on a submarine. The wheel turns with surprising ease. The hatch tilts open without effort, assisted by a large spring. There's a matching wheel on the inside of the lid.

The air that wafts from the underground reeks of dampness, mold and death. I shudder. For a second, I'm back in time. The dreadful moment I opened Sarah Sweeney's coffin.

I force myself to look down. A cast-iron ladder vanishes into the dark. I stare below, thinking, *Who in their right mind would go down there?* I'm reminded of something Mooney once said: "You ever have to go after a nutcase? It doesn't hurt to be a little nuts yourself."

As I climb down, I hear something. Voices. A man and a woman. I see that, beneath my feet, at the bottom of the ladder, I will drop into a dimly lit, earthen room. I go down the last few steps and plant my feet on hard-packed earth. The stench is stronger here.

The room is small and empty. There are two openings in the earthen walls directly opposite each other. Each is a tunnel. Coming out the left tunnel, a rubber-coated cable snakes around the floor and disappears down the opposite tunnel.

The voices have stopped. I hold my breath and wait.

Then the man is yelling. I still can't make out what he's saying, but I know he's somewhere to the right. As I head toward his voice, I see light emanating from a hole in the middle of the floor, twenty feet ahead. I go quietly to the opening. There's a second ladder. The stench is getting stronger.

The man speaks again. I make out one word: *country.* Then a panicked scream comes out of the shaft. *It's the scream I heard at the boathouse!*

I scramble down the ladder as quietly as I can, my body surging adrenaline, my mind popping off like firecrackers. *Why are you here? What are you gonna do with a rock?*

When I ease myself off the bottom rung and turn, I step into Eldrick Creech's nightmare.

56

Gone

At the far end of a long, dimly lit corridor, two women and a man are fighting. The women begin screaming.

The man is covered in blood. He towers over them. *Creech!*

"*No!*" I yell, just as he stabs one of them in the neck.

Creech jerks his head around and glares at me like an enraged animal.

"*Stop!*" I yell again.

Incredibly, all three stop struggling.

Creech squares his shoulders to face me.

The younger woman's neck is bleeding. Wearing a makeshift sling, she's clutching a dog to her chest. The other woman is tiny and looks as crazy as Creech.

I charge. Creech lurches toward me. When I feint left, Creech is slow to react, so I bring the rock around with everything I've got and smash it into his temple. His skull feels like granite.

Creech crashes into me. I hook his ankle and take him to the ground. Slam him into the dirt so hard, air explodes from his lungs.

Eyes half-open, his lids twitch then go still. I wrench the knife from his hand and toss it away. Getting up, I rush to the women.

The smaller one is leaning against the wall crying, "Oh God. Oh God."

The girl holding the dog slumps to the floor. Her eyes are huge with fear. I kneel next to her. She doesn't know I'm there.

"I need to see it," I say.

She doesn't respond.

I peel her blood-soaked fingers away from her neck. The cut is jagged, the meat separated. But the blade missed the jugular. I recognize her. *Amanda.*

The other woman yells at me. "Who are you?"

Ignoring her, I remove my jacket, then take off my T-shirt and tear it into strips. I make a pad from one piece and a bandage from another. Pressing the pad against the hole in Amanda's skin, I wrap the strip around her neck to hold it in place. I take her hand and place it against the makeshift bandage. "Keep pressure on this." She's still out of it, yet does what I ask. I pull my sweater back on and stand.

"My name is William Snow," I say to the older woman. "You must be Rosalie Tam." I nod at Amanda. "Her mother sent me to find her."

Amanda looks up. "Mom?" she says, and bursts into tears.

Rosalie Tam puts her hand on my shoulder. "Thank you. How did you—?"

I take her hand. "There's no time to explain. We have to get Amanda to a hospital."

"What do we do about that?" Rosalie points toward Creech.

"What happened to him?" I ask.

294

"I smashed his head in with a box. I guess I got lucky. He was unconscious for a while. When he came to, he had trouble walking."

In Rosalie's eyes I see a kind of frantic contentment. A glowing.

"We have to go," I say. "Now!"

We help Amanda to her feet, support her and the dog between us, and head for the ladder. Because of the narrow passageway, we have to pass closely by Creech. The instant we look down at him, his eyes open. We step back, but it's obvious that Creech is incapable of moving. His head is a ruin of gaping flesh and blood. His mouth is an open wound. Ignoring me, he stares at Rosalie and Amanda, as if bidding the women farewell. What little light there is in his eyes dims. His jaws slacken, and his lips slowly part.

Eldrick Creech seems to shrink before my eyes – a dissolving man, emptied of hope and purpose. Tears seep from eyes no longer black, their color blanched by the encroachment of death.

Creech tries to speak but no sound comes out. I can tell it's a question.

Maybe he's crying for the loss of all he's ever lived for. Maybe he's asking for his family. Or maybe he's grieving for the blood he's spilled, while his own blood flows unchecked into the earth.

I'm surprised by how it feels to see a man die that I first encountered just moments ago. Regardless of his horrific crimes, despite his insanity and his corrupted intentions, his death is a sad, intimate thing to watch.

As I lean down to pick up the knife from the dirt, a ghastly sound burbles in Creech's chest.

"Let's get out of here," I say. I take the dog from Amanda and the three of us go to the ladder to climb out of the subterranean hell.

We go through the tunnel to the second ladder. Soon, we're standing outside, bracing ourselves against the wind. We lean on each other to catch our breath.

Creech's empty house looks foreboding. Its wavering curtains beckon to us like fingers.

I hold Amanda upright with one arm. Rosalie leans her weight on my other side. I'm acutely aware of the lightness of Amanda's body, of the coppery scent of her blood as it soaks into my sweater.

I look out across the wide sea and take my first easy breath in fifty hours.

It's over.

57

Daylight

We go into Creech's house, out of the relentless wind. The women sit at the kitchen table.

Amanda's wound has stopped bleeding. I look into her eyes, but she doesn't look back. Trembling, fine beads of sweat cover her exposed skin. She appears to be in shock.

Rosalie's cut is superficial, and she appears to be in full possession of her faculties.

The little dog is underfed, gaunt, listless. I gently pass him to Rosalie. Ferocity burns in her eyes.

I check my cell for service. Still nothing.

"If not for you, we'd be dead," Rosalie says, stroking the dog's head. Her hand is shaking violently.

"You were both holding your own," I say.

Rosalie and I walk Amanda into the living room. When we bring the girl to the couch, she collapses into it and curls into the fetal position, her blood-soaked clothes staining the worn fabric.

Rosalie sits tenderly in a large wicker chair. The dog seems to be asleep.

I run upstairs and grab blankets from the beds.

When I cover the women, only Rosalie seems to notice.

Briefly, I tell Rosalie how I found them. She tells me about Creech. The dead man. The box. The knife. But when she tells me about the detonator, my heart races. *It's not over.*

"I have to go back down there," I say.

Rosalie almost leaps out of her chair. "No! You can't leave us. Please, let's just get out of here!"

Amanda turns her head. Stares at me from under her blanket.

"I have to find the detonator," I say.

"No. No! Just *leave* it!" Rosalie pleads.

"We're not negotiating," I say.

As I go out, I give the women a last glance. Amanda a bloodied bird. Rosalie a fighter, ready to fend the next blow.

I go down the ladder into the darkness. My eyes seem to adjust quicker this time. I follow the tunnel to the second ladder. Dropping into the bottom corridor, I smell blood. It's splattered on the walls.

And it's pooled on the floor, where Eldrick Creech no longer lies.

58

Done

Drag marks in the dirt. Wet with Creech's blood, they lead to an open door. With my back against the wall, I move silently to the door's edge. I hold my breath, listen, tighten my grip on Creech's knife.

From inside the room, a scraping sound.

"Creech," I say.

Nothing.

"CREECH!"

His voice is barely a whisper.

"*Yeah...*"

"Why don't you come out?" I say. "You need help."

Nothing for a few seconds. Then, "So. You're gonna help me now?"

I don't answer.

When he speaks again, his voice is stronger. "You really want to help? *Then come in.*"

I recall Creech lying at my feet, bleeding out. His skin had already turned gray. Why isn't he dead?

"Creech," I say.

I hear a guttural sound.

"*Creech?*"

"Jesus," he says. "Give it a rest."

I hear something like shoes scrabbling for purchase. But all this dense earth muffles sound. I don't know where it's coming from.

This time Creech's tone mocks. "Come on in, friend."

"Not a chance," I say. I look around in the semi-dark. Shadows everywhere. What I wouldn't give for a flashlight.

"Suit yourself," Creech says. "I suppose it doesn't matter. Except for the one thing."

"And what's that?"

"You said you wanted to help me, right?"

"No. What I said was, 'You need help'."

Creech coughs, clears his throat, coughs again, which sets off a series of wet gagging sounds, like his airway is clogging with blood.

"What's your name, friend?"

"I'm not your friend," I say, my heart banging. "My name is Snow."

"Snow?" Creech gurgles. "Like, *pure as*?" I can almost see his sneer.

He has another coughing fit.

It's quiet for a beat or two, then he spits. It's followed by a nasty sound, like a globule of blood plopping into the mud. When it's finally over, he clears his throat.

"You sent that email," Creech says.

His voice seems to come from the shadows – in front of me, behind me, gaining strength.

"What do you want?" I ask.

This time his pause is so long, I get a creepy feeling – like the man passed through the wall and is standing behind me now. I spin around, but there's no one.

Feeling foolish, I say, "I could just leave. Lock the hatch. Let you die here."

"Sorry," he says. "But that won't work, *friend*. I'll just go out the other way."

There's another exit?

"Besides. I'll bet money you're going to want to hear this. Hey, Snow. You want to hear something funny?"

"What."

"I push this button? You'll be *melted Snow*. Hah!"

The detonator.

"What do you want me to hear, Creech?"

Another pause, then, "My confession."

"I'm not interested," I say. "Come out."

Creech chuckles. "That's not gonna happen. And you're not gonna leave."

I say nothing.

"Yeah, I thought so," he says. "You and me? We got some things in common. You sink your teeth into something, you can't let go. Am I right?"

I say nothing.

"Otherwise, you wouldn't have come back down here. You would've gotten off this rock."

I close my eyes to prepare for the darkness of that room.

"Hey, Snow. On your best day, you couldn't touch me on my worst."

I inch closer. "This *is* your worst," I say. I listen carefully for the response. *Where is he?*

"Suit yourself." Creech's voice is low and close, like he's breathing in my ear. "Come on in, friend. Let's do this."

I curl around the doorframe and run into the room.

59

The Driver's Dream

Slanting through the side-porch windows, the afternoon sun feels warm on Eldrick's neck. He leans back and settles his bulk into his favorite chair.

"Honey?" he says, over the sound of the TV.

His wife doesn't answer.

"*Rebecca?*"

"What is it?" she calls out.

Eldrick knows Rebecca is reading a book in the other room. But he's thirsty, and he's feeling lazy.

"Lemonade," he says, hopeful. "With ice."

No response.

"*Please!*" he yells.

Before he can take two breaths, Rebecca enters the porch carrying a tall glass of lemonade. Sparkling yellow, with lots of ice.

"I'm way ahead of you, babe," she says, smiling.

Eldrick takes the cold glass, sets it on his side table and

returns the smile. "You're the greatest," he says.

Rebecca pats her husband's muscled shoulder and goes back into the house.

Eldrick takes a sip of his drink. As always, Rebecca has squeezed the lemons herself. It's perfect.

He adjusts the volume down. Doesn't want to disrupt Rebecca's reading. It's the third quarter. The Giants are murdering the Jets, 38 to 9.

With the outlook of the game assured, Eldrick Creech – rabid Jets hater – falls asleep.

"Dad."

Ricky shakes his father's arm. "*Dad?* Wake up!"

When Eldrick opens his eyes, the first thing he sees is the birthmark – the blue and purple smudge on the left side of his son's face. It's the first thing everyone sees.

When his grammar school classmates teased Ricky about the mark, Eldrick told his son to ignore them. Be the 'bigger man'. But when Ricky entered middle school, and a neighbor's kid began taunting relentlessly, Eldrick decided to put a stop to it. He went to the school, stormed into the classroom, stood at the front and glared at the little shit. Creech didn't have to say a word. No one in that school would ever bully his kid again.

"Hey, bud," Eldrick says, scratching the stubble on his chin.
"Hi Dad."

Eldrick's daughter, Judith, comes into the room like a spring breeze. Behind her, Rebecca, carrying a cake with lots of candles burning.

Eldrick beams while his family sings "Happy Birthday".

When the singing is over, he stands, makes a wish, blows out the candles, hugs his family.

Kisses the kids' foreheads.

"I love you, Eldrick," Rebecca says. "We all love you."

When Eldrick kisses Rebecca's cheek, her skin comes away on his lips.

60

Say Goodbye

Running into the room blind.
I stop. Crouch.

Shadow to my right. *Too small.*

I spin left. Don't see him, but...

Behind you!

I whirl and jab the knife into nothing but air. My foot catches. I stumble backward. The smell of decaying flesh crawls into my mouth and slithers down my throat. I roll off the corpse and end up sitting in the mud.

Directly across from me, right next to the door with his back against the wall, Eldrick Creech sits in the reeking darkness. All the time we were talking, we were on the opposite sides of the same wall, not three feet from each other. Eyes fully adjusted now, I see the hiked-up pants leg, the empty ankle holster.

In Creech's huge hand the snub-nosed revolver looks like a toy. Its barrel is pointed at my stomach.

"Hey, friend," he says.

"You don't look so good," I say.

"Nice to meet you, too."

Creech is even paler than before. Cheeks hollowed. Eyes gray and glassy. Face, hair, clothes, plastered with dried blood and filth.

"What now?" I say.

The gun wavers. I pray he lacks the strength to pull the trigger.

"I don't know," he says. "I'm a little under the weather. Not thinking too good."

Creech raises the gun and points it at my face. For an instant, I'm sure this is it.

His hand drops.

"Why don't you give me the gun?" I say.

"Fuck me," Creech says. "You got some balls on you."

He coughs, and a mist of blood sprays the air.

"Jesus," I say.

Blood is leaking out of his nose. It drips slowly from his chin onto his defiled shirt. This is an awful thing to watch.

"I just wanted to lay eyes on you," Creech says. "See who it is has the balls to come all the way out here and fuck up my day."

"You're dying," I say.

"You think?" he says.

His hand twitches. The gun barrel sways.

"Creech," I say. I lean forward onto my knees, so close I could reach out and touch him.

His lips coil into a grimace. He holds his left hand up so I can see. *The detonator!* "What's your pleasure?" he asks, raising his right hand and pointing the gun at my face again. "The choice is yours."

307

For an instant I don't see a gun, I see Paula. *I should have changed for her. I should have lived a normal life.* I reach out to touch her.

The explosion shatters Paula and blows me off my knees.

61

Flowers

I'm paralyzed, frozen in time, captivated by a single flower. I don't know flowers. Don't know this one's name. With its long stem and full, pinkish petals, it stands alone, fluttering in the wind.

'Flowering' is a term ballistic experts use when describing the way the skull and the tissues of the brain are atomized by the explosion of a hollow point bullet.

For some time now, Paula and I have been sitting, looking out at the world from the deck at the Butler Hospital psych ward. Between us is a little plastic table, on which sit two glasses of lemonade. Hers is almost empty, mine is almost full. I'm not sure how long we've been here, mainly because I've spaced out. Truth is, I've checked out completely. Because of the flower.

Paula had been updating me on Amanda's condition. The recuperation of not only the girl's body, but her spirit. It was then that my eyes fell upon the flower.

"William? Are you all right?"

When Paula touches my arm, I flinch.

"Sorry," I say, deflecting. "I was thinking about how important it is to stay in the present. How this moment is all we have."

I'm not telling her the whole truth – it's too fragile to share with her. Doctor Stuart says I'll know when the time is right.

She looks at me with concern, her lovely face framed by the soft curls of her sandy hair, her gentle blue eyes unwavering. "It must have been awful," she says.

"Worse for them," I say, my eyes falling again on the lone flower. "Rosalie and Amanda. They…"

My thoughts run off somewhere, leaving me without any words.

I wonder, does the flower know it's alone?

"William?" Paula says.

"Yes."

"What's wrong?"

"Nothing," I lie, again. "Rosalie Tam," I say.

"What about her?"

"What she did goes beyond heroism. Ninety-five pounds of pure fury. Creech underestimated that one."

"He didn't estimate either of them," she says. "And *that* was his undoing."

Hearing the admiration in Paula's voice, I look over at her and my heart erupts. When will my feelings rise above the sounds that bellow in my head? When will they drown out the chaos? Sabrina. Sarah Sweeney. Eldrick Creech's brains and blood.

Outside the realm of my storm, I hear the doctor's repetitive drone:

Time.

"Rosalie Tam," I say, dragging myself back. "She's gone on a *vision quest?* Is that really what she called it?"

"No," Paula chuckles. "That's what *Mooney* called it. He was being snide, but that's only because he's so 'blown away' – his words – by what she did. He called her a 'tiny little bad-ass'."

"She's driving across country," I say. "Alone."

"Yup. That day, after she came to visit with you? We went to the cafeteria and had coffee. She told she could never sleep in her house again. So, she called a realtor, put it on the market, then put all her stuff in storage. Maybe what she did down in those tunnels gave her the courage to create a new life for herself."

"She's a force," I say. "But I don't remember her being here."

"It's okay. She understands."

We don't speak for a while.

"The two of them," I say, taking my eyes off the flower yet again. "They're *both* forces. Incredible women."

Paula agrees. She tells me Amanda is suffering from Post-Traumatic Stress Disorder and is seeing her own therapist. Now that she's moved out of the garage and back into the house, she, Annie and her mother are healing. Their relationships are... flowering.

Paula reaches across the little table and cups my hand in hers. This time I suppress the flinch. But she knows anyway and withdraws.

I tell myself that I'm grateful for the warm day, the soft breeze, the fact that I'm alive. I look across the parking lot below. At the far end there are woods. I feel a powerful urge to run through them.

*

311

On our way home from the hospital, Paula doesn't say much. Maybe she senses that I'm staring down into the labyrinth of the unknown, the phantom underpinning of our lives.

I think intently about madness, about what being 'mad' means. I try to imagine it has an arc, a span that goes from 'here' – *sane* – to 'there' – *insane.* At what point along the arc does one go 'over the edge' and 'off the deep end'?

Everyone has a deep end. I watched Eldrick Creech sail off his in spectacular fashion.

Eldrick Creech haunts me. One moment I was facing certain death, the next I was watching the man's head explode. The horror of it left me with a recurring vertigo. Without warning my internal gyroscope shuts down. I find myself tipping. About to fall.

As we pull into the gravel lot, I look up at the hulk of my floating home. I wonder what possesses me to live inside an armor-plated tug. If I care about the ocean so much, why have I committed myself to *Paralus,* which, having no engine, is terminally stuck? Maybe I'll bring this up in my next session.

Paula and I hug in the parking lot. I want to say "I love you" but I can't get the words out.

I'll never erase the image of her floating before me, just as Creech put the gun under his chin and blew his brains all over me.

My footsteps echo throughout my steel ship. As I head for the catwalk above The Pit, I try to imagine the pain Creech must have suffered as he watched his family burn, as he *smelled* them burn.

I stand at the railing, look down two stories to Bradley's bed. She's curled up in her corner on her blankets. Her good eye cants upward and her tail thumps softly. I swear there's a smile on her crumpled face.

Then it happens – the vertigo – and I feel myself tilting toward a two-story fall. I grab the cold rail and hold on, my eyes squeezed tight. Everything turns black – then out of the black comes the image of my sister, Sabrina. A moment later, Sarah Sweeney materializes behind her, a ghost trailing a ghost.

My heart roars.

Beyond the images of my two lost girls, another appears. I've never seen this one, but I know who she is. Behind her, the shadow of a woman hovers. Behind the woman, there's a small boy.

Creech's daughter, wife, and son.

Creech. Why do I feel empathy for an abductor? How can I feel sadness for a mass murderer?

It's been said that within every person lies the potential for all human experience. Given the right or wrong circumstance, anyone can snap.

I blink. My vertigo fades, and the ghosts fade with it.

I descend the steel steps carefully, go to Bradley's bed and lie down next to her. So close, I can feel her beating heart.

The End

Read an excerpt from the next William Snow thriller, *The Man on the Moon*:

Dirt

Heather awakens. When she opens her eyes, the damp earth above her collapses, lodging her lids open. She screams, but the sound dies when a clump of earth tumbles in and clogs her windpipe.

Heather flails for her life – but the movements are only imagined, the fantasy of a mind gone mad. In truth, Heather can neither see, breathe, nor move – so complete is the embrace of her freshly filled grave.

Heather swallows more soil – she inhales it, ingests it. Her stomach wretches.

In Heather's final moments, an image of Alan appears in the darkness. He's smiling.

It is Thursday evening, May 1st, 1952, Heather's 18th birthday.

CPSIA information can be obtained
at www.ICGtesting.com
Printed in the USA
FSHW010440090621
82095FS

9 781781 329443